Alexander Cordell was botion in 1914 ?? ?? in North China. To date books, the first of which COUNTRY in 1959. MWelsh industrial revoluti living on the Isle of Man research.

Tunnel Tigers

Alexander Cordell

SPHERE BOOKS LIMITED

SPHERE BOOKS LTD

Published by the Penguin Group
27 Wrights Lane, London W8 5TZ, England
Viking Penguin Inc., 40 West 23rd Street, New York, New York 10010, USA
Penguin Books Australia Ltd, Ringwood, Victoria, Australia
Penguin Books Canada Ltd, 2801 John Street, Markham, Ontario, Canada L3R 1B4
Penguin Books (NZ) Ltd, 182–190 Wairau Road, Auckland 10, New Zealand

First published in Great Britain by Weidenfeld & Nicolson Ltd 1986
Published by Sphere Book Ltd 1988

Made and printed in Great Britain by
Richard Clay Ltd, Bungay, Suffolk
Set in Plantin

For my friend, Jim Turvey

Acknowledgements

I am grateful to many librarians for help in research; also to Mr Tom Jones, Mr Glen Moody, Mrs Audrey James, all of Pontypridd; Mr Gwyn Martin (NUM) of Porth and Mr R. Nichols, the Gwent historian. Mr E. E. Edwards of Rhymney gave me valuable assistance. I also wish to thank Mr T. E. Morgan, managing director of the historic firm Brown Lenox, and Mr Gareth P. Jenkins of the *Western Mail*, who made a helpful contribution. To the old gentlemen of Wales, again my gratitude. Without them, this book could not have been written.

There comes a crowd of burly navvies, with pick-axes and barrows . . . the hills are cut through, or the breaches between them spanned, we choose our level and the white steam-pennon flies along.

George Eliot

Book one

Chapter one
1839

Summer, bright with sun and perfumed winds, came dancing over the moors with mouse-ear chickweed in her hair, a dress of wild violets and a crown of foxgloves; my world bloomed with dog-roses, wayside strawberries and willow-herb. With the chops of the heifers decorated with gold dross, the whole munching country from Bradford to Glossop crossed its legs, lay back in the cornfields and dozed in a pot-bellied bumbledore June.

'Are you daydreaming again, Nick Wortley?'

'No, Miss Brandt.'

'Then please pay attention to what I am saying.'

'Yes, Miss Brandt.'

Officially, I referred to her as Miss Brandt the school teacher; unofficially, she was known to me as Ruth. Said she:

'I was about to tell you that words are jewels; that to call them scandalous names like "nouns" and "pronouns" is like calling dirty things after unloved people in the street. Do you hear me, Nicholas Wortley?'

Talk had it in High Doss that Ruth Brandt, the Owner's daughter, was after a man, and if she couldn't get a man, she'd go after the likes of me, aged fifteen.

'Yes, I heard you, Miss Brandt.'

It was difficult for me to understand why the old tripers in our High Doss Co-operative thought ill of her. The Devil himself dyes her garters, said Ma Bopper, and that one's no better than she should be, others claimed; and Mustapher, the Turkish rat-catcher who'd bite one in two for a quart of ale, reckoned that the mice looking up her skirts were as big as pint glasses.

'Nicholas Wortley!'

I thought: Jesus, why always pick on me: 'Yes, Miss Brandt?'

'Clearly you haven't heard a single word I've said this morning. The Athenian Republic may not play a large part in your education, but Dai Bando appears to find it of interest.'

Sod the Athenian Republic and sod Dai Bando.

I thought, too: O, sun, Oh sun! Just to lie with Miss Ruth Brandt in the Big Cornfield come July when the ears were gold and fanning live in the wind! Just to lie in her arms far from the dirt and stinks of High Doss; watch the lashes spread wide on her cheeks, and listen to the sounds of summer. Up upon an elbow now in dreams and look into Ruth Brandt's face; see her eyes startled before the first kiss. My duck, my mopsey, my love-pearl, which is what Old Soak whispered to Maria, his missus, behind the partition on a Saturday night after ten pints of Allsops. And his Maria, an Irish Jewess, dimpled fat as a boiling joint, would wave her plump legs in the air and whoop like a Cherokee Indian when Old Soak got her going. It was astonishing to me how God discovers different moulds in which to pour women: the one he used for Ruth Brandt must have been fashioned like the hanging baskets of Lebanon.

Miss Brandt taught us words – me, Dai Bando the cobbler's son, Binnie Tooley, Martha Higgins and Bridget O'Shea – in the evenings when we'd finished the Co-op shift up in High Doss. But how to describe Ruth Brandt with only words to use?

Her black skirt (sometimes it was brown and the seam was down the back) fitted her slim buttocks to perfection; the white silk blouse stretched tightly over her breasts told that these were unlike those of the blousy skivvers who worked naked to the waist at the fulling vats in the basement of High Doss – surely the breasts of Miss Brandt were covered with satin, each small enough to be cupped in my hand, but one only saw them between the months of June and September.

4

'Where do they get to in winter, mun?' Dai Bando once asked.

'Search me.'

And he made a face at the sun. 'I reckon they're there all the time, mainly speaking, but they cover 'em up with bales of red flannel.'

'Could be,' I replied.

He was wrong, of course; they shrink in the month of October.

Dai Bando was thirteen and I thought it bad for him to be thinking of such things at so tender an age; more, it was akin to a betrayal of Miss Brandt's virtue to be discussing her at all; it was an invasion of her privacy, but the temptations arose again and again. Even while calling myself a dirty little bugger, I'd lie amid the long line of snoring sleepers in High Doss and watch her enter the door by the iron stairs and move with delicate precision down the rows of snoring obesity until she reached Old Soak and Maria, who were two beds down from mine. And always, because Miss Brandt was not only generous but compassionate, she would pause at the pile of haunches and shinbones folks called Skin Crone, who was dying, and touch her emaciated face. And Plum Belly, a gin-soaked travelling actor, would declare from his mattress in his best Shakespearean voice: ' "My mistress's eyes are nothing like the sun; coral is far more red than her lips' red. If snow be white, why then her breasts are dun; if hairs be wires, black wires grow on her head . . ." '

'Are you there, Nicholas Wortley?' asked Miss Brandt, ignoring him.

And I would sit up in the bed and pull the blanket aside to allow her entry.

'You are late.'

'I was delayed. Do please make love to me quietly, Nicholas, lest it wakes the others?'

'Certainly, Miss Brandt.'

And there forged upon my loins a strength of iron as red heat forges, and reaching up I drew her down into the bed beside me and there was a dominance within me and little of pity.

'I love you, Nick Wortley,' said she.

I never replied to this – no woman in the world is having me as easily as that – yet it always seemed an outrage to her modesty that she should be forced to lie against the hardness of me and sacrifice her softness without apology.

'You promise to tell me if I hurt you, Miss Brandt?'

In the hazed moonlight from the cracked windows that shaft the dreadnought sleepers; on the blue-whiskered chins of Old Soak, Little Darby the Fuller and Plum Belly the actor are steaming the mists of dawn; within Po Betsy's grunts and Billo's groans the harvest of the night explodes in the bowels of Belcher, turning over seven beds down. But a rose of Sharon is present within the conjured picture, and behind the high cheekbones of my lover's face I see the scarred pattern of my canvas pillow: the plate-broken moon touches the curves of her golden mouth.

'Thank you, Nick Wortley, that was quite delightful.'

'You're welcome, Miss Brandt.'

'For heaven's sake, Wortley,' Miss Brandt cried now in the classroom, 'you haven't heard a single word I've said!'

'I have, ma'am, honest!'

My voice broke on the last syllable and I lowered my face in shame; half a man, even the voice, like other things, went up and down like a ninny. The other children giggled: Dai Bando, sod him, hooted at the ceiling. Miss Brandt touched her mouth with a little lace handkerchief, saying:

'The same time tomorrow, then? All six of you, after shift?'

'I can't come, missus,' cried Dai. 'I'm on night-drying-out.'

Miss Brandt consulted her register. 'Then might it be best to leave lessons for a day or two . . .?'

'Oh God, *no!*' I raised a red face, saying, 'I . . . I can come, ma'am . . .'

'Really! All right, then – providing you have finished *A New View of Society* by then.'

If it meant staying up all night.

'Excellent!' She clasped her small, plump hands together. 'Then you shall come, Wortley. But not here – up at the Big House after your dinner – say, about seven-thirty?'

'If there *is* any dinner,' whispered Bridget O'Shea, aged nine.

At the door Miss Brandt added peremptorily, 'Ring the front door bell and the butler will show you into the library, understand?'

'I reckon she's going to do you, Wortley,' said Dai Bando.

You never knew where you were with Dai Bando. Starved in childhood because he fell on stoney ground, he was a weed of a boy with a sunflower for a head, haricot beans for eyes and ears that guided him like a sparrow hawk.

With peeps and keyholes you never knew where you were with Dai Bando from minute to minute.

Like the rest of the family, he was either asleep, half asleep or wide awake with sparkling eyes; one moment dumb, next minute you had to shoot him to stop him talking.

Rumour had it that the family ate opium, which was knocking around High Doss about then. In the East, people chew betelnut, they tell me, to dilute the terror of their lives; and Dai had his Uncle Bobo, an old sea salt who had fought as a powder-monkey at Trafalgar and before that did the China Run on the tea clippers: Uncle Bobo brought the opium back with him, folks said, and the only woman in High Doss who had painless births was Mrs Bando; she turned them out as fast as rabbits with never a whimper. And sometimes even while you were talking to Dai Bando, the little beggar would drop off.

'With luck you might even marry Miss Brandt one day, then we'll all be in the money,' Dai said now.

'*Get off!*'

Chapter two

Six or seven parallel streets stretched down a hill to a valley; these, intersecting with others, formed blocks of rank-on-rank cottages leaning shoulder to shoulder against the wind; like tipsy navvies out on a randy.

In the middle of the square so formed was a ruined mill, once a thriving factory owned by Samuel Brandt, who owned most things around this suburb of Bradford, including us. But recently it had been taken over by the discharged workers of Sam Brandt's mills, – the sick, lame and lazy, as he was pleased to call us. And the people had formed a co-operative under Robert Owen's system, renaming it High Doss.

There was no moon that night, when I came home from Ruth Brandt's English night class: dusk had fallen over the canal that brought in the wool from Bradford, and the stars, weary at waiting so long for summer, looked faint enough to drop out of the sky. Twisted chimneys and a shattered roof glowered over the black, forbidding country.

Earlier, I'd been into Coney Wood for a rabbit; old man Brandt, Ruth's father, was a bugger for man-traps, but you had to take the chance on a leg if you were after a coney, and now the body of a young buck was warm beneath my arm.

I loved Coney Wood; it was filled with the same sun and music of the woods back home in Pontypridd, which were the dandelion days of my childhood in Wales, before they took me for the workhouse.

Ay ay, bluebells swarmed in the woods of Ponty, and when God smoothed them with his hands they sang to you the same elfin chorus as here. Those were the days when you could read a newspaper on the Old Bridge by the light of the little bloomeries, and when they tapped the iron cauldrons in the yards of Brown Lenox, the world caught

9

alight right over the Graig to Mountain Ash, and Mardy.

But that was eight years back, in 1831 when I was seven years old and my parents were transported for their part in the Merthyr riots of that year. And I can remember the Specials coming into our kitchen up by what was later Dan's Muck-hole in Ponty.

I was sitting on my mother's knee, waiting for Dada to come home from the level whcre Tom Clarke, who lived next door but three, was killed. In their spare time he and his missus made muffins which they sold in Ponty Market, and you'd toast them on a fork in front of the red-toothed grate, and when you bit into them the butter would run through your teeth and down your chin. He was a North Country booger, was Tom; sometimes I wonder if he's still selling muffins on the other side of a dream where there're no Dan's Muck-holes and no High Dosses.

Aye, muffins were bought when times were good, but when my people went up to Merthyr for the riots, the Specials came into our kitchen. And I can see their batons rising and falling and the blood on my father's coal-grimed face. Then the neighbours joined in, like they do in Ponty, with the Welsh landing hooks and the Irish swinging boots, and you couldn't see Specials for dust. But then the Military arrived with khaki and buttonsticks, and my mother laid into them with the copper stick and put one on the Sergeant-major, which didn't do us much good, for he was lying on our kitchen floor like something embalmed.

Dada and Mam went to the Assizes and I went to the workhouse until the master there had the bright idea of sending me north in the workhouse cart with sixty other kids, and folks in High Doss took me in. That, like I said, was eight years back.

'What's your name?' asked somebody.

And a woman's voice said, 'Don't cry, lad, you'll be all right now Gwen 'as got you. What's your name, ye say?'

'Nicholas Farrer.'

She was a North Country missus without fourpence to

her name, but she hugged me to the ample breast. Another two seconds and I'd have been a corpse.

'Now you're 'ere with Joe and me, we're calling you Nick Wortley. All right?'

'Ay ay, missus.'

She had conceived and aborted five times, had Gwen Wortley: a woman hungry for a son.

'Look, Joe, I got a little lad,' said she. 'Ain't he lovely?'

'Mother o' Christ, I don't know how we're going to feed him,' said Joe.

Now, going down the cellar steps in High Doss, I was accosted by a gaggle of ragged women, and you had to watch this lot for a word out of place and they'd blacken your bits and pieces.

'Where you been, Nick Wortley?' asked one.

'I tell you that, missus, you'll be as wise as me.'

'He's been on lessons with that Brandt piece!'

'Your ma's been asking for you, my son.' This from a young, bosomy slut with eyes of wild surprise, and her name was Patsy O'Hearne, as Irish as the shamrock.

'And she ain't in the best of health and temper.'

'The poor soul's labourin' cruel.'

I pushed through them and continued down the cellar steps.

This was Gwen's sixth attempt, and if she birthed properly it would be a miracle, said the midwives. Patsy bawled after me:

'Your mither howling blue murder and you're out sparkin' that Brandt bitch. What's she got that we haven't?'

'Ach, forget him,' said another. 'If she showed him an inch it'd drive him bloody topsy. Get on, ye randy little begger!'

At the bottom of the steps was the fulling basement, a place of steam and bubbling water; condensed water streamed down the walls, yellow slabs of fungus clad the ceiling.

Here worked the fullers who boiled the grease out of the wool before it was taken up to the ground floor for drying on tenterhooks, dyeing, willying and teasing.

High Doss, for all its dilapidation, was self-contained, its seven floors serving every process of woollen manufacture.

Robert Owen himself had organised this co-operative, paid money to institute it and more to old Sam Brandt to keep him away from its meagre profit margin. And the venture was working, my pa, Joe Wortley, told me; it was working so well that soon Doherty of the Combination up in Shipley would be down to organise a branch Union. The only fly in the ointment, said Joe, was Sam Brandt bringing in the new machine to do nap shearing: he was getting away with murder in his Ramsdyke mills, and if he brings in machines like this and links them to the mechanical water flow, it will be the end of High Doss.

Pity they can't invent a machine for having babies, said Gwen Wortley now, and she gripped the edge of the squatting labour tub till the knuckles cut white on her fingers.

'Jesus,' said she, 'it's a murderin' labour, is this one!'

'How ye doing, Mam?' I asked her.

Gwen looked up. Her eyes were puffed up and heavily shadowed in her tortured face. 'Where the hell you been till now?'

'Came as soon as I could, Mam.'

'Aye, that's it, isn't it?' She spoke North Country. 'Nobody bloody cares. Me husband's up in the attic talkin' murder with anarchists and you're prancing about the schoolroom with Sam Brandt's daughter. Jesus, Mary and Joseph, if this is childbirth you can have the next.'

'Sorry, Mam.'

I pitied her. Gwen was naked, but for some sacking thrown over her shoulders. Within sight of a hundred labourers she was sitting on the tub, sometimes obliterated by the wreathing steam of the fuller vats, while the fullers – men, women and children – naked to the waist, scurried about her, pausing only to plunge their stirrers into their concoctions of bubbling water, wool and grease. Weeping, Gwen sat, her slack breasts upon her bulging stomach, and as I knelt beside her she tried to cover herself with the sacking.

'Got a coney for you, Mam.'

'Sod you, Nick Farrer.'

'Don't call me that, Mam, I'm a Wortley like you.'

'No, you anna, you'm a Farrer, or you don't leave me to fend like this. Jesus Christ, Nick, look at me.'

'Sixth time lucky, Mam,' I said.

'I'd give me life to get me hands on your father.'

I held her, and she wept.

'Don't leave me with these heathens, will ye?'

'I won't leave you,' I replied.

Later, Gwen's pain subsided and she sat patiently while the fullers, their bodies streaming sweat, did their dance of the fulling vats: stirring and plunging the boilers, creaming off the wool grease, and bawling to Gwen as they began the Weavers' Chant:

Poverty, poverty, knock, me loom is saying it all day. Poverty, poverty knock – come on, Gwen, give it a go – gaffer's too skinny to pay . . .

Some were fat to obesity; most were skinny and gaunt of face, their drumstick limbs tenting their skeletal bodies. For this was a human mass production line devoted to the business of manufacturing skeletons: most of them moved wearily, their bones calcined by heat; the children drooped with the inherent maladies of poor constitution, born to hunger from hungry parents. Some, too, being new to the game, were full-busted and merry; young Amazons who had arrived without suffering the watered meal of the travelling workhouse carts that brought the starving of the south to learn the apprentice trades of wool in the north.

13

'Give it a bawl, Gwen!'

'Two out and start counting, eh? One for Joe Wortley and one for Sam Brandt?'

'Were it really old Joe? I didn't think he had it in him.'

Gwen's nakedness, I thought, was refined by her pain: also, it meant nothing to me; I had often seen her naked. Soon, I knew, her labour pains would quicken and there'd be women crowding around the tub; some on all fours, others hauling up pails of water from the vats and tearing up old petticoats for rags. Young wives, biting at their fingers, would group around the door, wondering at their lot: oh aye, if one woman birthed in High Doss, another fifty had it with her, a few actually holding their stomachs in pain. The labouring men didn't heed it at all; nowt to do wi' us lads. And then would come the cheeping scissors, the shrieks if the birth was a bad one . . . and then the first unearthly cry – girl or boy? Next the sweeting and cooing and 'Ain't he lovely?' for a baggy, blue-faced, inarticulate creature sent to High Doss to keep people awake.

'Bloody hell,' said Gwen, and drummed her heels upon the floor.

'That's my girl,' said the woman called Patsy. 'Give it a shove.' She stared up into a young girl's face. 'Ye see what I mean, kid? Keep your legs crossed.'

I feared this Patsy O'Hearne; she had a blemish on her face. Talk had it that she worked spare time in the beds of Bradford, and I resented her immorality in the face of Gwen's pain.

The sight of these women should have fashioned pity in me, yet all I knew was loathing. I could accept the endorsement of their poverty and exploitation, but not their animal docility: the filth of their homes, the state of their beds. Patsy herself slept single in High Doss, six beds down from me, and you could have grown potatoes in her straw palliasse. We had fleas and lice, but when other bugs arrived they took to Patsy first. I resented their acceptance more than anything: if only they would turn and fight the

14

endless succession of lodgers who invaded their lives; the lusts of their menfolk and the beatings they took with the fortitude of donkeys. The very book Ruth Brandt had given me – *A New View of Society* by Robert Owen – proclaimed the inadequacy of these High Doss women.

Now Gwen turned up her scarlet face to mine.

'Go now, Nick.'

'I want to stay with you, Mam.'

'Go! I canna have you here when they open me legs.'

Bending, I kissed her sweating face, and Gwen's eyes opened wide: she stared at me as if it were an assault, for I had never kissed her before. The fullers stopped work and stared in the silence; women about us moved their feet uncomfortably.

'Jesus,' Patsy cried suddenly. 'Ye'd think he were the father!'

Even Gwen laughed, and I thought: Not far from here is the Coney Wood and beyond the woods the harvest is stooked; I had seen Miss Brandt coming out of the Big Field last June and her arms were bare and brown with summer. A lark was singing and she was laughing at the sun.

At the door I turned to Patsy, and asked, 'Who's delivering her?' Patsy tightened the rope girdle at her waist. I added: 'It's not an exhibition – you keep them fellas off.'

'Dear me, listen to it!'

'Run along now, son,' said Gwen.

I pointed at Patsy. 'And you wash your hands before ye touch her, understand? You wash your hands or I'll be down to see to ye!'

Patsy stared, affronted, then cried, 'Did ye hear that? Sod off, will ye, you cheeky young booger!'

The Weavers' Chant started up again as I went up the cellar steps, diminishing into silence as I reached the ground floor:

Poverty, poverty knock, me loom's
a'saying it all day and night.

Poverty, poverty knock, knock, knock,
we'll give Old Brandt a fright.
Tuner should shackle me loom, but
he'd rather sit on his bum. For
he's far too busy a'courting our
Lizzie and I can't get the bugger to
come. So, poverty, poverty knock,
knock, knock, poverty, poverty
knock, knock, knock . . .

Vaguely, I wondered if Ruth Brandt would ever have a baby; would she sit on a labour tub and sweat and groan like Gwen? It was insufferable to accept that she might endure such pain and indignity; I once heard somebody say: 'White, black or yellow, in palace or in shanty, women know the dance of pain after the dance of life.'

Now, outside in the alley of the back I heard a woman scream; a single, piercing cry. Stopping, I listened and then heard Patsy's voice, 'That's right, Gwen, let it go. Mrs Hardacre over in Fenton had the bloody roof coming in.'

Another voice said, 'Aye, but ye know Ma Hardacre – easy births and strong in the vocal chords is her trouble, mind.'

Gwen screamed again.

I think I knew she was going to die.

And even as I listened I heard her give a sweet, sad sigh, like the ending of the day.

Chapter three

I knew where to find Joe Wortley, my adopted father, before Gwen told me he was up with the anarchists; it was the easiest thing in the world to find him on a Saturday night when ale was trickling out of the publics. Not that he drank a lot because he hadn't the money, but it was in the inns and publics that they made their plans for the woollen trade. This time, though, the meeting was in the High Doss attic. When I came in and put the book on the table, three men stared at me in the light of the lamp, and one was my father, who said:

'Where you been?'

'Down to see Mam.'

'O aye, I mostly forgot.'

'She don't, Pa, she's having the baby.'

It hurt him and was meant to. One of the two men said: 'How do, son?'

'How are you?' I dropped the rabbit at Joe's feet.

'Happen you been down Coney Wood again, eh?'

'Happen,' I replied, taking him off.

I owed a lot to Joe Wortley, but not just then: just then he should have been downstairs with his Gwen.

Joe said: 'Rolly Hill and Benno Oldroyd, Nick, come down from the Union up with Doherty's lot in Shipley –'

The man called Benno interjected: 'Tell him the truth, for Christ's sake, Joe. Ah don't rightly know what's happened to you lately.'

'He's frightened of getting his fingers broke,' I said.

'Is he now?' said the man Rolly: he was squat and fat with an inner obesity, more round the collar than Ruth Brandt was around the waist. His companion, Benno, wagged a scrubbing-brush face upon the body of a lath. He said, bending to me:

'Speakin' like that! If I was ye pa I'd be knocking me hands about you, my son.'

'What do you two want with us?'

The two men stared at me, and I added, 'Because one thing's sure, you ain't from Shipley,' and Joe Wortley said:

'Maybe not, son, but they spoke to the Huddersfield Combination before they come down, you know.'

'Did they now!'

'And the Huddersfield mob said that if we break Sam Brandt's machinery, it's all right with them.'

Joe trembled inside and out with pathetic frailty, and I pitied him. Yet I knew that the truly courageous human is the one who achieves his aim, though afraid.

Life had seized my adopted father by the hair, held him up to public ridicule and thumped his body into skin and bone. Yet, despite his nightmare visions of scaffolds and broken fingers Joe still retained a desperate desire to vindicate his heroic visions. Joe Wortley of the High Doss Wool Co-operative, selected by Robert Owen to lead the way in Bradford, would one day show the world of wool the meaning of co-operation.

I said quietly, 'No disrespect, Pa, but if you had any sense you'd send these two buggers back where they come from.'

Nobody reacted to this, so I added, 'Meanwhile, you ought to get downstairs to Mam, she's having a bad time.'

'After we've done up here,' said Joe.

'What's this old book about?' asked the fat man, and picked it up and flapped its pages.

I answered, 'It's Robert Owen's plan for a new form of society.'

'Who gave it to you?' asked Benno, the thin man.

'Miss Brandt, the school mistress.'

They regarded me with surly contempt. 'That's what we come down here about, really speaking. What's she to you?'

'His business,' said Joe.

'Ay ay, but ours directly, Wortley. Especially if he's

frame-breaking up in Shipley wi' the Combination lads. How old is she?'

'Knocking twenty-five.'

'And your lad aged fifteen? That ain't healthy. A Jew, isn't she?'

I asked, 'Weren't Jesus one?'

'Aye, but he weren't a mill-owner.'

Joe said wearily, 'Listen. Sam Brandt's an old sod and he takes all he can get off the workers, but the daughter's a different kettle o'fish. She gives bread, she teaches our kids, and she don't hold no brief for her old man. So let's get down to talking. If you break the Ramsdyke shearers down here, I'll find a gang to break for you up at Shipley, now come on!'

And Benno replied, 'We would if your lad weren't mixed up with the Brandts, Joe Wortley. If our Gaffer Ludd breaks down 'ere he won't be foolin' around, so your boy best keep his arse this side o' the Gentiles, for Gaffer's bound to know – nowt gets past him. I've seen him beetroot red at the sight of a Solly. Tell us what ye want of us.'

Joe said, and I saw he was trembling again, 'You see these hands?' and he spread them on the table. 'They've done every task in wool for thirty years, they have. They've sheared it, scoured it, oiled it, carded and spun: woven and weeted it with piss, stretched, teasled it and raised the nap – now listen. When I crop the nap, I do it wi' hand shearers, and I can crop close, down to a billiard table, my lads, and I been at it since Mary had a baby. But now Sam Brandt's bringing in mechanical shears on waterpower, and if he does that proper we're finished in High Doss.'

'So you want his shears broke?'

'Ay ay, like the Luddites did twenty year back.'

'And in return, you'll break for us up in Shipley, for we've got a bugger up there called Horseferry and he's ten times worse than fookin' Brandt.'

'You're on, mates,' said Joe. 'Me and my son and about four others, that right, Nick?'

I turned away. 'Count me out.'

'In the name of God, what's wrong with you?'

'I'm not breaking frames up in Shipley!'

'But that's the bargain, lad,' cried Joe, swinging me to face him. 'We break up there, the Combination breaks down here, that right, lads?' he appealed to Rolly and Benno.

'It isn't what Robert Owen goes for.' I picked up the book.

His anger flared. 'Sod Bob Owen. Where d'you think he is getting us? We're on our own for Owen's finished! Lad, listen to me. For the past hundred years, we've been breaking frames up north. Christ, we had to, for I can remember the time when kids of four were pieceners on the domestic system, with the slubbers beating 'em to keep them awake, and getting their brains knocked out wi' shuttles. Do ye want those times back? For the Brandts and Horseferrys will see ye get 'em.'

'I'm not breaking frames, Pa.'

Benno said, 'Jesus Christ, he's got it real bad with Sam Brandt's daughter, ain't he!'

Joe was shaking with an inner fury and he seized me by the shoulders, shouting in my face. 'This Co-operative were doing all right before Ramsdyke got the mechanicals, and unless we break them, son, the babbies will be starving come winter. It's sense, ain't it? We break up in Shipley, these lads break Brandt down here – nobody farts on his own doorstep. There's no risk, is there, boys?'

'None, if this snapper keeps his trap shut,' said Rolly, and he sweated ominously, wiping his red face with a rag.

'It anna so healthy, Joe Wortley,' added Benno, 'with your lad sparkin' the Jew girl. Prattling kids can give a lot away, ye know. Remember Danny Botley? He swung up at York through a whisperin' kid.'

I said, 'I'd not prattle, Pa, but I won't break frames neither, because decent men like Owen are against it. The last breaking was in '33 up in Barnsley, and if we start it again it'll be the end of High Doss.'

Joe said nothing, just when I expected renewed anger. Then, 'Mind, you're risking it, lads. Our Nick's right for all he's a lad. Tom Meadowdale had his fingers broke, for he told his missus so before they hanged him. And Rusty Evan the Welsh lad shouted before they dropped him, "They broke me fingers to make me tell, boys, just look at me hands," and he yelled with pain when the hangman tied him.' Joe shivered and put his hands under his armpits.

'Bloody hell,' whispered Rolly, 'you're a bright pair you are, an' no mistake. You're the same, son. No guts in ye, like your pa.'

'Broken fingers don't worry you if you're dead,' I answered. 'Me Pa's ill, can't you see? Get back to Huddersfield and tell them we'll manage, that we're not breaking frames, neither here nor up north.'

At the door, Benno said, 'Aye, we'll go now, but we'll be back when Joe Wortley's over his fears. Meanwhile, keep your tongue buttoned with that Brandt piece, or we'll have it out of your head.'

After the men had gone, I stood by the attic window and looked at the moon. Joe was ill; the fever had been coming on him for days, and I didn't know what to do for him. Soon somebody would come up from the basement and tell me about Gwen and the baby. When the baby came, it would cry all night and most new babies started up here in the attic, to save the off-shift keeping awake. So that's what I'd do, I thought. I'd go down to the dormitory and get the straw beds and settle the family up here for a spell.

Joe was on the floor at my feet. His bare feet were stuck up and blue with cold, and in his sudden fever he kept blowing on his fingers, holding them up like claws.

'You're all right, Pa,' I said, and took off my coat and put it over him. 'Our Gwen will be up here directly, and she'll see to you, she always knows what to do.'

After a while I sat on the floor beside him and held him in my arms, giving him the heat of my body.

Later, while Joe was sleeping, I lit the lamp and sat at the table reading Owen's *A New View of Society*. But now, with the book closed I stared through the attic window at the moon.

Seeing the moon with its embracing light, I thought of Africa where the trees grow upside down; of the sweltering deserts and the bare-back acrid stink of withered bushes and the mirage of stagnant pools. I thought of the ice-caps of a lunar world of snow and fire, the boiling springs of long-dead volcanoes and great eruptions within the core of the earth. Tiger's-eye and ivory glowed upon the camel trains of the old silk route of Kamazan; ornate, jewelled swords flashed amid the cries of innocents and blood. And there grew within me an urge to escape from High Doss into the enormity of a waiting world. Beyond these stinks was a flowering land; vital, resurgent, it beckoned in my veins. The sudden promise of the wilderness brought a sensuous beating of my pulse, and I rose and went to the window, standing within a self-made vacuum that snatched me up, suspending me in Time.

Faintly in the distance, labouring Bradford was beating its fists on the bowl of night like a caged bird seeking freedom: she glowed and shuddered on the cloud layer above the hills in vivid colours of light and shade. And beneath this glow, working in a metallic darkness of hammer and spike and loom and shuttle sat all humanity in the eye of my mind. Yes, and beyond the city – beyond that and still beyond – were the spluttering fuses and the thunderous detonations of the railway mania; the cascading earth that the navvies called muck; the roaring clatter of the great End-On, the track-laying method.

Brunel, Stephenson, Joseph Locke and Vignoles – these

were the magic names! And under them 10,000 laboured in a foul-mouthed and terrible comradeship, changing the contours of Britain. Vulgar, abusive, they blasted and shovelled and dug, lifting above their heads their giant earthworks, greater in bulk than the Pyramids. Later they dwarfed by their labour the enormity of the Great Wall of China.

And of the monuments to their genius one finger pointed in my mind, a finger within my reach which I could grasp – the great Sheffield to Manchester, the railway which, defying even Stephenson's science, was preparing to butt a path of steel under the Pennines. There was talk of this in the newspapers, men laid bets upon it in the publics: for had not the great man said that he would eat the first locomotive that showed its face out of such a tunnel? But this was the cone-charge of Vignoles' genius: he would sweep away every obstacle in his path by the labour of a selected few.

Tunnel tigers! That's what people called them!

Enclosed or confined places had always frightened me, but this call was greater than my fear and the name snatched me up; I stared out of the window to a land beyond the glow of Bradford. And I gripped my hands and said:

'Aye, all right. I'm coming . . .'

'What you say, son?' asked Joe weakly, looking up from the floor.

'Nothing, Pa. Sleep now, sleep . . .'

'Aye, you wait for me, man,' I said to Vignoles in my mind, and went down to the cellar to see how Gwen was getting on.

She died at half past ten that night.

Chapter four

Gwen had been buried six weeks and Joe was up and about on his feet again – in more ways than one, said Patsy O'Hearne.

'The fella's out and away again, Nick,' she cried. 'Don't tell me he's courtin' already!'

'Pa's business,' I answered, 'not yours.'

'But do you see the spite it brings to us women? With one scarce cold in her grave wi' her babbie, he's out for mounting another.'

'You leave my pa be!'

Hands on her hips, Patsy breasted up, pushing the other women aside. 'Or could it be that he's travellin' with the anarchists?'

Another said, 'Old Sam Brandt had a water-wheel broke night before last, you heard?'

'Not by me feyther,' I said. 'He weren't even here.'

A quiet woman said, 'Don't have to be, do he? The Combination breaks machines down here, Joe Wortley breaks 'em up in Shipley. That's the rules, ain't it?'

I didn't reply to them. Squatting on my palliasse I was sewing the tail of my shirt across the shoulders; time was my Gwen used to see to things like that.

'Shall I do that for ye, me lovely?' asked Patsy.

'I'll manage.'

'Eh now, hoity toity, eh? Come on, my charmer, shift you over,' and she pulled her skirts above her knees and squatted beside me like a roadside gipsy, but I hung on to the needle.

Give Patsy your shirt and next she'd have your trews off.

Summer was lost to us, booted over the hills by a scraggy old matron with a long red nose and an icicle, and her name was

Autumn. Peering around the hedges for folks in ragged clothes, she shrieked down the valleys like a child being mutilated, stinging our faces with needles of pain. And Joe Wortley, my pa, was still coming and going, meanwhile talking in his sleep beside me and blowing away the agony of his mittened fingers. Sometimes he would wake the whole of the dormitory, begging someone for pity on his broken hands . . . but still he went up north at the weekends, and other things began to break down here in Ramsdyke Mills, with Sam Brandt purple in the face with fury and special constables and the militia riding their stallions around the yards of High Doss.

I knew what was happening, of course, and the deception forbade me going to school to sit under the accusing eyes of Ruth Brandt: she was no fool, either.

'It's your feyther, ain't it?' said Old Soak accusingly. 'Come on, Wortley, make a clean breast of it!'

'It's no more me feyther than me!'

His Maria came then, breathing gin all over me. 'Sam Brandt'll have the lot of us because of him, you see!'

'He'll pull down High Doss over our heads,' cried Little Darby, who was four-foot-two.

And Plum Belly, the actor, oiled with Allsops, smoothed his brewer's goitre with slow, careful hands, saying, 'No good will come of your father's activities, mark my words, young lad.' While Billo and Belcher, hairy and immense, just looked and said nothing, but if High Doss closed down because of Joe, they would take it out on me.

'Sod you Wortleys,' said Patsy. 'The curse o' Mary's children be upon you if ye take the bread out of our mouths.'

All this I feared, but it was that last day of September that I feared the most.

It was dusk, I remember, and raining, but it did not just rain: it bucketed, it tub-washed, it sprayed torrents of water through the shattered roof of High Doss and set us all baling and mopping like survivors in a sinking boat. I was on my knees scooping up water around my bed-space when Dai Bando came.

Dai was look-sad and dozey and I reckoned he'd been at the opium again, for his Uncle Bobo had come back from the wars . . . he who ate opium to ease the pain of his shattered face, for a red-hot cannon-ball had winged him and he had no jaw. He were a terrifying sight was Uncle Bobo.

'You've got a visitor,' Dai whispered.

'I've got what?' I sat back on my heels, and he leaned his face on mine like a revolutionary with a bomb.

'Miss Brandt. Down in the yard, come after your body,' he whispered.

'Ach, go to hell!'

But Dai persisted. 'Down in the yard, I tell ye, lookee here . . .' and he held up a bright sixpence. ' "This is yours, Dai Bando," she said, "if you go and fetch Nick Wortley." '

'Jesus!'

'No, mun, it's you she's after. Go quick, the old girl's soakin'.'

Patsy sat back on her heels, too, I noticed, as I made my way out of the dormitory. The spawn of the Devil, was this one, and in some unaccountable way I knew that her destiny was linked with mine.

Ay ay, her destiny, mine and Dai Bando's – linked.

The Doss yard was being swept by the wind; its cobbles ankle deep in water and flying in sheets to the river. A pale, fractured moon stared sullenly into the face of Ruth Brandt; she was sheltering under a gable, her eyes bright, her cape flying about her shoulders.

'Follow me!' she cried.

Now, in the loneliness of the Big House library, I steamed in my soaked clothes amid a sea of vellum, gilt and scarlet binding; from floor to ceiling the chandeliered room was crammed with books.

'Sit down, Nicholas,' said Miss Brandt, entering.

She was wearing white; it was the first time I had seen her in white from head to foot, except in lusty dreams. Her hair was down and plaited over her shoulders; she looked like a young girl going to her lover.

'I'm soaked, ma'am.'

Behind me was a chaise longue of red and gold; the Persian carpet spread a widening stain under my bare feet.

'Then stand if you like. I have bad news for you, I fear. Your father has been taken somewhere up north.'

I did not reply. It was something I had been expecting.

'Arrested by the militia,' she added. 'You know what this means?'

'Yes, Miss Brandt.'

'It appears he was one of three men from High Doss; they have been breaking machines near Shipley. This is ridiculous, for the Luddites are dead and gone; there's no need for frame-breaking today. But there's worse than that, I fear.'

I raised my face to hers.

'A man has been killed.'

'Killed? Joe Wortley wouldn't kill no one, ma'am.'

'A Mr Horseferry, a friend of our family.'

'Couldn't have been me feyther, ma'am. Old Joe wouldn't hurt a fly.'

'Perhaps not, but he has been breaking, and in the process somebody has died. You know what will happen, don't you?'

I nodded. Despite the panic of my thoughts I knew an absolving sense of calm, and this was fashioned by her serenity and dignity. Never in my life was I likely to know again such dark beauty; it built a cherishing that was never to be lost to me. She spoke again, but I did not hear her. Then she said:

'It is amazing! You just don't appear to appreciate the seriousness of what has happened, Nicholas. Are you even listening to me? Your father will be hanged, but you are also involved, aren't you?'

I did not reply.

'Perhaps you haven't been breaking machines, but you are under suspicion of it. My father's new mechanical shearer was smashed last night . . .'

'Not by me.'

'But you know the people from Shipley who did it, don't you?'

'No.'

'The names Oldroyd and Hill mean nothing to you?'

'Yes.'

'You have met them?'

'When they come down here weeks back, ma'am, but I don't know about them breaking Ramsdyke shearers.'

'My father has three mills. How did you know the one at Ramsdyke was broken?'

No chance with her; too clever for me. Miss Brandt began to pace the room, floating from place to place for I could not see her feet.

She said, 'Nicholas, there isn't time for long explanations. If you don't leave High Doss at once, you'll be arrested. Your father has already talked; you have been mentioned. Look, take this money,' and she went to a sideboard, opened a drawer and took out five sovereigns.

There came to the room the silence of unspoken thoughts. The fact of Joe's arrest did not appal me – I had expected it, soon or later. The danger of my own situation did not concern me, either. I knew only that I was within the presence of one I loved. And the expression of gentleness in Ruth Brandt's face told of an unspoken bond between us. She said then, her voice low:

'You should not be in High Doss, Nicholas; you should not be in this stupid position. There is within you a great

28

potential. I don't know what it is, but it is there. You will continue with your studies?'

'Yes, Miss Brandt.'

'Your poems, too . . . Remember you told me about your poems?'

'They ain't nothing, ma'am.'

She said, 'How strange it is. You talk like all the others in High Doss, yet when you write it is as if another person is speaking. Did you write this poem?'

She took from the same drawer a scrap of paper that I recognised and held it before me.

'Ay ay.'

'You surely must have copied it from somewhere – come, be truthful.'

'Didn't copy it, ma'am,' I said, and she held the paper higher, and read: ' "Were you to leave me, I would not die or make grief a trumpet to shatter the sky . . ." ' She took a breath. 'Come, Nicholas! You copied it!'

I asked, 'Where did you find it?'

'In your exercise book, in your desk.'

'I got a lot more you can see if you like.'

'To whom did you write it? Binnie Tooley, perhaps? She's about your age.'

'Not Binnie Tooley, ma'am.'

'Who then?'

I returned her stare. Surprise was in her face, and something of compassion. She said, 'I'm ten years older than you, but it is near enough for me to remember the business of growing up. We all go through it, Nicholas . . .'

'Yes, ma'am.'

Miss Brandt moved indecisively; keen to make off somewhere if somebody hadn't taken her legs. She said, looking past me:

'You are gifted. I want you to promise me that you will continue to write – anything – little poems like this one, for instance. Read, read, read everything you can lay hands upon. And keep a diary, understand? This will force you to write something every day. You will do this?'

'Yes.'

At the door I said, 'Thanks for the money, Miss Brandt. One day we'll meet again, perhaps?'

She smiled brilliantly, her head on one side; her hands out to me.

'For sure . . . One day, Nick Wortley. Go now.'

I don't think she saw Patsy O'Hearne looking through the library window, but I did. You couldn't do anything without peepers in High Doss.

Chapter five

On the road to Glossop, I opened my eyes to the stars of morning: Orion the Warrior was flashing gold and silver, Venus making the Sign of the Cross. Down in a nearby valley, hidden by the gullies and gulches of a lunar land, cockerels were crowing in a spiked, evil chorus. Getting up, I brushed myself down, picked hayseed from my hair and looked about me. In threats of imminent downpours, great black clouds barged and shouldered their way across the caverns of the heavens, as if in haste to drown the earth.

In an abandoned shippen below me, a farm cart raised accusing arms at its rejection by humans; the pond beside it was slimed with green water; the rain puddles looked lifeless, as puddles do when they have been out all night.

I was about to leave the ruined barn by a rickety ladder when I saw a girl crawl from under the cart. Pulling off a ragged shift as she went past the cart, she tossed it on to the footboard; then with feet spread wide she stooped, cupped up the pond water and began to fling it over her face and body, and the dawn, breaking across the sky in a quick cut-throat redness, turned the water into droplets of blood. I watched. Presently the girl straightened and tossed back her hair, caught it with a professional flourish and tied it at the nape of her neck with string. I was standing at the foot of the ladder by now. Turning, the girl surveyed me. I judged her age to be fourteen – a year younger than me, which was the age of her body; but her eyes, slanted so high at the corners that I thought they were never coming down, made her into a woman.

'I thought I'd let ye know I was up there,' I called to her.

'*Arrah!* I knew ye were, fella! I saw you come in last night.'

Irish – her music was such I'd heard before.

She said, 'Now away wid ye while I finish me washing.'

Within ten seconds I was at home with her. In my dreams of childhood, I had shared her place with Mary's children; knew their hungers, the plaintive melodies of their chants, and the bawling of the babies they had sixteen to the dozen in the courts and cellars of Pontypridd. I used to take my uncle's bait tin down to him in Brown Lenox and often saw them there, stripped to the waist in the molten heat of the bungs, rodding out the ashes from the fire-boxes. But now the woman was down to her garters, and scarcely a glance she gave me as I wandered away, which was a waste indeed, for the dawn redness was now upon her body, and her hands moved in wetness, changing her from a white woman into a red one; her hair, down again, was blowing about her head.

As I saw her then so I will always remember her: an elf washing herself all over under a scarlet sky. Her lilt had reborn in me the windy acres of Connemara where my mother was bred. And one thing's sure: if you come across a spare rib that calls itself Irish, it's best to be Irish too. So I put my fists deep in my pockets when I saw she was dressed and came back to her with a cheeky Irish face and whistled to loosen my front teeth, and she said as I came up:

'Sure, you're all right, fella. You didn't look, because I watched ye.'

'No odds to that. I've got sisters back home and you've got nothing different.'

'Are you Irish?'

'Like the shamrock,' I lied.

'Are your sisters Irish, too?'

'Now wouldn't they be if they're me sisters?'

'What's your name, then?'

'Nick Farrer.'

She put a finger in her mouth and looked at the sky.

'Now there's a lovely music in that . . .'

'What's yours?'

'Abby Nothin,' said she. 'Where are you bound?'

'Woodhead tunnel on the Sheffield–Manchester. I'm tramping for a navvy.'

'Now, isn't that queer! I'm going there, too.'

If she was, it was a mighty strange coincidence, as I knew later. And while she wasn't a patch on the lovely Ruth Brandt, it was better than travelling alone.

Abby Nothin, I thought. What a name! It's amazing what a travelling fella turns up.

We walked and rested that day on the moors, and come evening the sky darkened and mist began to swirl in the peaks and valleys. The walking had been hot, but the Irish girl did not falter, and we promised ourselves that, come nightfall, we would be close to the town of Glossop, which was nine miles off Woodhead.

Boozies were outside the taverns of Glossop, mostly half-naked giants with muscled backs and thighs, parting their beards and tipping in ale without a swallow, with their little scrags of women whose beauty had gone hanging on their arms. And a floss-headed boiling joint of a woman in a pink Hungarian blouse was dancing on the cobbles to an Irish fiddle, showing enough of the Great Divide to straighten the Leaning Tower of Pisa.

Worn mules and horses, scarred by whips, trudged past us, head down in moody discontent: a fine big Shire stallion now, straining at a load ankle-deep in mud; now a dwarf handspringing beside us, pausing to beg in his rags, hollowed by hunger. And the locals, taken over by the navvies who were thrusting the railway through to Woodhead, sloped the alleys with a miserable acceptance of their fate, for everybody seemed in the family way, including the local vicar.

In a little quarry west of Hey Edge, we rested and watched in silence as the sun went down over the rim of a musical world, for blackbird and thrush, linnet and skylark had joined in a vast orchestral chorus. Some of these I answered, my hands cupped to my mouth, as I used to do back home in the woods of Ponty. And Abby Nothin listened and laughed; with her little hands clasped around her crab-apple knees, she flung back her head and laughed, and there grew within me a small sense of comradeship.

But because I didn't need so close a companion, I got up and left her.

'Where are ye off to, fella?'

'I'm answering a call of nature.'

The Sheffield-to-Manchester was already running to the south of the Woodhead reservoir and heading for the Pennines, and although it was funeral quiet on the newly built line, the Miller's Arms was crammed to the door with clients, for it was pay night, the end of the eight-week wait, and the navvies were hitting up the wallop for a randy.

I'd seen some outings among the shuttle-cockers back home when folks like Old Soak and Plum Belly got going, but never one like this.

Shoving a path through the coloured waistcoats of the navvies I got to the bar counter and hammered it for ale. The floss-headed barmaid smiled up.

'What's your pleasure, ye gorgeous thing?' she asked. 'Can Cushy Cuddlecome do anythin' for a fine set-up fella like you?' and I recognised the bouncing bosom we'd seen dancing in Glossop.

'A pint,' I said, 'and a little less old tongue with it.'

She leaned over the bar, made no eyes to speak of, and said, '*Diawch*, ye a marvellous creature. Hey, me big hairy fellas, there's a Taff from the mountains of home come in!'

As Welsh as a leek. God help us.

Nobody took any notice; few of the navvies heard her for a cock-fight was going on in one corner of the bar and a pair of terriers were at each other and handfuls of money were chinking and bets being laid, and you've never heard such a rowdy since they raised the Tower of Babel.

The barmaid yelled above the bedlam, 'Where you from, then?'

'Pontypridd.'

'What are ye doing in this God-forsaken place?'

'Travelling for a navvy.'

'Tunnel tigers?'

'Ay ay.'

'You need your brains cropped, lad. Six foot up and handsome, you should be kneeling on a hassock in a chapel back home. Who let you loose among this bloody lot?' She poured me a pint and I blew off the froth and I just got my teeth into it when a dance started on the floor behind me and the crush flattened me against the counter. Pewter in hand, I watched.

Three big navvies and their women began a Lancashire clog dance, arming each other around a little old bug of a man whose skin was as blue as a blackberry. In tatters, champing his toothless jaws, he put a farthing on the floor and danced upon it while the others circled him and clapped the time, and soon the watchers were clapping too, and an Irish fiddle ringing out an air, and the old man sang:

I've met a lot of women and liked 'em all a spell.
They drive some men to drinking and other men to Hell.
But I've never met her yet, the woman hot who can
learn a trick to dear Old Nick and a lusting navvy man.

And the crush of men around me bawled in chorus:

Roll her round, lads, pat her tum,
Wiggle your hips and waggle your bum.

Amid shrieks and hurrahs the dancing navvies wagged their rears, their women pulling up their skirts to show bare legs and garters.

The old man sang, and the entire place was clapping and singing with him now:

I don't go for the ladies grand or those of high degree.

A winsome wench who's willing is just the one for me.
I'll drink and whore where 'ere I can till life runs out its morta
   span,
The end of which is a roadside ditch for a Peto navvy man.

And the chorus roared:

So roll her round, lads, pat her tum,
Wiggle your hips and waggle your bum .

The chorus was repeated, battering off the walls of the taproom, with the women showing their drawers, and tin whistles and a melodeon going and somebody banging holes in a drum.

'Bloody hell,' I said, and tried to get into my pint, but a navvy barged into me and I spilled it down my front.

'Now you can see what you've come to, boyo?' shrieked the big Welsh barmaid. 'One thing's sure, mun, you'll never see the like in Pontypridd,' and she ducked under the counter and joined the dancing gnome in the middle of the navvies, and the pair of them kicked up their legs while the tempo quickened. She cried to him:

'Beware the Man in the Big Pew, Ezekiel. He had you once, remember!'

'Ay ay, and he'll have me again if I have my way!' He tried to get a hand down the front of her, but laughing, she pushed him away, crying as she danced, 'And round and round we go, me great big lovely fellas, round and round we go!'

You couldn't drink a pint in here, no chance, so I shouldered my way through the packed room and stood outside in the sweet, clean air of the peat-bogs. Somebody had chopped up the big harvest moon into stars and put them glowing in a lanterned sky, and for the first time since I'd left High Doss, I wondered what I'd set myself up for.

And for the first time, too, I thought about Joe, my adopted father, for whom all terrors would soon be realised:

machine-breaking had stopped since the Barnsley riots six years back. God help him now, and his comrades. They'd break more than their fingers. No so long back they broke six necks in a public execution up in the city of York.

And where, I wondered, was Ruth Brandt?

It seemed, standing there, that I was alone in the world for the first time since the workhouse cart had dropped me off years back in High Doss. But I wasn't alone, for the sound of a voice turned me; I heard it but faintly above the din of the revelry of the Miller's Arms taproom.

It was Abby Nothin.

'Where did you get to, for God's sake? Ye rotten damn rapscallion, you left me flat, so you did!'

'Yes,' I said to her. 'I don't need you, Abby Nothin, so get away – get on, get off.'

'But I need you, Nick Farrer,' said she, and her elfin face peered up. 'For I'm starving to drop me teeth out. Will ye give a penny to feed me?'

'Aw, Jesus,' I said, and pushed her along in front of me. 'Come on.'

Chapter six

A night-jar was shouting in the wreathing mists of Pikernaze Moor when I went in search of a rabbit, and within five minutes I found one, a big buck with his ears tuned high for stoats, so I didn't disappoint him. His ball eyes watched me with terrified intent in the moonlight as I walked around him in ever decreasing circles, and he stamped the ground to warn his doe and the young ones, but couldn't move an inch to run. Reaching him, I belted his ear and put him under my coat.

'Sorry, son.'

With the church clocks striking the hour of midnight on the wind from Glossop, the rabbit was skinned, gutted, skewered and roasting on a fire of twigs and peat; its soul rising to the heaven where all bucks go with nothing on their consciences. And saliva was lying on the mouth of Abby Nothin as she watched.

Later, when the moon pulled up her harvest skirts and shone her big round bottom over Pikernaze, I awoke because the girl beside me was shivering; so I rolled over and pulled her into the warmth of me, which is what we did in High Doss when winter was thumping into us – one body warming another. And I saw in a rift of Abby Nothin's hair the shine of distant stars, and knew that the life of High Doss was over and that life, for me, would never be the same.

I felt within me a greater sense of purpose, a confidence, an inner joy and a boundless expression greater than myself. As the chameleon sheds its skin, so I had shed the old Nick Farrer: as if my Irish mother was calling me from the grave, I felt vital, renewed. And at that moment I saw, with the girl's face now against mine, a hare watching us from distant gorse. And suddenly, as if beckoned by an unseen hand, a hawk dropped like a stone out of the moonlight and I heard the shriek of a taloned crucifixion; and saw in a waving of vetch grass, which is the hair of the bogs, the victim eaten alive in a fluttering of feathers as the hawk ripped and tore.

'For God's sake, Nick Farrer, what ails ye?' cried the girl, and leaped to her feet and gripped her hands, staring down at me.

'I . . . I had a dream . . .' I put my hands over my face, staggering up.

'Ye had a dream? Jesus Christ, man, you were screaming for murder!'

And I think I knew then that what I had dreamed was not a dream, but reality: that such a passing would be my fate when all were safe and dead, leaving me to suffer it.

'Are you ill?' She was trembling, her hands out to me in ragged supplication, and she made a soft lamenting sound.

I waved her to me. 'Come back to sleep.'

Dropping to her knees beside me, the girl said, 'As God's me judge, Nick Farrer, I thought it only the likes of me that comes dozey in the head when the moon shines full.'

'You can always tell the age of a female by her knees,' Joe Wortley had once said, when he was telling me the facts of life. 'Mark my words, young Nick. A milking woman can be as flat as a washboard above the waist, ye see, but you can still lend her out for wet-nursing, so it's not the size of the things that count . . .'

'Pa, go on with you!' I'd replied.

'Aye, but it's true, son,' he had continued. 'Splice a female under an unreasonable age, and you're in trouble wi' the law, for most of these have crab-apple knees, horrible little wrinklies. But if a female's knees are round and smooth, especially with a dimple, you ain't against the law. And if her lips are red and full and not hard and cracked come winter – specially if she's lost her big buck teeth – you're in. It's much the same with horses.'

And Gwen had shouted, 'You'm a dirty old begger, you are, Joe Wortley, talking to the lad that way.'

'No, I ain't, missus, I'm teaching him the facts of life,' and he'd added, 'Mind you, young 'un, there's other things as well of course, but I ain't seen one of those since a year last Sunday.'

The sun was up, bright and golden in the sky above Pikernaze now; and Abby Nothin was walking in front of me, with the hem of her ragged shift doing a curtsey against the back of her legs, so I hurried up a step and bent and took a look at her knees in the front, and it frightened me to death because they were crab apples: no smoothness, no dimples, just wrinkled little crab apples.

'What you lookin' at, Nick Farrer?'

We reached Cock-Foot Quarry when the sun was overhead and rested on the side of the Etherow River, whose steep banks, forsaken by the dry summer, shone in shoals of brilliance – the mother-of-pearl crustaceans of a million tragedies before the world was ice. Here we washed off the dust and sweat of the day side by side, and I knew again the intimacy of this girl's presence.

'What did you do before you took to the road?' I asked her.

'I was working for me Aunt Cassandra.'

'As a servant?'

Abby nodded. 'Aye, she ran a Bible agency in Manchester, but she couldn't get on with her parlourmaid, so she sent a letter to Connemara, and I left home.'

'So you came from Ireland to work in Manchester?'

'Yes, but I left after a month, for I couldn't get on with me Aunt Cassandra, neither.'

And she stretched out her bare legs on the riverbank and looked at me like a cat after cream, saying, 'She was a fair blossomy piece, me Aunty Cassandra, and she always wore white so she could walk like a queen with a crown on her head. When me mither was alive she lived with us in Cashel, till Tom Sparrow the game-keeper met her walking naked in the woods and playing on her violin, so Squire sent her to Manchester.'

'Where she opened the Bible agency?'

'But the trouble is it was no Bible agency, for me aunty used to dress herself up in finery and sit at the window of the bedroom tapping on the glass. And the fellas who came up the stairs for Bible lessons got more than they expected.'

A little wind moved and it was warm upon our faces and the dried-up river begged for the sweet benediction of rain.

'A bad house, was it?'

'Ach, it was no place for me, with me poor mither always warning me to stay clear of such wickedness.'

'So you left?'

'Aye, but not straight away, for Aunty had no cook, ye see. The last cook she had boiled her Christmas pudding in one of her old man's socks, so Aunty put the skids under her, which only left me. Ye can't leave a relative in dire distress now, can ye?'

'No,' I said. 'So you stayed for a bit?'

'I stayed for a month, but she never paid me. "Aunt Cassandra," I says to her, "I love you truly, but you canna expect me to stay alive on oats and bones and you eating three square meals a day," at which she got into a festivity of temper and said she wasn't earning enough to feed the two of us . . .'

I lay back on the grass and listened to her music, my eyes clenched blood-red under the sacred journeying of the sun, for the early October day was beautiful. 'Go on, go on,' I said.

'Ay ay, but it was so sad, you see, for though me aunty could have any man she pleases, it appears she don't please so many, and trade was dropping off.' Abby Nothin rolled up on an elbow and looked into my face. 'I ain't never going to get old, Nick Farrer. I'm going to cut me throat the moment I'm thirty.'

'Hurry up with the life story. So you left her?'

'Jesus, how can ye leave a body in such distress? "Just put on the mantelshelf the amount you think I'm worth," she says to her last client, and the fella left sixpence, which meant that the pair of us would starve to death. So I decided to take a hand in me aunty's affairs . . .'

This brought me up on an elbow as well, and Abby Nothin smiled at the sun, saying, 'So Cassandra went down to the kitchen in the basement while I dressed up in her finery, sat in the silk armchair by the bedroom window and tapped at the glass.'

'Good God!' I said.

'And the first one up the stairs was a great boast of a fella with a top hat and a cape and a coach-and-pair outside on the road, which meant we were going up in the world.'

'You didn't!' I said to her.

'I did, fella; what's more, I was passable good at it, for he left a golden guinea on the mantel and sent all his bosom friends, and within six weeks we were in the money.'

'So you became a prostitute!'

'Bless me soul to Hell!' she snapped. 'The Devil will never tug the tail o' your shirt, will he? It anna the first time the legs have saved the stomach, so don't look so saintly. Though me ma will beat the ass's reins off me when I get to Heaven, for following the wickedness of me Aunt Cassandra.'

I said, getting up, 'All that's fine and dandy, Abby Nothin, but it sounds like you enjoyed it.'

And she winked up at me from the grass. 'It's better 'n a winter sneeze, Nick Farrer. You ever done it?'

'No,' I said, fretful.

'Blessed are the pure in heart, my son, for the others don't know what they're missing. We're away now, are we?'

I nodded and she got to her feet and stood before me, smiling into my face and I knew the witchery in her, some of the wickedness, but also some of the humour, and she said, winking again, 'Are you sick and sore at Abby Nothin because she's a wanton? She's a nasty little bitch is that one, I expect you're thinking.'

'Likely so.'

Gathering up our bundles we started off again and did not talk for a while, being contained within our thoughts, then touching my hand, she said:

'Walking out with you, Nick Farrer, whatever you're called, is like tucking in the ends of a winter scarf. Don't think bad of me.'

'I'll do my best.'

Reaching the railway line to Manchester, we walked together along the bright new rails and knew that we were in Vignoles' country, the engineer who was butting a tunnel under the Pennines.

'Do you know anything about navvies?' asked Abby.

'Not much.'

'They're rough, tough chaps, and rowdy, and they'll land you a black eye as soon as look at ye, but they're comradely.'

I grunted.

She continued: 'And the pay's good. They'll put you on tippers for sure, and a tipper lad can get eight shillings a week and three bob oat-money for his horse. Are you sharp on your feet?'

'When there's wild women about.'

'You tip with the navvies, you got to be sharp, son, for if the horse don't get you, the wagon will, and the next thing you know you've only got one leg. But they train you easy till you get the hang of it. And there's a fortune to be made if you can raise a butty gang.'

'What's that?'

'A big hefty chap like you is all the rage with navvies. You've got brains too, and if you've got brains you can raise a butty gang. Raise ten men or so, give the cost of a bit of work and the big contractor will hire it out to you.'

'Sub-contracting?'

'Ay ay, like Edward Banks.'

'Who's he?'

Before us now was spreading the hand of desolation; the earth had been turned up as if by a vast explosion. Peat and rocks were jumbled into peaks of confused refuse, turning the wilderness into a pockmarked landscape, and we walked slower, picking our way towards the cone-charge of destruction – the end of the railway line.

Abby continued:

'Jesus, Mary and Joseph, everyone's heard of the great Ted Banks! He was hired out to a farmer with straw in his mouth – one-and-six a week. He left Scotland with two shillings saved and two shirts to his back, and one shirt he kept in his pocket. First he navvied on digging the canals, then he became a ganger with his butties, then a small contractor. You talk of Vignoles, but he's small kippers compared to old Ted Banks, for he built bridges, railways, station yards and tunnels. Now he lives in a castle, and the bugger couldn't even read or write.'

I stopped and looked at her. 'How did you get to know all this?'

'Because I've worked on the railways. I've been a skivvy in a hut since Jesus was a baby. I was born in a brat-cage on the Stockton-Darlington. My mither was a navvy skiv and me pa worked under the big Sir John Rennie down Sheerness way.'

I stared at her. 'Then what about this other yarn you told me – born and bred in Connemara and living with your family in the Irish town of Cashel?'

This stopped her dead and she scratched her ear, so I added: 'And all that yarn about a Bible agency and window-tapping to save the life of your Aunt Cassandra – was that all lies as well?'

'Aw sufferin' God!' Abby exclaimed, staring into my face. 'You'll be havin' a dull old life, me lad, if you believe every word folks tell ye!' and she sidled up to me.

I cried, 'You spin a fine old tale, but you look more like fourteen to me, just a kid.'

'A kid, did you say? I've got hair under me arms!' She was outraged.

'I had hair under me arms when I was twelve,' and I pointed a finger in her face. 'You're just a damned liar, Abby Nothin!'

'Ay ay, son, but it were a gorgeous Irish tale, you must admit, and you're a very beautiful fella maybe for fiddlin' with me garters.'

'You go to hell!'

'Wait for me, son!' she cried as I went off. 'Father deliver us, the man's really going . . .'

And although she was half a mile behind, I heard her voice above the beating heart of the railway, for the navvies were at it now and going like marrow-bones and cleavers on the shining railway line before me.

'Wait for me, Nick Farrer, wait for me . . .!'

Later, I heard she was over at Dunford, at the other end of the works, but I didn't see the going of her now.

I'd had enough of Abby Nothin to last me a lifetime.

Chapter seven

'Hi away there!' shouted Little Bert. 'Swing her, mun, swing her now, and *trip!*' and he shoved in the wooden sprag and the wagon wheels jammed with sparks flying. Racing alongside Betsy Mare, I saw the cross baulks coming up, swung up the hitch-pole and unshackled her, bawling, 'Up, up, up, Betsy!' and the old horse went right, I went left, Little Bert put the sprag in and the muck wagon hit the baulks with an almighty crash, rearing up, tipping and flinging out its load.

Were I to paint a son, I would make him like Little Bert, for his eyes were dark and filled with shadow; his hair was black and parted in the middle – a miniature man.

'Right!' called the ganger. 'Get that horse round and hitch us back.' I seized Betsy's bridle and, slipping and sliding in the clay, pulled her round and stationed her back where she'd come from, and Little Bert tied her to the wagon shackles and we levered it back on the line for the next load down.

'Well!' cried Little Bert, 'you're pretty good, for I only told you once. And lively, Gaffer, did ye see him hop?'

The ganger, silent and enormous, wiped sweat from his face with his rag. 'He'd better be, lest he does it on one leg.' And he gripped me as I went past him and hauled me back to him: he was six foot up and bearded black, and his yellow teeth rolled drunkenly in his muddy face. 'Who sent you in, lad?'

'Mr Purdon the engineer,' I replied.

'Did he now! You one of his relatives?'

'Come off the tramp, Gaffer. Asked for a start and Mr Purdon saw me and took me on.'

'Where you livin'?'

'Mr Purdon put me to Shant Five.'

'With Old Peg the skiv there?'

'He'll do all right with Old Peg, Gaff!' cried Little Bert, my spragger: he was bright-faced and quiffed and born in a brat-cage down Middleton way, or so he said. 'She feeds shant-men good.'

The ganger asked, 'You got tommy, son?'

I looked at Little Bert, who said, 'Grub, bait, food, he means.'

'No, sir.'

The man grunted with surly discontent; once he'd been a top ganger, Little Bert said, but the ale got him; he was a right good gaffer till he got outside a gallon o' Allsops, then God help ye. You stay on the right side o' this big sod, said Little Bert, or he'll kick your arse over the Pennines, never mind under 'em.

'What's your name?' asked the man.

'Nick.'

'Nick what?'

'Nick Taff,' I replied.

'What sort o' fookin' name's that, then?'

'It's all I got,' I said.

'And right for you, mister!' cried Little Bert, and the sun was on his face. 'I got no second name, neither!'

The ganger's eyes were steady on mine, and he said, 'Listen, Nick Taff, or whatever you calls yourself: if you're in Shant Five wi' Old Peg, you're in with a grasper, for she'll slide your dinners under the door. And I never knowed such a set o' nipple-suckin' toddlers as inhabit that place, for it's a two-storey layout and sports a brat-cage. It's got fleas and lice, and Cat Eating Scan who goes for kittens, and if ye don't get bitten to death, you'll get thumped to death.' He nodded, sober serious. 'You couldn't 'ave done worse – Purdon's a bastard wi' the new lads, and he's seeing to you special. You Welsh?'

'Aye, sir.'

'He do speak funny, don't he, Gaffer?' cried Little Bert.

'I wondered so for I heard the music, but I thought you might be Irish.'

'Welsh,' I repeated.

'Stay that way. If Cat-Eating Scan thinks you're Irish, he'll eat your sister-in-law.'

A whistle went down the line; an army of picks and shovels went shoulder high in a sudden orchestra of pips and squeaks. The big man turned away, and Little Bert said, gripping my arm: 'Blow up! Blow up!' and the shout echoed down the line of wagons. 'Here we go! That's us,' cried the boy. 'Shall I see ye over to your shant, Nick Taff?'

'I can manage.'

No escorts. I intended to start the way I was going on.

My body ached and I'd only started at the end of the day shift. Ten minutes of lessons from Little Bert and I'd become a trained tipper-lad, which was the way most young 'uns started, he explained.

Though the work was hard, the sense of it was easy, if you managed to stay in one piece. For the trick of it was to dump the wagon full of muck and fill up the hollows for the railway to go through: you had to run with the horse, break him into a trot while you did a gallop alongside the rails, hook his harness clear of the wagon at the last minute and let the five tons of earth upset itself into the hollows. If you didn't jump clear, you could end up under the horse – a lot of horses and tipper-lads were buried in the cemetery, short of a leg, said Little Bert.

'Horses buried in cemeteries?'

'You go under a wagon, mun, they can't tell horses from tipper-lads.'

'Jesus.'

'But you'll be fine and comfy with Old Peg. She'll act like she was your mother.'

She leered up as I entered Shant Five, this Old Peg, and I

wondered if Baal could spare her out of the pit of bones where he kept old hags: I'd seen Skin Crone dying in High Doss, and she looked the picture of health beside this one. Her drumstick limbs projected obscenely through her ragged dress: she was toothless, and her chin was held up by a filthy bandage tied on the top of her hairless head: give her a broom and she'd been round Manchester chimneys.

'What ye want?'

'Come for lodging, missus.'

'Have ye now? Who sent you?'

'Mr Purdon the engineer, missus.' I stood decently before her because she was old.

'Why didn't ye say?' It lifted her and she rose from a three-legged stool and swayed before me – nigh six foot up was she when she stood. I judged her to be seventy, but men told me she was only forty, a well-set-up woman with a family down Liverpool way, before her death by men.

'You got tommy for me to cook?' she asked.

I shook my head.

'Money?'

'Sixpence,' I lied.

'You got a ma?'

'One time.'

'What you doin' in this bloody place?'

'Sod me,' I said, 'you don't want to know something!'

It pleased her. Her faded eyes momentarily shone, and she gripped my shoulder with a taloned hand and led me to a cooking-bucket in the middle of the room.

From its simmering stew came ten strings, and Old Peg said, 'You see these strings, mun? This is Old Peg's cookin', see? For I'm the hut skiv and the fellas depend on me, understand? Lookee . . .' and she pulled at a string and half a rabbit emerged from the stew – one glazed eye staring at me through the steam. 'This is half a leveret and it belongs to Educated Ifan – he's an Irish who calls himself a Taff, for they don't like the Irish round here . . .' and she winked a bruised eye at me. 'And on the end o' this old string is a

49

peg with three notches on it. Look now, see what Tom Ostler's got – he's a right bastard is Tom Ostler, so you keep clear of him . . .' and she pulled up a bullock's heart out of the simmering mess. 'And on the end o' that string is Cat-Eater's sign – six notches on the peg.' Old Peg straightened. 'They're very particular gents when it comes to grub. Pull up a peg for the wrong chap and someone gets a head bashed in – me especial. Now then, you'll get no bait come supper unless you intend to eat. How does it?'

It was then that I noticed the thick leather belt around her waist with keys hanging on the end of it, and Old Peg saw me looking.

'While the men are out, I'll give ye a tour of inspection, for you're only a lad for all the size of ye. These are me ale keys for the barrel in the corner, see, and I got to wear them night and day lest they 'ave them off me and squeeze the barrel.' She peered up at me with her sad, rheumy eyes, and straightened to her full height. 'You understand, son?'

'Ay, ay, missus.'

She said, wiping her bruised eye. 'I likes you, lad, because you treats me respectful. So for tonight I feeds you free. What's your name?'

'Welsh Taff.'

'How old are you?'

'Sixteen,' I lied.

She stared past me through the door. 'Sixteen, eh? Jesus gentle, can you imagine that? Oh, and one last thing, for if you're Welsh like Educated Ifan you'll be a passionate chap. So if you fancy me in the middle of the night, fancy you've 'ad me, for I'm finished wi' all that caper now.'

'Yes, missus.'

'Being a well-set-up woman I'm pestered no end, and I'm only here for the cooking.'

'I understand.'

With that she left me and went to the door and I saw beyond her the navvies coming towards Shant Five for the ending of the shift, and Old Peg turned to me in the sun, and said:

'Mind you, you'd be shiftin' some to corner me for a few years back, when I were sixteen, too.'

'I can well imagine that,' I said.

'Can ye now? Ach, you sweet thing! God bless your heart, lad, I'll feed you like a dandy.'

Slide my dinners under the door, eh?

Mind you, I never did see the bottom of that bucket, and if you felt like a mess of mushrooms for breakfast, you reached out of your truckle bed and picked them off the floor.

Chapter eight

There were twelve navvies in Shant Five including me: there was Little Bert, Alf Posh, and Ezekiel, the blue-berry man I'd seen dancing in the Miller's Arms; there was Educated Ifan; Jake O'Hara, who was an ex-sailor – he shared his bait with me, for a navvy would always share his tommy with a mate. There was Tatty, Byron, Tom Ostler and Cat-Eating Scan who pulled kittens to pieces and I knew I'd have trouble with him; and there was Gaffer, the ganger of Shant Five whom I'd met coming in plus Dandy Dick who came later. I awoke next morning lying in the truckle bed beside Gaffer.

'Lie still,' said he, and I obeyed.

The shant was alive with activity, mainly from Old Peg who was racing around with the handle of a broom, threatening the sleepers, crying:

'Yo ho! Yo ho! Come on out, ye lazy set o' bastards, up!' And she brought the thing down on anything handy, shrieking: 'There's me been skinnin' me fingers since cock crow and you lot jumping beds wi' the trollops. Come on, come on!'

I made to move.

'Don't go,' said Gaffer.

'Out, out, out!' shrieked Peg. 'Out with ye and bum the tucker. There's a quart of ale and half a loaf for the first fella at the table!' Now she stood at the bottom of the truckle, the broom handle up. 'Come on, Gaffer, show a leg. Ain't it Old Peg's task to get ye up?'

But Gaffer only folded his hands behind his head, saying, 'Get em all out, woman, I want to talk to Welsh Taff.' And he shouted down to the bustling men: 'Scan, come here.'

Here was a man, half-ape: no more than five feet tall, he was as broad as he was long, his movements ponderous, drunk with strength; one eye was a red socket, the other burned in his high-boned hairy face; Asiatic. His moleskin trews were yorked at the knees, his navvy waistcoat, once scarlet velveteen, was caked with mud. Gaffer said:

'Get 'em going End-on. I'll be out directly.'

The man did not move; his single eye was fixed upon me.

'Christ, go on!' bawled Gaffer. 'Or Purdon will be about and you'll be down the road on the ticket!'

'I've got to go, too,' I said quietly. 'I need a slash.'

'Cross your legs,' said Gaffer.

Lying back on the bed I watched the activity. Nobody washed, and now I knew why I'd been scratching all night. Sullen, half asleep, men lounged on the floor or sat at the long board table served by forms, pushing handfuls of oatmeal bread into their mouths or tearing at the remains of last night's supper with their strong, white teeth, for most were young. And in their sullen silence the treble voice of Little Bert kept piping up as he ate excitedly, snatching at scraps thrown to him by the rest. Around them, filling their pots with ale or pulling the tops off her cottage loaves which she baked in an outside oven, Old Peg ministered to their needs like a guardian angel, being rewarded in gasps and grunts. She shouted at me:

'Remember, I want bait off you today or you don't eat, my son!'

'Leave him,' commanded Gaffer, and sat up on his bed. To me he said, 'There's a brook outside – you want to wash?'

'Aye.'

'Be sharp about it, I haven't got all day.'

Later, at the table, Gaffer said, 'Welsh Taff they call you, eh?'

I nodded, drinking the weak ale Peg had set me.

'No other name?'

I shook my head.

'Where you from?'

'My business.'

He drank, too, watching me over the mug. 'You learn fast. Last night I saw Purdon. He tells me you can read and write?'

I nodded again, and he said, tossing a paper on to the table before me, 'Read that,' and I read aloud from the paper:

'It is of importance that some daily record be kept of the institution under which all navigators are employed. Sooner or later an affiliation will be made with other apprenticeships. The repeal of the Combination laws of fifteen years back . . .'

The man nodded and took it from my hand. 'All right, all right. And if you can write as good as that ye can be of help to us.'

Rising, he went to his bed-space, pulled out a ledger and set it before me. 'This is a diary. You know what that is?'

'Aye.'

'Any fool can dig and shovel. You've seen a sample o' that this morning with this dirty batch. Jesus Christ!' Turning away, he ran his fingers through his mop-black hair. 'No brains, nothin'. Just work, ale, women. Sometimes I think there's no hope for us, that the Combination was born dead.' Swinging around I saw the sudden fire in his face. 'And you'll be as bad after a few months here. Have ye even heard of a Combination?'

'Yes.' I returned his glare.

'Then explain it. Six foot up don't mean brains. Most of this lot keep them in the arse.'

I said slowly, 'Are you talking of the Tolpuddle Martyrs? I know of them. And that's what they got for trying to form a Combination. My pa marched with the Consolidated Union protest on the day Cubitt locked out workers for not signing the pledge.'

He stared at me. 'God Almighty!'

'Aye, God Almighty. Back in cotton and wool we've been

hammering for a union of workers before you lot here knew where Tolpuddle was, and we've been stretchin' our necks up in York before ye thought of killing off tommy shops. You're not the only ones under the boot.'

Old Peg was listening at the door.

I said, quietly, 'We ain't alone, you know.'

'She only understands one word in ten. Who are you, for God's sake?'

'No odds to that, but I'll want to know more before I set myself to a diary in this fookin' place. Are ye done with me now?'

There was a long silence; the big man wandered the room. Then turning, he said from a distance, 'Christ in concrete, do ye believe in God?'

'Not much.'

He smiled and wiped his bearded face with the back of his hand. 'Like all the forsaken bloody radicals! Jesus!'

'I tell ye one thing, He ain't up in Bradford.'

'A revolutionary are ye?'

Now he was weighing me.

'No.'

'We can do without those sods.'

'Listen, Gaffer. I come for work, not politics.'

'You'll always have politics while you've got these conditions.'

'Ay ay, but I saw what happened to me feyther, so I'm leaving 'em to somebody else.'

'How old are you?'

'Sixteen, I told you,' I lied again.

'Where did you learn such talk?'

'Robert Owen.'

'*A New View of Society?*'

'Could be.' It surprised me.

He said, earnestly, 'We need you, son. We need young 'uns to help straighten out this God-forsaken country.'

I said, 'It's not forsaken. One day it will all be swept away. One day it will be different, like my pa said. But I don't come for talk, Gaffer. I come to be a tunnel man.

He said, grinning widely, 'You're on! Meanwhile, watch yourself on tipping lest you break a finger. I got you on ledgers.'

'Try that, Gaffer, and I'm off!'

His expression changed and he turned up his face. 'Jesus, gentle, you do drop 'em in the most unexpected places,' and he held out an arm to me and I stepped within it while Old Peg's eyes went big in her shattered face. And in this fashion, like father and son, we went through the shant door and down to the railway.

'Purdon told me you come in with a woman, that right?'

'Could be.'

'Ye don't give a lot away, do you? Are you always so clammed up?'

'Mainly,' I said.

Chapter nine

'Right you now, ye set o' scroungers!' cried Old Peg next breakfast. 'It was eggs for supper, every man jack, but all you got is bread again; the cocks 'ave got bad feet chasing after the hens. Hallo, me little Welsh fella.'

'You're a good old girl, Peg,' I said.

'Yours is the only hen on lay, me darlin',' and she rolled a duck egg out of her sack apron and put it on my plate.

'Hey, bugger you, missus!' cried Alf Posh. 'I paid for my egg. Why has he got one free?'

'Because I'm bigger than you,' I said, elbowing him away.

'Leave him be,' said Gaffer, sitting down at the table. 'He's got to have extra, being a growing lad.'

'He'll have extra one day,' said Cat-Eating Scan, and his evil eye glowed red at me across the rim of his mug.

I didn't mind him; no business of mine what went on under his hat, but I wouldn't have tried him for size; not one there fooled me, not even Gaffer, and he was six foot three. But Cat-Eater came different. We didn't like each other; he knew it, I knew it. I said, grinning at him over the table:

'Any time I come rough with you, Cats, you can run and tell your auntie.'

'I'll tell my auntie on you one day, ye little sod.'

He made sweeting noises at me across the table.

'Well done,' I said. 'Now do it with your mouth.'

'Why, you little bugger . . .!' He got up.

'Hold it!' said Gaffer, and I lent Cats a wink, poor old lad.

Educated Ifan said, coming in, 'One day, Welsh Taff, Cats'll bloody 'ave you.' He sat down beside me. 'He has been known to pull kittens to pieces, are you aware of that?'

'He can have a go.'

'Ach, dear me,' said Jake O'Hara, who came from Bantry. 'I'd rather be scratchin' a beggar's arse back home in the lovely land than quarrelling with each other in this fookin' place. What you say, Byron?'

And Byron, a club-footed, near-deaf-mute whose weasel face glowered under heavy brows, snapped at his bait tin like a dog at flies. Since I'd been in the shant he hadn't given me a look. Jake added, gulping down his ale, 'If anyone's coming to bits and pieces, it's me. When are we finishing this bloody End-on, Gaffer?'

'Tomorrow, lads,' Gaffer answered. 'I've sub-contracted out for an air shaft.'

'Into the hill?' I asked.

'Into the hill, from the top. An air shaft.'

'How much?' I asked.

'Purdon's signing for it, but it looks good.'

'What's it to do with thee, any road?' asked Tatty, who was Lancashire.

'He's in the butty gang and he's got a right,' said Gaffer. 'A pound a foot, says Mr Vignoles, and that's fair. Ye won't do better, none of you, on four shillings a day.'

'There's five air shafts coming,' said the little man called Ezekiel.

Someone said he'd been struck by lightning while fulfilling a normal function, but I didn't get the truth of this till later: it had had a profound effect on him, said Educated Ifan, for when thunder clouds were gathering, you wouldn't see Zeke for dust.

Gaffer said now: 'I tendered and got the first air shaft; a pound a foot, and a bonus for quick work.'

'We'll have to move some,' mentioned Tom Ostler, sucking at his clay.

I never saw Tom without that clay pipe, and down in Hell the baccy burns quicker, he used to say.

'When do we start?'

'Tomorrow. The End-on is just into the hill. And this will be some tunnel. With gangs digging – from Woodhead and Dunford – three miles under the hill will take a year in millstone grit.'

Three miles of tunnel through millstone grit. The longest in Britain to date.

Great is the ingenuity of man that he digs a hole through the belly of a mountain and goes in dark places where no eye has seen, that he can pick and shovel and blast with gunpowder and shake hands with his fellows in the bowels of the earth; grovelling in the light of flickering candles.

I shivered, and Cat-Eater saw me. 'Don't fancy it, eh? It goes one better than writing things in letters, don't it, Little Fan?'

I didn't reply. Not many things scare me, only the pressing, oppressive surroundings of blackness, the claustrophobic sensation of the totally enclosed space. Better the End-on, the galloping horse, the whining of wagon wheels and the orchestra of picks and shovels. I sweated inside, but nobody saw this. I fought the fear and drank my ale.

Educated Ifan said at nothing: 'Some folks don't like it, being underground. I knew a collier once; he worked the same stall with me da. Every time the cage went down he did it in his trews. In the end he went to see the district nurse. She fed him arrowroot, then he never went at all, poor sod. Her name were Menna Price.'

'Where was that?' asked Tom Ostler, blowing out smoke.

'Merthyr Vale.'

'Menna Mad, you mean,' said Alf Posh, smoothing down his hair with Macassar oil. 'I knew her. Big titty piece. She used to court my brother-in-law.'

'When do we start the air shaft, Gaffer?' I asked.

'This time next week, God willing.'

'Let's hope he is,' replied Ezekiel. 'I ain't done much good so far when it comes to God.'

'It's the weather I'm worried about, not God,' said Gaffer.

★

Let me be clear on this: the proposed tunnel under the Pennines was to be three miles and thirteen yards long; a single railway, standard gauge, from Woodhead Station to Dunford Bridge.

Gaffer said, quietly, 'That piece you come in with, Welsh Taff, didn't she finish up at Dunford?'

'Search me. She don't tell me her private business.'

'What was her name?'

'I don't remember,' I replied.

Yes, the Pennines in that area are solid millstone grit and a mile a year in that stuff is good going.

'Good going even for an engineer like Vignoles,' said Gaffer.

The night was hot, the shant stuffy with the stinks and dirt of soaked, dishevelled navvies, and Cat-Eating Scan was snoring for pounce thunder, with his boots cocked up and his belly swilling with ten pints of homebrew. Threepence a quart. 'I don't know where he puts it,' said Old Peg, and she locked and barred the Allsops and tied the key around her waist again lest someone got at it in the night.

The moonlight was blue and there was a nip of winter in the wind as Gaffer and I wandered. He said:

'Old Peg was all right when we worked the same shift, but she won't stand up to three-shift feeding, and that's what it means when we start the air shaft. End-on laying's one thing; vertical sinking is another. She's got to go.'

'Where to?'

'Workhouse in Glossop.'

'That ain't Christian, Gaffer.'

'She shouldn't be here at all, poor cow. That ain't Christian, either.'

'Eat or be eaten.'

'That's it, and that's why we're going to change things. She won't last the winter, any road. Give it till after Christmas and this bloody place will be the Arctic Circle. Do you realise that Vignoles will have four hundred navvies living out in the open in the middle of winter?'

He was right. Talk had it that Vignoles was after tents to shelter us, for the sleet came horizontally over Pikernaze during the winter gales, but Lord Wharncliffe, chairman of the Manchester Railway Company, said the shareholders couldn't afford them: so the gangers and gaffers spread the word that we would have to build shants. Our gaffer had done this. But now our butty gang was sinking an air shaft up on the hill above Woodhead Station, so we'd be sleeping up there in coffin holes, each man covered with a corrugated iron sheet.

'But it won't always be like this, lad. Things'll change when we get the Combination.'

'You and your bloody Combination!' I retorted.

His face was square and strong in that eerie light, 'It will, I'm tellin' ye, Taff, if every man does his bit. So if I catch it sinking air shafts, will you carry on the diary for me?'

'Aw, don't be daft!'

'No, I mean it. The new Union lads up north are waiting for it – six reports from six railway divisions, and Woodhead's one. I . . . I've made a will, ye see . . .'

'Ay ay! To me Aunty Nell I do leave the cow, to Uncle Ned I leave the back rent,' but his fingers were like steel on my arm.

'I got a queer feelin' about me, Welsh Taff. If I snuff it, will you carry on me diary? It's for the apprentice boys coming on, ain't it . . .?'

'All right, all right. The way you're going, you're six feet down.'

Later, Gaffer said, 'She's over at Dunford, you know . . .'

We were back at the door of the hut. Flo the Pig came out to greet us, smelled the cold and went back in. It wasn't that I minded sleeping with Flo, since your standards drop after you've slept with humans, but I didn't go much on her eighteen relatives.

61

I looked at Gaffer. 'Who you talking about?'

'That piece you came in with. She's working at the Dunford end. I just found out.'

'Ay ay? Am I her keeper?'

'Well, you young 'uns get around, don't ye?'

'What does that mean?'

Gaffer made a face at the moon. 'Well, with Old Peg leavin' we need a personal recommendation, don't we? And wi' lads like you hatching chaos in the bunks, we need a woman with all her working parts.'

'Don't tell me you've got that in the Union rules!'

'No, but things'll get worse up here before they get better, and the harder men work the more they chase the randy.'

'Go on.'

'So I've been thinkin'. You can buy a wife for a gallon of Allsops over at Dunford, or borrow one for the night for two quarts – that's the going rate. And they tell me there's a fella running a full-scale brothel at Dunford wi' girls coming in from Warrington – he's got a barn for it set up on George Hall's land by the Stanhope Arms. And so I thought . . .'

'That if we had our own woman with working parts, we'd keep the lads at home.'

'That's what I reasoned,' said Gaffer.

'The missionaries won't like it.'

'Sod the missionaries. They've got their own women – they don't go short on nothin'.'

'I thought you approved of God.'

'Aye, I do, but he's nowt to do wi' missionaries.' He rubbed his bristled chin. 'How old is she, that piece?'

'She says she's sixteen. Mind, she's got hair under her arms.'

'If she's got hair under her arms, she'll do for me,' said Gaffer, 'for that's the sign of the woman. First thing in the morning I'll get meself over to Dunford.'

Then he knelt by the truckle bed and fished out his diary;

laid it on the table before him and wrote in a slow, careful hand:

December 18th, 1839. Vignoles promised us tents but Lord Wharncliffe won't give the money. The men are soaked and shivering. If we don't dig for cover soon . . .

Later, I got into the truckle and hinged up beside him for warmth.

'See you in the morning, Gaffer,' I said.

And he interfered with me something terrible with his snores.

Chapter ten

And so, even before I'd got settled into navvy life, we left Shant Five and climbed the hill one squally Sunday morning and the twelve of us stood in the rain watching the surveyor and his staff man peg out the ten-foot-square shaft.

'What's the vertical?' asked Gaffer, his face turned from the storm.

'Four hundred and fifteen foot down through the hill.' He was a little ferret of a surveyor with a face like a spotted dick, but he knew his calculations. In the event he was wrong: when we hit the horizontal tunnel months later, he was three inches out.

The rain was storming now, soaking us; the wind was a wild thing trying to blow us over.

'Right, first we've got to make a shant for cover,' said Gaffer, so we began.

It took us four days to dig the grave up on the hill. It was twenty-eight foot long and sixteen wide; the wet sods we cut from the top we used to build up walls for the sides; the roof was of tree beams covered with schist which we manufactured from blown-up boulders, and it leaked like a sieve; the floor was made of earth beaten flat with cinders. You went up six steps to get to the door, which we built windward; there was a square window either side of the door for light. In the middle of the shant we made a Scotch stove fired by peat; after the smoke had blackened everything, it went out of a hole in the ceiling.

At each end of the shant were bunks to sleep six; in one corner was a double bed for the skiv plus entertainers. Educated Ifan, who knew of such things, knocked up a ten-foot chest of drawers; Little Bert, to our astonishment, made a decent table, for we'd left the other one behind. We had newspaper clippings from *British Workman* and cartoons from *Gospeller*, paintings of George Stephenson's new engines, hooks in the ceiling to hang our boots, hooks on the walls for our kit, those who had any.

We brought Old Peg's ale keg and bits and pieces, for she did herself well between hidings, being fond of objects under glass, like stuffed parrots and embalmed pets. She had a looking-glass hung on a peg for seeing to her black eyes, for there's nothing like a bit of belly pork to bring down a swelling, she used to say. She had a Japanese clock that didn't tell the time, and a five-gallon chamber-pot for going under the bed. 'Never repeats what he hears,' she used to say, 'Never mentions the little things he sees,' but Educated Ifan did:

'You have Old Peg on that chamber in the middle of a storm and you've got Handel's Water Music,' he reckoned.

Lastly, our prized possession: Tatty, who preferred his women from the waist up – 'You can keep their legs, mister' – hung his oil painting of a duck dying in a storm, which sent Alf Posh into tears after twenty pints of old and mild in George Hall's Casbar over at Dunford.

All things considered, we were a very happy community, but all work and no play makes Jake a dull boy, as Tom Ostler mentioned, and what was really needed in this happy little place was a lady with good working parts.

'I've already told ye, mates, I'm seeing to that,' said Gaffer.

We were a butty gang now. Counting Old Peg, we were thirteen, three over the odds, for a starting butty gang like us was usually only ten.

You had to have capital to start a Butty, and clearly, Gaffer had got this from the Combination: a gaffer starting small didn't need a lot of money, providing he had a good sub-contractor who'd advance him interim payments as the work proceeded. And old man Purdon wasn't so bad; certainly I've known worse when it came to fiddling the butties, or getting big cash advances from the engineer and then sloping off with the money.

Later, when Woodhead tunnel had been on the go for months – about the time Joseph Locke replaced Vignoles on the job – two main contractors were appointed to handle the tunnel: Tom Nicholson had the Dunford bore; Dick Hattersley handled Woodhead. But up to 1842, everything was worked on the small contractor system, and these split themselves down into butties.

Mind, they were professional boys, these small contractors. The really big men like Brassey and Peto, millionaires of their time, treated their navvies fair: often they called them comrades; knew them personally, saw to their ills and ate with their families. But that didn't apply at Woodhead the Slaughterhouse. Break a leg here and you'd wait two days for a doctor, for Mr Pomfret, our surgeon (we paid him twopence a week per man voluntarily) lived in Hollingworth, eight miles off.

He were a good old stick, this Henry Pomfret, and we liked him, but you could bleed to death with a leg off under the wagon or a smashed arm spurting under a ten-ton boulder before old Pomfret got on his horse. Like I heard young Toby Atkinson say when the rockfall pinned him, 'Chop it off, Sam, go on, chop the bugger off and haul me free.'

'I ain't chopping it orf, young 'un!' cried his ganger. 'Mr Pomfret's on his way, and for Christ's sake, do stop howling.'

'I'm howling for me mam, Ganger.'

He had a right, said Ezekiel, the poor little dab was only twelve.

In the end, they chopped his leg off above the knee.

'Upon my soul,' said the ganger, 'I never did hear such a bloody palaver. You gotta do better 'n that, young Atkinson, or Hattersley'll see you pensioned off.'

He did. In the middle of December, and Toby Atkinson waved to us on his way to Glossop on his home-made crutch. Later, I heard he was in Manchester workhouse, and that Dick Hattersley had sent him five pounds' compensation. He were a right good chap was Hattersley, a self-made man who started as a labourer on the Stockton–Darlington. Fellow feeling makes one kind, I suppose.

In his time he'd been a tipper-lad as well, the mean bastard.

Meanwhile, in terms of compassion, I was worried about Old Peg, for I knew she'd die of fright when Gaffer told her she was off down the road. But there was more to it than just being old: she were a dirty old faggot, was Old Peg, and cooking dirty, too. For who wants Cat-Eater's kittens in with the main stew? Such things don't appeal to normal people. Besides, she weren't tidy in other ways: you could skate to Manchester on her dishcloth, and I've seen her drying pots on her last month's drawers.

'What shall we call our sod hut now it's finished?' asked Dandy Dick, a new fella just come in.

'Just call it "Sod Hut",' suggested Tom Ostler. 'It's made of sods and bad sods live in it.'

'Call it "Ashes of Roses",' said Alf Posh, and he sniffed at Dandy Dick's armpits. 'You got scent on, mister? If so, you can cut that bloody caper.'

'What about "The Hermitage"?'

'Now, that's a good one!' cried Little Bert, enthusiastically. 'Come to think of it, we're all hermits, really speaking.' —

It met with general approval, but with the prospect of Abby Nothin's arrival, I wondered if it was timely.

Actually, Ezekiel was the one I couldn't make head or tail of. Blue as a blackberry and without a hair on his head, Zeke was a God-fearing chap who worked on the basis that nobody ever went to Hell on his knees. Now he flung his blue-veined hands upwards, crying:

'The dew of Heaven is falling among the cornstalks of

Woodhead. All the drunkards have been sobered at a stroke! A mighty Pentecostal wind is blowing over Pikernaze . . .!'

'For the love of God, will you give up?'

Years back old Zeke had got a milkmaid in a wheatfield. All legs and petticoats was she and calling for her ma when a storm blew up; and the lightning struck old Zeke in the middle of the back, turning him blue. He'd never been the same man since, said Alf Posh.

Some queer old people lived in The Hermitage, excluding me.

Chapter eleven

It was morning that Cat-Eating Scan went off the ale and sewed his mouth up for a week, which, according to Gaffer, he did when he ran out of cash. Like women have their ears pierced for earrings and black folks put rings through their noses, so Cats had special holes in his lips for sewing up his mouth. Of course he kept little places at the sides for poking in bits and pieces to keep him alive till he saved more beer money, but the only way he could sup ale was to sniff it up his nose. And that, said he, is no way to treat a brew like Allsops.

Naturally, I was all for this because it stopped him talking. And since old Cats ain't the soul of discretion, as Ifan mentioned, this was the right time to bring a new woman in.

'How do you intend to do it?' I asked Gaffer.

'Bust into Shant Fifteen over at Dunford and fetch her out.'

I said, 'Suppose the comrades in Shant Fifteen don't want to part with her? Good skivs are hard to come by.'

'Then that'll be too bad for the poor sods in Shant Fifteen,' said Tom Ostler.

'I still say you're making a mistake,' said I. 'Old Peg has her faults, but you catch Abby Nothin, Gaff, and you've got a tartar.'

'We tame lion-tamers in by 'ere,' said Alf Posh, 'never mind bloody tartars. Go and get her.'

There were several ways of getting a good skiv on Pikernaze when you paid the old one off.

You could kidnap a Glossop wife when her old man wasn't looking, but that always caused a palaver, with special constables poking under truckle beds looking for female underwear and distant relatives laying out navvies with knobkerrie sticks.

Another way was to snatch a skiv already employed in somebody else's hut: Old Peg, with tremendous pride, reckoned she'd been snatched five times. Or you could do it by direct confrontation: bust headlong into another shant, beat up the occupants, grab their skiv and drag her off in the middle of the night.

Lastly, it could be done by stealth while appealing to her better nature and the chance to improve herself. But for this particular method it needed a Romeo, said Gaffer, to turn Abby Nothin into a shanty Juliet.

So they sat, all of them, and looked in my direction. Nobody said anything; they just looked.

'Oh, no ye don't!' I cried.

Little Bert cried happily, 'She's your woman, ain't she, Welsh Taff? Go on, be a sport!'

'She isn't my woman!'

'You brought her in!'

'I did not. I was on my way here and stumbled into her . . .'

'You bet!'

Alf Posh said, his eyes closed, 'We've got to have her lads. I've seen her, and she's a right bit o' crackling.'

Then Gaffer rose and said with fine authority:

'While you was out, Welsh Taff, the butties 'ave been discussing the case. You're about this woman's age, you're the best-looking fella here, though that anna saying much. You've travelled with the lass already, so she trusts ye; and we'll only get violent if we can't get her legal – it's all in the Union rules, my son. Tonight you goes and fetches her.'

'God willing,' said Zeke.

'It's up to you,' added Tom Ostler. 'We gotta have a skiv now that Old Peg's left us and gone into the workhouse.'

She had . . . on the end of someone's boot.

Five air shafts were being dug on the hills in the three miles between Woodhead and Dunford, ours, The Hermitage, being the first.

According to intelligence reports, Abby Nothin was the skiv in Shant Fifteen, which had just been built near Grip Hill Slack above Dearden Moss, for the navvies at Shaft Five. And I was lazing on the truckle bed that I shared with Gaffer when people started coming and going with pails of water, towels and carbolic soap.

'What's happening?'

'You're having a bath,' said Gaffer.

'I am *not!*'

'Can we send you wooing in that bloody state? You stink to high heaven, mun!'

'What chance would ye have with a decent woman?'

'A dash of Macassar oil on your locks and Jennings' Flea Powder under your arms.'

'I could fancy you myself,' said Ifan.

They came at me from all sides, but there was a physical confrontation before they got me in the bath.

They held me down, stripped me naked and put me into the big tin bath, and the wind outside was howling with icicles: they scrubbed me raw with mops and brushes, hauled me out, dried me, and dressed me in new underwear bought special in Glossop. Grey flannel shirt, red stockings, and a set of real wool back-flap combs.

'Mind you,' cried Ezekiel, falsetto, 'you gotta watch Shant Fifteen, they tell me, for there's a two ton foreigner called Tabor lives in there – eighteen stones and a foot between the eyes, and he's right fond of this skiv, Abby Nothin.'

'Now you tell me,' said I.

Poofed up, powdered and light of step, I set out for Dunford and Abby Nothin when the moon was high.

Over the Round Hill I went to the second air shaft on the line of the tunnel. Here was a circle of shanties like ours at

The Hermitage, but more of them – at this height the dig was 600 feet.

The shanties squatted like toads ready to spring, their little square windows glinting as I passed. Melodeons and fiddles stirred the frosted air; a skiv was getting a hammering somewhere, for I heard the thumps and screams.

Drunk navvies beat their skivs because they were there; sober, they beat them for sport. Head bumps, cut eyes, split lips, black and blue all over, this was the lot of skivs in the age of heroism, as historians called it. Mostly ancient crones like Old Peg, of course; the young ones got out quick because they could run. Cat-Eater used to hammer Old Peg out of habit. And that was also in the Combination rules, apparently, for Gaffer used to sit smoking his gum-bucket and do nothing about it.

Stopping for breath on the upward climb, I saw behind me a yellow pulse on the clouds above Woodhead – the reflection of what was happening underground.

There, a man-made lance was being driven into the bowels of the mountain; the grass beneath my boots protested at the rape below. And the moon sat, plump and full after her heavy meal of summer, and watched.

Beasts writhed in cavern darkness; the virgin earth bellowed to the agony of the penis in her vitals.

'Bad cess to any fella working underground. The earth don't like it,' said Abby once, and I reckon she was right.

Now, remembering her, I patted myself for courage, for she was a tricky customer if you put one over her, with more suspicion than teeth. The great thing to remember when you're after a woman, of course, is not to appear too keen.

Now, I'm not a chapel bugger myself, but I've respect for those that are; and looking up at the stars I felt myself one with the great pavilions of the night where God was dozing on his couch after shift. For the thought was striking me that I could do with God just now, since there were six-foot navvies in Glossop town with boy soprano voices: walking proof that the comrades in Dunford were likely to take umbrage if you snatched their skivs; but also a living fact, if any is needed, that while we in Woodhead were cultured chaps, the navvies of Dunford were largely heathens and thieves.

Really, when one stopped to think of it, I was rescuing little Abby from a fate worse than death.

With this in mind I plodded on to Dunford.

The night shift on Shaft Five was going like the clappers, with the shaft itself some 100 feet down. A big horse gin they were working was swarming with carpenters and hempsters, this last being the device turned by horses for raising and lowering the muck buckets.

At least fifty pickmen and shovellers were labouring on the shaft itself, working back to back, so nobody got a pick up his private property.

They worked in silence, save for grunts, throwing the muck over their heads into carts. Later, like us, they would lay a narrow gauge for a quicker turn-round on railway wagons, and every navvy would be expected to fill seven or eight of these a day. This meant that the average idiot (we were then on fourteen bob a week) would lift twenty tons of earth a day.

I've seen men bleed from the nose, mouth and eyes. Dead at forty, alive at fifty if you were lucky. This was why we worked in silence, leaving the metal to make our music.

In the middle of this sweated labour burned a gigantic bonfire, shooting its sparks up into the sky, a drum-roll accompaniment to the symphony of picks and shovels . . . pips, squeaks, rasps and growls, like a big Welsh Orphean choir.

I stopped under cover, listening to the phenomenon, then strode on.

No more delay if I was snatching Abby Nothin.

It were different when I got near the Dunford shanties.

Here a little sea of tin roofs, wet with night mist, shone their sadness at the moon; phantom mists from pools of stagnant water writhed like bedsheets round crippled chimneys. And although the moon was full, it was as black as a witch's gown in Finger Silence Street.

A little wind kissed my face with wetness and I heard above it the sound of a man singing, and his voice was bass and pure.

Being Welsh, I listened, and this must have been my downfall:

I've navvied here in Dunford,
I've navvied down the south,
Without a drink to cheer me,
Nor crust to cross me mouth.
I fed when I were workin',
I starved when on the tramp;
A stone 'as been me pillow,
The silver moon my lamp . . .

And then burst forth such a racket I've never heard since Pru Knock-Twice in Ponty paid the rent with a shillelagh – mouth organs going and Irish fiddles screeching, I was so taken with this that I suppose I didn't see a curtain move over a Shant Fifteen window.

I peeped through this window and saw fifteen navvy occupants fast asleep, heard the snores coming up, saw the ale-mist rising. On tiptoe, I entered, and the second thing I saw as I crept into that hut was a half-open door and beyond it an iron bed, and on it the lovely sleeping face of little Abby Nothin, just like Sleeping Beauty.

Now, it's not every shant skiv who gets a corner to herself, partitioned off for privacy, nor a big double bed and a chair and table, with pictures on the wall, so I knew at once that they thought a lot of this particular skiv in Shant Fifteen, and that there'd be the devil to pay rent to before they parted with her.

On tiptoe, I crept along, nearly knocking over the bloody table as I gently closed her partition door.

Since we'd parted, the marvellous creature had grown into a woman, and the face of Abby Nothin that night, with the moon painting up her high-curved brows, would have brought delight to the heart of a eunuch.

'Abby . . .' I made myself whisper.

Nothing happened; and then she stirred in sleep and the moon faded upon her face, bringing us to blackness.

'Abby . . . *Abby Nothin* . . .!'

She was breathing like a woman embalmed, and I wondered if she was dead. Then, suddenly, without warning, she opened her eyes and stared, as people do within the vacuum of waking and sleep.

'Jesus, Mary and Joseph preserve us!' she exclaimed, sitting up, but I put a hand over her mouth and pressed her back on to the pillow.

'Nick Farrer! What are ye doin' here?' she whispered eyes switching.

'Ye darlin' thing,' I whispered back, 'from the moment ye went I've been starving to death for ye.'

She sat up, and her voice was low and disdainful. 'Starving, is it? Ye went off, you damned rapscallion, without the grace of a word, leaving me to fend!'

'Sure, and it was the greatest error of me life.'

'It will be if Tabor finds ye here. He's a big ape of a fella and he'll pull ye limb from limb. Did anyone see ye come in?'

I shook my head.

'What do ye want with us?'

She was pert now, her senses flowing, and she pulled up the neck of her nightie as if I was halfway down it.

I said, going Irish, with her small hands in mine, 'Abby Nothin, I treated you bad and you didn't deserve it. But if you come back with me to Woodhead I'll fuss you like a dandy; I'll work me hands to the bone for ye, I'll build you a kitchen fit for a queen, with coloured curtains in the bedroom, knitted shawls on the bed, and walk you in silk and finery.'

'Bless me soul to hell, is it marriage you're offerin', me darlin'?'

'Ay ay,' I replied, 'but not directly,' and she narrowed her eyes and looked at me in the moonlight.

'Dear me, ye sound like another bloody Irishman,' and she held my hands against her, adding, 'but there's a terrible longing in me for you, Nick Farrer, and I'd rather be a rag doll living the hungers with you than behave like an animal in this terrible place. There's sixteen heathen navvies in this hut. Do ye know what they expect of me, apart from the cookin' and cleanin' and washin' and mendin' and the hammerings I get every pay night?'

'You poor darlin', I can well imagine.'

Close to tears was she, the poor thing.

'I've been thinking of ending me life,' said she, 'and then the door opens, ye sweet soul, and you come in.'

'That's right,' I said.

I knew I'd got her now: it's all a question of honeying them up and playing the right cards. I added, 'So I came especial, to take ye back with me this very night, Abby Nothin, and I can give ye a roof in Shant Hermitage until the wedding celebrations. Will ye come?'

She clasped her hands together and whispered at the ceiling: 'God bless ye, love, I'll be ready directly. But I've been sick and sad for you these past months, so will ye not slip in between the blankets for a trial run? For I love ye to distraction.'

'A trial run? Here?'

'Ach, get the wickedness out of you, Nick Farrer! Just come in and hold me like you did on the moors that lovely time when we first met – remember? I don't mean nothin' more.'

76

'Suppose someone comes in?'

'Ach, no! They're off shift, mun, and dead to the world, so they are,' and she pouted her lips for kissing and opened her arms to me.

I said, reluctant, for it was a three-mile slog back to Woodhead and coming up for dawn.

'I'm not clad decent for sleeping out, ye know. All I've got under here is me back-flap combs.'

This put her double, with two hands stopping her giggles.

'Ach, your combs will do fine, lad – when we marry I'll see ye wearing less. Arrah, me lovely little fella! Come on in with Abby?'

And she opened up two white arms.

I might have known.

You learn the important things in life too late.

For the moment I was beside her in the bed, she flung those arms right around me neck and yelled at the top of her voice:

'Tabor! *Tabor!* There's a fella in here tryin' to wrong me, and he's got me in the bed!'

Good God!

Levering her off, I was out of that bed in a single bound; snatched my boots and trews off the floor and flew through the door like something scalded.

And I went through the mud of Finger Silence Street bare-foot in my combinations, with Tabor the ape-man and a dozen navvies after me, and every time the flap in my combs blew up somebody landed me one in the arse that shot me along that street like a bloody rocket, and I didn't stop until I reached the road to Woodhead.

Chapter twelve

All that winter we sweated in Shaft Five, doing the skivvying ourselves for our luck was out to find a wench of reasonable proportions. All we seemed to collect were the rags and bones, poor old relics from the bins of Glossop; lift their skirts and you'd find birds' nests.

But it wasn't only the miss of having a female in the shant, although a lot can be said for the sight of a woman when a man awakes on a winter's morning. It was the choring and skivvying, the washing and mending, and there weren't anyone to thump when the call was on you, said Cats.

It was a vicious winter on Woodhead that year, coughing and sneezing like a black old sow, with wild nights blowing the Arctic gales and the hunchback trees of Pikernaze hammered double.

Your hands would freeze to the shovel in the air shaft; the only warm place was in the bucket down the hole, for we'd reached a hundred feet by now.

Then one night there arrived a plump, hardy wench from Sheffield. It was a wet bitch of a night, I remember, and every dog in Woodhead was howling when she came; but we howled that much louder in our shant before she left us: her name was Bess and she did nothing but eat and laze around with her boots cocked up, a gum-bucket in her mouth, and a bust full of erotic emotions, so we gave her a bob and sent her down the road. The woman went out and the bugs came in for warmth, little black buggers that fed hard on blood; under your arms, between your legs, fighting the fleas who considered us their property.

Men go to pieces when there's no woman around. Maybe she's a broken fiddle or someone's grandma, but she's a woman, and she's there.

A lot of the old girls in the tiger shants were decent people, turned out by their men for younger pieces. And, as the shants went up and the contractors took on more navvies, so the trickle of women into the Woodhead shants changed to a flood as the word went around the towns.

'Supply and demand,' said Educated Ifan.

The superintendent reckoned that wife-lending and wife-selling never happened, but it did. He wouldn't have it that they'd got a Casbar over at Dunford where you could buy a woman for a quart of ale, but it happened because I saw it when I went to Dunford again looking for Abby Nothin.

It was as if she had disappeared off the face of the earth.

Just having her in mind was worth it; just thinking that one day she might turn up was a consolation, like having an extra set of false teeth in the coffin.

'She'll come one day, don't you fret,' I used to say.

'Not while you're around,' said Dandy Dick.

'Especially while I'm around.'

Strange – she turned up when we least expected it.

Meanwhile, spring booted wailing winter out of it and the Pikernaze moor changed her colours with the speed of a chameleon. The old currant bun came up red and raging. Warm winds blew forgiveness from the south. The rock buttresses, once icy to the touch, became hot water bottles for the backs of resting navvies, and a girl called April came dancing over the moors on dandelion feet. In pity for the louse-ridden, flea-bitten navvies she came; we were reborn, alive.

But she had no pity left for Gaffer who was killed that month.

'I've never known a man go so difficult,' said Ezekiel, 'and I've seen some good men die.'

If this is the spring that killed my Gaffer, give me bloody winter.

★

Things were to change a lot in the tunnel between 1839 and four years later. Vignoles, the first engineer, would be replaced by Joseph Locke, a man to be compared with Brunel and Stephenson. And it was Locke who changed the system of small contractors like us in butty gangs. But, come or go, we still had Purdon over us, and that's what mattered to us in the butty gang now.

'All the time we've got Mr Purdon,' Gaffer used to say, 'we've got the butty system. Don't you worry, he'll see us through.'

He did, by God.

For my part I never went a lot on Purdon. Folks said he was a site engineer that Hattersley couldn't do without but God knows why Gaffer approved of him. True, he'd been good to me, had Purdon; he had taken me on, but that was only because I could read and write. Perhaps Purdon was something to do with the coming Combination, but I never got the truth of it, for he broke every rule in the Combination book.

Later, when the accident rate at Woodhead became ferocious, it was Purdon they blamed for the rise in deaths.

'But that ain't Mr. Purdon's fault,' Gaffer used to say, 'that's financial. You want to blame somebody, blame Lord Wharncliffe, him and his shareholders.'

Maybe, maybe not; but a lot of the blame I put on Purdon, and a lot more than that I put on the navvies themselves.

Like Snicker Donkey over at Dunford: a clever dick was he, for he used to smoke his pipe on an open barrel of gunpowder. Or take Bill Bloap at the tunnel entrance over at Edgehill: he used to undercut – that is, hack away with pick and shovel to get an earth 'lift', as we call it – burrow like a mole and hope the muck stays firm. Well, it didn't for Bill Bloap. Fifteen tons fell on him and his bowels shot out of his body.

That was on the Liverpool-and-Manchester, way back in '27, of course, but thousands of muck-shifters had been killed that way since then.

Aye, engineers like Purdon might have killed a lot of us, but we killed so many ourselves they called it mass suicide. Bravado chaps, trying to make an impression: 'Leave it to me, my son, it'll be all right.' Drunken men, men who had worked too long; old men who should have been off the job and took short cuts; young men who were trying to prove something. These were the folks who killed us.

Mark me, there were other things as well, like sunstroke, smallpox, cholera (we had this in plenty at Woodhead), consumption and the runs, which was why we kept back-flaps in our trews. And the missionaries who came in on horseback, these Holy Joes who promised us everlasting fire because we worked on Sundays. They took a toll as well.

But nothing took such a toll in me as the time when Gaffer died.

Few liked Mr Purdon: women ran from him, sharp objects fell from the sky when he was around.

Squat, hairy Purdon now bent his cane over his stomach with kid-gloved hands.

'What's happening down here?' he asked.

'Got this old boulder, sir,' said Gaffer, and all four of us – Purdon, Gaffer, Tom Ostler and me – stared at it in the light of the helmet candles. We were all in the bucket; above us, the shaft shot up to a pin-point of blue, the sky, the chain snaking up to the winding gin above. It was like standing in the barrel of the longest gun on earth.

'Get rid of it, then,' said Purdon.

Gaffer said, 'It'll need digging out.'

'No it won't, ye fool – blast it.'

'It's soft here,' I said. 'The sides will come in.'

'Who are you, then?' Purdon peered at me.

'Welsh Taff, sir,' said Gaffer. 'The lad who can read – you took him on, remember?'

'Are you the gaffer of this butty, then?' Purdon asked me. I shook my head.

'Then speak when you're spoken to, or I'll send you down the road.' And he tapped the boulder with his cane again. 'Blast it out,' he said.

Purdon went up in the bucket to the top. Gaffer sent Alf Posh down to the tigers at Woodhead to say he was blasting, and he, Tom and me went back down in the bucket with fuse, gunpowder and drills. I said, when we sat the bucket on the boulder, 'I reckon this is going to shake things up down in the tunnel.'

'That's right,' said Tom. 'I say split it gentle and haul it out; or it'll make one hell of a hole.'

'Jesus,' said Gaffer, 'you're worse than bloody Purdon. Of course I'm going to split it.'

'It's tricky, mind,' added Tom, who was our shot-firer.

'That's why I'm doing it myself,' said Gaffer. 'You two get back up.'

You never argued with him, so Tom left his drill, iron rammer and powder keg on the boulder, and he and I went back up top in the bucket.

At mid-day we were waiting up there with our snap, in the sun. The ground trembled beneath us and a finger of smoke and dirt shot skyward out of the shaft like a bullet out of a gun.

Tom and I went back down in the bucket, and we found Gaffer sitting on the boulder with blood on his mouth. Two red sockets had replaced his eyes and the iron shaft of the rammer, flying out of the borehole like an arrow, had pinned him through the stomach against the air shaft wall.

'Jesus Christ,' I said.

'Is he dead?' whispered Tom.

'Not at all,' said Gaffer.

He lowered his head upon his chest and said, and his

voice was firm and strong: 'Nick, lad, keep the diary. For the Combination boys, eh? The Miners' Association, remember?'

'Yes.'

'Somebody up there will read it. Doherty? Owen? I forget, but keep the diary, son, and everything under my bed.'

I wept.

'Christ, none o' that,' said Tom Ostler. And he tried to pull the rammer out but it stuck firm, and Gaffer said, raising his socketed eyes:

'Leave it, Tom, leave it. But don't bury me down here – take me up?' And he died.

I held him.

'Bloody hell, don't take on,' said Tom Ostler. 'Pull this old rammer out and let's get him up.'

Tom Ostler was whistling as the bucket took us up; with Gaffer in my arms and his blood on my face and hands, I realised the futility of life.

'Gaffer's stopped it,' said Tom, as the bucket reached the top.

'Ain't you got a soul?' I asked him, for he just kept on whistling.

'Jesus, no,' said Tom Ostler. 'I'm a canal man, I've seen hundreds die.'

'He's still got his head on,' cried Alf Posh. 'Come on, lad, stop the bloody snivelling.'

When we got back to the shant I went to Gaffer's bed-space and found the diary.

The trouble was I couldn't stop crying.

'You're still only a boy, really speaking, b'aint you?' said Ezekiel.

'He's a fookin' nance, that's what he is,' said Cat-Eating Scan. 'The fella's dead, ain't he? He ain't a workhouse fragment, is he? What more do ye want?'

Chapter thirteen

Hope, who makes an unhappy bedfellow but a good breakfast, was up and about next morning, and we put Gaffer down with solemnity.

Sporting black favours, the whole of Woodhead downed tools and walked in procession to the station. Here we put Gaffer on a wagon flat, laid out proper and clean, said Alf Posh, which is more than happened to Willie Wedlock, poor sod, when he caught it on the barrow runs of the Great Western Railway.

'We raffled him,' announced Posh.

'Ye what?' asked Randy Dick. Quiffed up and polished was he, his face shining with soap, boots to shave in, a starched collar to cut his throat and a favour in his buttonhole big enough to bury him. Most of the time Dandy's feathers stayed in the three-ball pop, but he fetched them out for weddings and funerals.

'I told ye, we raffled him,' said Posh. 'Two hundred of us bought tickets at a tanner a time. I was treasurer and it landed me with five quid for a randy. Down Southampton way, it was, and we didn't have a leg between us at Yo Ho!'

'How about the poor bugger who won him?'

'He were all right, for he put Willie in cold storage. "Give him a fortnight and he'll walk out on his own!" he told the constable who came following his nose.'

'What happened?'

'The parish took him over. I mean, ye can't have stiffs lyin' around in a civilised community, and the parish priest played Hamlet. He never got paid for the service, but the organisers had a marvellous booze-up on the draw.'

'I don't believe it. I think ye made that up,' said Abby from the door.

84

'Stone the crows,' whispered Dandy. 'Who's she?'

Abby Nothin it was, standing there in a ragged pink dress with frills and foibles, hair down her back and an expression on her face to bring a sigh to Satan.

As one door closes, another one opens, my mam used to say back home in Ponty. Gaffer goes down – Abby turns up.

Ezekiel, being old, just looked, his jaw dropping. Educated Ifan, who was stirring the bait bucket, raised his bowler. Cat-Eater, smoking his clay, cleared his throat and spat, which was the nearest he got to intelligent expression. Tom Ostler whistled. Tatty never got lower than the fine swell of her bosom, and I stood up.

The child had turned into a woman.

'What do you want?' I asked.

She dimpled at me and put her finger in her mouth and I knew that we were bound for trouble.

'Now, isn't it a question of what *you* want, me big hairy darlings? For it's all over the county that you're after a skiv.'

'Take my word for it,' said Jake O'Hara, leaping up. 'I'll hit hell out of anyone insultin' her. Have ye a name, my lovely colleen?'

'Ye can call me lover if you're referring to me,' replied Abby. 'Would it be Connemara you hail from, sonny?'

They was words coming out of the past: called by my mam to a passing collier; on her knees at our front door was she, scrubbing her white half circle into an uncaring world. And the thought raked me from my sullen disinterest into one of regard, awaking within me a new respect for the girl before me, and something of affection.

I said, 'Come on, come on, what brings you, Abby?'

'Mainly the economics of the belly, for the madmen over at Dunford started coming free with me, and while I don't mind a couple, I draw the line at sixteen.' She looked around the shant. 'Is it clean in here?'

'It will be,' cried Jake O'Hara. 'Sure, I'll build ye a hide-away in the corner over there and scrub me fingers to the bone for ye.'

'You'll not be bothered in the nights,' I said.

'Is the tommy good?' she asked, starting to bargain.

'You'd have ye stint sharp on pay day.'

'Right on the nail,' said Dandy Dick.

'Like Resurrection Day,' added Ezekiel.

Abby wandered about, picking things up and slapping them down. 'Aye, well it seems you're needing a woman around, for the only clean thing in here is the pig,' and she put her boot behind old Flo who'd come wandering in with her new litter, and she sent her out squealing. 'That beggar's out for a start. Have ye lice?'

'Armies.'

She shivered, holding herself. 'Dear me, you're a dirty set of savages, aren't ye!'

'How much?' asked Cat-Eater, returning to the economics.

'Ten bob a week every eight weeks on pay day.'

I nodded agreement, and she added, 'A wall partition in that corner,' and she pointed. 'A bed wi' a hair mattress new from Glossop, a table and a chair, and no interference with me personal property. Me ha'penny belongs to me.'

We looked at her, and she added. 'Which means I sleeps alone, and no peeping Toms.'

'Dear God!' said Tom Ostler. 'A Glossop virgin.'

'She's not!' ejaculated Jake O'Hara. 'She's a little Irish darlin', aren't ye!'

Byron, of the club foot, sat unspeaking, but his dark eyes were brooding a small, malevolent lust. Trouble would come if we took this beauty on.

Little Bert came in then with gusto, not realising we had a visitor, and skidding to a stop with firewood under his arm, he surveyed the apparition.

'Mornin', ma'am,' and he tore off his cap and screwed it

against him, skirts always making an impression upon his adolescence.

'That makes twelve, doesn't it?' asked Abby, looking past him.

'Thirteen, including you,' I said.

'You the gaffer here, then?'

'He anna the gaffer really,' said someone, 'but he holds the money – we buried our gaffer this morning.'

'So I heard,' said Abby. 'That's why I'm here.'

I never got to the bottom of that remark, but I knew one thing: Gaffer used to have a remarkable interest in George Hall's land and the Wilson Casbar over at Dunford.

That night, with Abby Nothin asleep behind a temporary blanket in her selected corner, I pulled out Gaffer's diary from under the truckle, put it on my knee and wrote my first entry:

April 10th, 1840: This morning we buried Gaffer, the keeper of this diary. My name is Welsh Taff, and I'm carrying on with it, which is what he asked. He left me £30 twelve shillings which is Sick Club money, and this is my receipt for it. Nobody wants the job of gang butty, so I'm taking it on. After Gaffer's funeral we took on a new skiv and her name is Abby Nothin. She were done up in Sunday savageries, and now she wears a pink dress and a flouncy hat like the ladies in Manchester.

Nothing in Woodhead was ever idyllic; when the testament of Man's labour is written on the scrolls of his inhumanity, the tunnel under the Pennines will stand at the head of the queue. But, having Abby Nothin around for the next two years lifted our spirits in Shant Five and made life bearable. Just having a woman for the next two summers and winters made all the difference, for the tommy was good and the companionship improved; the comradeship, of course, was always there. And she was a skiv and a half was Abby: the lice took to their feet, the fleas hopped, skipped and jumped with her after them with Glossop flea-powder. And we had to stand in line morning and night while she dusted it under our arms and other such places.

Meanwhile, she patched and sewed and mended: in winter she dried our clothes, soaked from the tunnel, on a fire guard around a great Scotch stove she bought from Manchester; in summer her washing flapped on the line outside for all the other skivs to see, and these took hammerings because they weren't up to Abby. She even nursed us when we went down with feverish colds; she could tie up a graze and tourniquet a bad cut as good as any nurse.

And I'll say another thing for her, the woman could cook – and house-proud? – listen to this.

She pulled down the rags we called curtains and put up army blankets dyed scarlet; the mice and rats ran for their lives when she brought in a big tabby tom cat she called Persian. Fair's fair, I told them in the shant – she's the best thing to come our way over the past two years, and with our air shaft now poised to break through into the tunnel below – we were about to meet the tunnel tigers coming through from Woodhead – then for a bonus, said Lord Wharncliffe – a sovereign a man on the day the first air shaft breaks through.

'I'll believe that when I get it,' mentioned Cat Eater.

'Ay ay,' added Tom Ostler. 'Like we asked for a woman with working parts, but I anna seen none yet. The tommy's fine, but all this scrubbin' and cleanin' anna good for the health, my ma used to say.'

'No offence intended,' said Alf Posh, 'but things ain't been the same since you took over, Skiv. Time was we could bring women in, but now it ain't allowed.'

'In many ways, things ain't what they used to be,' said Dandy Dick.

'That's because for the first time in your life you're living civilised,' said Abby Nothin, flouncing off.

'It's a crying waste, you know,' complained Tom Ostler.

'In the old canal days, if you got a woman wi' working parts she shared 'em around.'

'Aye,' replied Alf Posh, 'and there's more to a woman than lookin' – there's cookin'. Ye can't have it all ways.'

'All the girls 'ave got it and all the girls hang on to it,' said Little Bert, glum. 'Just look at me eye,' and he held it up to the light and it was black and blue and sparking.

'Who handed ye that?' I asked.

'Cushy Cuddlecome, the barmaid down at Miller's Arms.'

'Ay ay,' said Abby, coming back in, 'I heard about that: make the same suggestion to me and I'll land you with one to match it.'

So we were as pure as the driven snow in Shant Five. You could walk a mile around Woodhead and never find a shant to compare with us: a gathering of virgins, monks and nuns; hard graft, hard lying, long hours and piety; all we lacked was oil for our lamps. And she drove us nutty, me in particular, for Abby Nothin was suddenly, unaccountably, at peace with herself; and she was suddenly, unaccountably, beautiful. The goose had turned into a swan and I was in love with her. Head over heels in love – me. And when she knelt to scrub the floor of our shant, her breasts capered and cavorted under her chemise like a pair of Green Apple Toms.

'Ought to be locked up,' said Cat-Eating Scan.

Chapter fourteen

Summer was into us again, full and splendid, and Pikernaze put on her brightest clothes for the thousand navvies now labouring on her breast.

They were days of bee-hum and streaming sweat, with the sun beating down on the backs of Pharaoh's slaves, and Purdon and another six like him out with whips. Rumour had it that the Manchester Railway Company, right in the middle of the second railway mania, was going bust; that Lord Wharncliffe had threatened to shoot himself and the shareholders had threatened to shoot Lord Wharncliffe.

On, on, *on!* From 'yo-ho' to 'blow-up' the pace was increased. No less than fourteen separate gangs were tunnelling horizontally. All over the country it was the same, a fizzy-fuzzing of labour.

From the time Victoria ascended the throne to the year she was twenty-one, the London–Birmingham and half the Great Western Railway had been built. And in the decade from 1830, nearly two thousand miles of track had been put down, with cuttings carved from solid rock and valleys filled with earth embankments; viaducts were constructed of massive arches, tunnels like ours lanced through towering mountains.

Six years after that, Britain boasted five thousand miles of railway line – five thousand miles painted scarlet with blood, smashed limbs and amputations, blindness by gunpowder and death by its fumes: eyes were put out, empty sleeves and trousers tied with string.

Men died under galloping horses, under wheels of lumbering wagons; they were crushed beneath a million tons of muck; they died under the soaring viaducts, in the stagnant pools beside the lines, to make this heritage.

They died slowly by poisoning: coughing up their lungs with consumption; from pneumonia in their thousands; from bronchitis (we called it 'brownchitis') – a fifth died because of their lungs. Name it and we died of it, including the pox, cancer through knocks, heart failure through strain, Bright's disease, non-stop bleeding, typhoid, scarlet fever and diphtheria through the damp; cholera through bad drainage and drinking burial-ground water.

Mass graves followed big accidents. Out on the windswept moors, discharged or sick navvies, with no place to shelter in winter, wandered soaked and starving; these died of exposure. Nipper Tandy, aged fifteen, was roasted alive one Sunday morning, when a wagon of hot ash buried him. Nobody officially wanted to know; the contractor sent five pounds to his mam in compensation.

Most died with their mates around them, which was the way we always wanted to go, but Little Bert died alone. Most left the name of a relative and someone who could write would drop a line, such as: 'Sorry to tell you that your Aldie passed on,' or 'Like as not your Harry's in Heaven about now. Yours faithfully . . .' But nobody wrote a letter for Little Bert, for he'd come down, like me, in a workhouse cart.

Alf Posh said I should have written to the master at Sheffield workhouse where the lad was born, but I said it was daft to send condolences to the master of a workhouse, and anyway, the one in Sheffield was a notable sod. 'Fook him,' growled Cat-Eating Scan – he had a soft spot for young Bert – 'we're his mates, so we'll take care of him. Fook 'em all, includin' you, Alf Posh.'

'I were only suggestin', mind,' protested Posh.

'Well, don't suggest. Just shut your gob.'

The shant was at odds with itself when our Little Bert died, and Abby Nothin wept.

'We'd best go and fetch him in then, hadn't we?'

'Fetch what?'

'Fetch what's left of Little Bert.'

'There's nothing left to fetch,' I said. 'The charge went off and he evaporated.'

With the five air shafts over the hill completed, all gangs were digging horizontal like mad things in the Woodhead-to-Dunford tunnel, so when we were through the millstone grit we'd link the cities of Manchester and Sheffield. This would allow the tie-and-collar beggars to ride through on scarlet with their office cases under their arms; gentry ladies with summer hats and parasols to wave lace handkerchiefs at the butty gangs along the line.

Sunday-outing chairmen of the boards would travel in state, their top hats polished with Guinness, and beery stockholders, their noses polished with gin. The rich and elegant, the puffed-up aristocrats, the squireen gentry who proliferated around these particular parts – people like Wharncliffe who didn't give a sod how many men died boring his fookin' tunnel as long as the shareholders were paid.

Ay ay, and people like Brunel as well, for if it comes to a comparison, give me Peto or Brassey – they can keep their bloody Isambard. Put him on a ship and send him to Portugal. When told in later years that 150 navvies were in hospital with serious injuries after nine months working on the Great Western Railway, he said the number was small.

I say it again – when it comes to death and disaster, give me Brassey who comes on the job, and eats with his men, not a walking calculation who spends his time at a drawing board.

In terms of carnage, our tunnel at Woodhead was a front-runner, and will be long after the railway mania is over and forgotten. Perhaps men will one day fly in the sky as easily as they sail the seas, but if that day comes and we dispense with railways, we will remember Woodhead as the biggest peace time charnel house of the lot.

That night I wrote in the diary:

June 10th, 1842: Today we lost a nipper lad. We called him Little
Bert. Purdon keeps shortening the fuses to save working time and
somebody forgot the warning bugle. Nothing to bury. No
relatives. He was a workhouse lad, aged fourteen. Our skiv
gathered flowers and put them in the middle of the shant, and old
Zeke, our God-botherer, said a prayer.

'I'll kill that Purdon for killing our Bert,' said Cat-Eater.
    'Let's pray he dies of cerebral palsy,' said Ifan.

Before we got into the truckles that night, out comes Abby
with the keys of the ale barrel in her hand.
    'I reckon we'd better have a drink on the soul o' Little
Bert,' said she, her face still wet with tears.
    'Go on, missus,' said Cat-Eater. 'Don't be daft.'
    'That's a Christian idea,' said Jake. 'Who's on the splice?'
    'We'll take it out of the kitty,' said I.
    'Fine and dandy,' and Abby stood in the middle of us and
held up her hand for silence, saying, 'I laid his place at table
just the same, see? For I do reckon that although he ain't
here to take his bait, he's here in spirit, understand?'
    This was a shivering thing to say, for navvies are scared of
weirdies and hobgoblins, but we sat at table in our combs
and drank Allsops out of the kitty, and after two quarts
apiece we were glad that Little Bert had passed on so that we
could have this particular randy. And we fell to discussing
the virtues of the little chap, and the games he had at Zeke's
expense . . .
    'What happened?' said Dandy, he being on shift over at
Dunford at the time, and Abby said:
    'Well, old Zeke had come in from the pugs, and done up
proper, remember? And he fetched in a big rooster he'd
stolen off Shant Nine down near Salter's Brook –
remember, Zeke?'
    Ezekiel answered, 'I didn' steal it, I acquired it.'

'Go on, go on,' said Dandy, urgent.

Abby continued: 'So I was featherin' and guttin' the rooster for the bucket, and I'd taken out the innards and put 'em on the table, including the neck, and in comes Little Bert and sees the rooster's neck lying on the table.'

Lifting her pot she drank deep, wiping her mouth. 'And there's old Zeke with his chin on his chest and snoring for a grampus, out to the wide, so Little Bert unbuttons Zeke's flies, puts in the rooster's neck and slips away sharp.'

We hammered the table; we filled up the pots; it was a night for a randy now Little Bert had gone. Abby was rocking at the table and I was seeing two of her.

'Ach, come on, missus, tell us, tell us!' cried Dandy.

'Well,' said she, spluttering, 'there was me preparing the rooster and there was Ezekiel with the neck sticking out of his trews, when in comes Flo Pig, takes one look, and snatches at Zeke's flies. "Good God!" I yells. "Flo's got Zeke's cock," and I fell over backwards and hit me head on the table, and the bucket went over and raised the shant.

'And there was Flo Pig going like the clappers with Zeke's cock in her mouth and Zeke on the floor, his boots waving her goodbye.

' "What's happened, woman?" he cried. "She's got your cock," I yells. "She's got what?" and there he is peering into his flies. "Bloody hell!" says he, "She has an' all," and he went at a gallop after Flo Pig, with her squealing to wake the dead of Glossop, and half the neighbours in the air shaft after her with billhooks and choppers!'

And while Abby told the tale, I looked at her. She was better than a man for telling a yarn, with her little hands expressing it before her face. Seeing me looking at her, her smile faded, as a woman's does when she knows she is wanted. There grew within me again that magic affinity. The laughter at the table died and the others knew the secret that had been born between us.

That night, which was the day that Little Bert died, I got up from the truckle bed and went to the door of the room where Abby slept. And found her wide awake as me, with her eyes wide open and her hair like a black wreath on her pillow.

For many seconds I stood there. Neither of us spoke: to have spoken would have broken the bond between us. And I think I knew at that moment that soon, perhaps even before the winter, I would jump her over a broom with me and take her as my woman.

I went outside, I remember. The stars were winking at me from the black vault of Heaven. Then I went back to my bed and dreamed – but not of Abby Nothin.

I dreamed of Ruth Brandt, which was very strange behaviour.

Chapter fifteen

September 9th, 1843: A navvy on the travelling newspaper came in today and told us the latest news.

Romeo Antic, a spragger on the Eaton barrow runs, lay drunk over the line and the shunt cut him in half. Dan Yoke and his twin, Dai Double, were washed away in Dover, and sunstroke killed Cheshire Gorge down at Bath. Cholera has come to Blisworth on the Up-and-Down, and six died there so far, through drinking burial ground water which the clergy said was good enough for savages. Cholera has come here, too. Sam Fourpence went first, withering like a dry stick with his feet on the back of his head; it scared the tunnel gang no end. That's ten we have put down this month alone. Nobody cares. I asked the ticket navvy if he had ever heard of a Union, and he said no chance, lest Jesus gives us a hand. 'The clergy, you mean?' I asked him, but he didn't know what they had to do with Jesus. Abby Nothin and me are marrying tomorrow, Jesus willing.

There's a little field of corn set like a golden sovereign in the purple moors just below Grains Moss. One shift a month I spent up there, doing odd things like lying on my back listening to the skylarks, or filling up the diary like Gaffer would have wanted. And I sometimes thought, lying there, of all the lovers who have lain in this same place; of how many kisses have been taken and given beside the brook called Black Grough. Men of swords and clubs have waited here; women in the skins of beasts and the purple robes of migrants who longed for love like me.

War and lovely bare-footed sunsets such ancient people have known. They, too, drank of summers, dreaming of fierce Italian sunlight. And when the sap rose and brought the pain of emptiness, I would sometimes turn my face away and think of Ruth; and the thinking sharpened my desires as a knife is sharpened within the loins.

Shame was an edifice that arose before me then, that I had happened upon such thoughts. For this was the path of the adolescent, I told myself; the man must grasp control. Yet the pain poured on; the hotness of it was in me and I knew of a sense beyond myself that was life and death entwined, a suffocation by ecstasy, and conscience wagged a bony finger in my face. With hands gripping the corn, I lay immersed in gold.

Crows were discussing September. Kingfishers, sweeping over Black Grough, were bragging about the colours of the willows, on the day that Abby came, wearing her pink dress. She stood at my feet, smiling down, inflated by Nature to exactly the right proportions. God help her if she'd arrived ten minutes earlier.

'Good afternoon,' I said.

'Dear God, hark at hoity-toity!'

'Sit down by 'ere,' I said, patting the ground.

'Down by there?' asked she, mimicking my valley Welsh, 'I'm not that daft. Besides . . .' and she made a young girl's face, 'I'll be creasin' up me foine pink dress.'

'Then take it off, there's nobody about,' and I folded my hands behind my head, for you can't do a lot until you get them horizontal.

'I'll bother you to moderate your suggestions,' said she.

This was her charm: she swept along from bawd to lady.

Through the crooked, clandestine years I remembered Ruth, and Abby said, 'If I come down there, Welsh Taff, ye'll sow me six childer, and I anna ready for the midwife.'

I sat up. 'Things have changed, haven't they? What about the Tabor fella and the butties in Shant Fifteen?'

'Jeez! I wouldn't touch them with ten-foot barge poles!'

'That isn't what you said before!'

'That's because I didn't love ye before.'

'You mean you want me?'

The sun came out of hiding to help me, bowing between us.

'Why do ye think I've come?' asked Abby. 'The moon will be standing on his ear before I'm done with you, Nick Farrer. Shift over.'

We didn't get back till dark, which speaks for itself, and when we reached the shant, the first one I saw was Cat-Eating Scan sitting cross-legged before the cooking bucket, sucking the bones of something tasty.

'What you got there?' asked Abby. 'I've come back to cook the supper, ye bloody comedian, didn't I tell you?' but Cat-Eater didn't stop to hear more, he was off. And Abby dropped to her knees and picked up the cat's skin lying on the floor.

'Jesus, Mary and Joseph! Just look what he's done!' and she howled at the ceiling. 'He's eaten me bloody Persian!'

'Dear me, so he has,' I said, and this enraged her. Leaping up, she brought her fist down on my head and belaboured me with everything handy, then ran down the shant overturning truckles and kicking everything movable, and she shrieked:

'D'you think I'm settling in this filthy place? For you're villains, every man jack of ye. Glory be to the saints of God, he's eaten me lovely Persian!' and she opened her arms and came down the room to me howling like a child, and I held her while she wept.

'I'm sorry in my heart for what's happened, girl,' I said, 'and I'd walk the roads with blood on me feet if you give me the chance to make it up to you.'

'Christ, ye change your mood with the change of the moon! Do you mean it?'

'By this time tomorrow I'll have turned you into two,' and I took her into my arms and kissed her.

Well, we didn't marry on the morrow, nor the day after, nor

the day after that, for Abby was striding around giving everybody hell because of Cat-Eating Scan's defection. 'You've got to admit it was a terrible temptation, for I ain't never seen such a lovely meal on legs,' said Educated Ifan.

But on the fourth day after the murder, with Cat-Eater still absent from home, Abby got up early, heated a pail of water on the Scotch oven and hauled it into her private corner. There, with Dandy Dick and Tatty peeping through holes in the partition, she stripped off down to nakedness, according to reports, washed with scented soap and lathered up her hair like nothing's been seen before, and combed and curled it special. When she came out, she looked like the Princess Gloria.

'Tomorrow I'm marrying Nick Farrer,' she announced to the room.

There was a whoop of joy, a single discordant shout, and you couldn't see people for dust. When they had gone, I held Abby in my arms.

'I'll treat you respectful,' I said to her. 'I'll earn for you and give you shares and I'll never be a sadness to you, Abby Nothin.'

'Will ye buy me another cat, lover?'

'Yes.'

'And hit hell out o' that savage when he crawls back?'

'You can dance on his grave,' I said.

Chapter sixteen

And so, in the middle of September, with the rooks shouting their heads off in the elms of Glossop, I married Abby Nothin and took her to my heart; I was eighteen, she was seventeen, or so she said. But of one thing I made sure – she had smooth, dimpled knees.

The day arrived on the wings of morning with a gentle wind fanning Pikernaze and the dew sparkling on every leaf and bough. The old bun put his brass belt on and was doing it with mirrors, slanting rays of golden light; the moors rose and fell in the haze like the breast of a sleeping woman.

Everything was happening at once in The Hermitage, with people rushing around in blue and red waistcoats with glass buttons, and white scarves knotted like Jack tars. Cat-Eater, now received back into the bosom of the family, was wearing big leather boots, sheepskin trews and a patch of white ivory over his empty eye; Ezekiel was done up in hunting breeches stolen off a gentry wash line, blue woollen stockings and boots to shave in.

And I was dressed like a dandy: brown velveteen jacket over a yellow waistcoast and buttons of mother o' pearl.

Abby, as befits a prospective bride, was hidden behind her stud partition with six other women, being powdered, combed and told the facts of life. Alf Posh was smarming down his hair with Macassar oil; Jake O'Hara was climbing into green, being Irish, and Dandy had gone into debt for a new khaki coat sewn with seven glass diamonds.

Down at Salter's Brook where the celebration was being held, they'd got combs and gazooters, fiddles, melodeons, three sets of Irish bagpipes and a big bass drum.

Talk had it that Joseph Locke himself was attending and that Lord Wharncliffe had expressed the desire to see a navvy wedding, which meant half the gentry in the county would be there, even as a heathen ceremony, it kept the clerics away.

Glory to marriage, I thought. Glory to a little bride in pink and white with a green Irish shamrock on her shoulder. Glory to the law that brings lovers together when the world keeps people apart.

That old September sun had a wide grin on his face and the clouds over Pikernaze must have gone through God's weekly wash: as blue as bag-wash was the sky in that splintering light. Always will I remember it. Always will I remember my girl.

She is gone now, light years stand like ghosts between us, but I see her now as clearly as I saw her on that September day, with her black hair down her back and tied with ribbons.

I went to the shant door and waited, and the Abby I knew came slowly out of the clutch of navvy matrons and stood before me.

'Will I do, Nick Farrer?'

'Dear God!' I said.

Seizing Abby's hand I ran with her down the hill, stopping to walk decent at times, bowing right and left, for navvies and their scrags of women were flocking in from all points of the compass, with urchins sucking toffee-apples and others done up in fancy dress and doing cartwheels of joyous expectation.

Mrs Ceinie Meltz, the Jew woman who ran the Tommy shop, was there in silk and finery, she who made a fortune out of us by charging 30 per cent over the odds.

You could buy anything from a pin to a shroud at these Tommy shops, but God help you if you hit the sack on debt, for she'd have the drawers off your gran for payment. I promised myself that, one day, if ever I hit it big on sub-contracting, I was coming back to places like this and close them up.

A word about these Truck or Tommy shops, while on the subject:

The main and sub-contractors, the owners and railway companies took some stick over the existence of the tommy shops. Mainly though, it was the poor exploiting the poor, but not all contractors, even people like Brassey and Peto, were saints in this connection.

Every nine weeks at Woodhead we were paid out in the Miller's Arms or some other cocked-up place where ale was flowing. This meant that since the paymaster was usually late, you could drink your advance wages away on tick; more, some hag-men – butty gang heads like me who sub-contracted – made more out of truck than they did on the job, for they were in league with people like Mrs Meltz.

And, as I've said, since her goods were often 30 per cent higher than the same goods nine miles away in Glossop, most navvies dealing with her were paying 40 per cent over the odds.

All right, folks said at Woodhead, we'll buy in Glossop, but you spent even more on boot leather than you did paying thieves like Mrs Meltz. On top of this, the truck shop-keepers often fiddled their books.

A navvy wife could settle her tommy debts on pay day, then find she'd got ten bob left for the next eight weeks, since some unforgivable husband had been pissing it away on tick – and he'd probably hand her a thumping, too, for even suggesting such a thing.

I tell you this. When we stand at the hand of St Peter on Judgment Day, truckers like Mrs Meltz will be pitchforked to the left with tritons up their rear, for I've known shop-keepers who were criminals, and drunkards who were saints.

We did have compensations for the likes of Mrs Meltz in our midst. We had Cushy Cuddlecome, late of the Miller's Arms, eased out by Meltz because she wouldn't go along with the frauds. You couldn't miss Cushy; she was the first one Abby and I saw as we came racing down to Salter's Brook.

Done in summer braveries was Cushy, sporting a wide-brimmed pink straw hat and a flounce of frills and fancies, ribbons and bows. A fine figure of a woman was she, about sixty round the bosom and eighty round the shanks; another inch of arse and it would drop off, said Abby. But beneath the ample breast beat a heart of gold, for she ran the local lay-me-down in Glossop in her spare time, and if it was close to pay day, she'd knock off twopence in the bob. Talk had it that she'd opened the new Casbar up in George Hall's land at Dunford, too, and brought in Wilson's Turkish Delights from Wakefield purely for local comfort. Very thoughtful.

'Virtue do have its own reward, my lovelies,' Cushy would say. 'Handsome is as handsome does. Give me a six-foot navvy and I'll conquer the world.' And she spun her white parasol as Abby and I came running up.

'Hallo, hallo, my charmers! Bride and groom, is it?' (She came from Swansea.) 'All ready for the greatest adventure of your lives?' and she slipped a sovereign into Abby's palm, whispering:

'Give 'im a good time, my precious, men don't get a lot from wives, mainly speakin',' and she curtseyed deep as Mr Purdon, our engineer, came up, fixing Cushy with gimlet eyes. Severe in black was Purdon, twice to church come Sunday, God save the Queen, and fornication a long way down the list. Yet he had twelve kids back in Birmingham, they said. Prim in public and amorous in private, that's his trouble, said Cushy.

'First thing tomorrow – I'll see you in the office, Farrer,' said Purdon, black as thunder.

'Not if he sees you first,' said Cushy.

The people barged about us in smells of carbolic and hot cloth; new boots were squeaking, a sure sign they weren't paid for, and Cushy was giving off lavender in fumes worse than a London fog.

'What can Purdon want with ye?' asked Abby.

'Ach, nothing much – something to do wi' the job.'

'You're due for a piece of his mind, I reckon.'

'You always get that from folks who can least afford it,' said Cushy. 'Come on, kids, forget him. It's your weddin' day, ain't it, Ham Bone?'

And Ham Bone, one of her six-foot bodyguards, grunted bassly from the recesses of his primitive mind and nodded ponderously in another direction.

'Oh, no . . .' whispered Abby. 'Here comes Sven Tabor!'

This was the giant ganger from whom I'd tried to steal Abby. Rumour had it that he was coming to the wedding to settle old scores, and she mentioned it now, for he was approaching with measured tread.

'*Diawch*, no *cariad*, don't you worry,' cried Cushy. 'My Ham Bone and Swillikin' Jock'll see to him,' and she gave her chaps the elbow. 'Go and pull off his leg or somethin'.'

Waiting until the sun was directly overhead, Blackbird Chapel, our unofficial clergyman, stood up on a barrel and opened wide his arms to the crowd. Short and fat, with a watch chain over his stomach like the chains around Parliament, he turned down his palms, blessing us. Very touching, very holy it all was.

Abby and me, the marriage candidates, faced the people. Cushy was already in tears, snivelling into Ham Bone's spotted red handkerchief. The sun burned down. It was so quiet you could hear the rush of birds.

'Friends all!' shouted Blackbird. 'We are come here to celebrate the wedding of our two young people, Welsh Taff and Abigail Nothin . . .'

I looked around the watching faces.

The burly faces of thick-necked navvies, I saw; side-whiskers sprouting black and gold. The emaciated bodies of the old were there, the hopeless resignation of the prematurely aged. Bright expressions of young wives contrasted the sickly adolescence of wives-to-be. Stalwart young men stood there, whose strength was overflowing. The stringy forms of those half dead, the burned-out relics

104

of the old canallers and the eager faces of those who were building the railways. But all were intent. Many were already tipsy, red-faced boozies trying to stay upright on the edge of the crowd. All were full of respect when it came to a funeral; all were full of mischief when it came to a wedding.

Blackbird bawled, 'Right! Let's get into it!' And we turned our heads to him. 'Do you, Abby Nothin, take this Welsh Taff to be your man?'

And the crowd bawled in chorus: '*Aye!*'

'To see to him proper and feed him good?' cried Blackbird.

'*Aye, aye!*' replied the people.

'To love, honour and obey from this day on?'

'*Aye, aye, aye!*' chanted the crowd.

'Right you!' called Chapel Blackbird. 'Bring the brooms!'

And Shadows and Bones, the local undertakers, walked around, weighing us up. The people roared: 'Skirts, missus, skirts, *skirts!*'

I looked at Abby, seeing her for the first time, it seemed: for within all that noise, the shouting people, the cat-calls and the obscenities, her eyes sent a message to me. Always will I remember her sweet beauty that day: her ragged pink dress tied with a silver girdle, her arms burned brown by sun and wind, and the little hat of plaited daisies and honeysuckle she wore on her hair, and her eyes were as blue as the sky. Like a little girl she looked on the day of her marriage.

Stepping forward, she lifted her skirts while Shadows and Bones stooped, holding their brooms in front of her.

'Jump, missus, *jump!*'

Abby pulled her dress above her knees and jumped, and a bellow went up that they must have heard in Manchester. I jumped, too, and took Abby into my arms, and her feet came off the ground and her skirt made a halo of colour in the sunlight as I swung her around.

'Kiss the bride!' the crowd roared again. '*Kiss the bride!*'

Breathless, I did so, whispering, 'Now run for it, kid. Run for your life!'

Ducking under the blessing hands of old Blackbird, we raced off hand in hand with the crowd in pursuit. They caught us within yards, of course, for big-shouldered youngsters were there to block escape, but the rite was being fulfilled, and the cries went up:

'The chairs, the chairs! Bring the chairs!' and Abby was towed off in one direction while I was taken in another. The chairs were placed and we were sat on them and hoisted up on to the shoulders of clamouring young bucks, and I saw Abby swaying and shrieking laughter, till a tipsy put his hand up her dress and she fetched him one that would have dropped Dan Mendoza.

Then the band started the *oompa-oompa-oompa* and Irish fiddlers were prancing along beside us doing antics, and I was near enough now to reach out and grip Abby's hand.

Casks of ale were carried up to the shant plantation. Bottles of Allsops were gurgled up to the sun, beards parted for foaming Guinness and the old girls wiped the tops of blue ruin, and I knew, come nightfall, that nobody would have a leg under them.

On, on, on, up the hill now to the place of execution, with Cushy and her apes running beside the chairs and sweating like colliers. It was a magical exhilaration that day I married Abby Nothin! Never will I forget it.

Now they had us outside The Hermitage and a truly grand reception committee composed of Tom Ostler and Dandy, Ifan and Tatty, Zeke and Posh with Flo Pig in attendance with relatives, their necks tied with pink ribbons. Even the doors were decorated with wild flowers, and the table set pretty with coloured paper and an aitchbone the size of a bullock's rump. I thought we'd eat first, and sat down, but they pulled me away and took me to Abby's big double bed, which they'd set in the middle of the room.

Everyone stood around, official; silence reigned, and then Cushy, now in charge, shouted:

'Right, me lads. In they go!'

And we were seized anew, one each side of the patchwork bed.

The young bucks undressed me, the women undressed Abby.

Off with my coat; Abby's pink dress was pulled over her head. Away with my splendid waistcoat, and off with two linsey petticoats from Abby, the last one flannel. Away with my braces and belt, down with my trews and I was there in combinations. Abby's stays were unlaced now, the top of my combs were pulled down, Abby's vest was pulled up and she was there in frilly drawers.

Though the room was packed, nobody spoke; no sound but the wind playing his tonic sol-fa in the eaves of The Hermitage and two half-naked lovers facing each other across the bed. Only Tatty made a sigh on seeing Abby's superstructure.

Off with my woollen stockings, Abby's worsted black ones were rolled down: except for boots we were there in the Garden of Eden. And Abby smiled at me, I remember, in the moment before the madmen whooped and the women screamed. With her head on one side, as naked as before the midwife, Abby smiled, gay and charitable.

Cushy yanked back the blankets and shrieked: 'In with 'em. In with the varmints!'

The old crones seized Abby, the young bucks seized me: flung us both into the big iron poster and pulled up the sheets – real sheets, said Abby, special for our wedding night.

And then the mob left us: the barrels were carried in, the ale-pots brimmed, gin was going up, whiskers foamed as the tankards went down, and they danced and made music into the dawn.

We could have been a couple of head-nits nipping in a wool sack, for all the notice anybody took of us.

I kissed Abby Nothin and moved over into the warmth of her, then stubbed my toe.

'Don't tell me you've still got your boots on!'

'Ach, Nick Farrer,' said Abby, and her arms went about me hard and strong, 'you're a magical chap indeed, so ye are. I only saw two of us get into this thing, but now I'd swear there's three.'

'How are you two love-birds doin'?' asked Cushy, three sheets in the wind.

'Passable,' said Abby. 'But he's no great shakes as a lover.'

'*Ach-y-fi!*' Cushy ejaculated. 'Passable's no good to a fertile young girl. Let's hope he rises to the occasion – good luck to ye both,' and she kissed us.

Later I heard tell that she left Woodhead and took up residence with her paramours down south in the Vale of Neath, but I didn't have the proof of it.

Chapter seventeen

In the morning, soon after Yo-ho!, I went down to Salter's Brook where Mr Purdon had his office. When I got back after the interview, I wrote in my diary:

September 13th, 1843: Perhaps I will soon take Abby away from here. Mr Purdon says I am too young to be a proper gaffer, so he is bringing another man in. And I've been doing it for two years! But also, I am under suspicion, although no charge is being made against me. Therefore, it may not be possible for me to continue with this diary. But let me now record that it is men like Purdon who are killing us. To save waiting time, he is still ordering that gunpowder fuses be shortened.

Yesterday Tom Ostler lit one of the shorter fuses – he being our shot-firer – and made to run, but slipped, and the roof came down and it blocked his way. So he went back to the charge and calmly lay over it, snuffing out the burning fuse with thumb and forefinger, because there was no time to get to safety. Another thing: I keep asking Purdon for copper stemmers, but he says they are not efficient. They're too expensive, that's the trouble. Gaffer died through using an iron stemmer, and talking of dying, here is a list of deaths and injuries since I've been at Woodhead: 28 killed: 19 compound fractures, 62 simple fractures; 110 cases of blast burns, concussions, lacerations and dislocations; a man called Punch was blinded; Rainbow, a chap from Wales, lost his arm and half his face: we've had over 300 minor accidents such as broken limbs and smashed fingers and toes. Little if no compensation is paid. And this is only the Woodhead end of the tunnel. God knows what is happening over at Dunford. Yesterday week I asked the surgeon, Mr Pomfret, to speak to Purdon about having copper stemmers, and now I know the outcome of that. Bugger iron stemmers; this is how our Gaffer died.

★

Earlier, I had stood before Mr Purdon's big desk in his office at Salter's Brook. God, they do themselves well, these folks. I'd never been in his office before. Like a little palace it was; mahogany desk with a green top, carpet and three armchairs; whisky and claret in bottles on a sideboard and a frisky little parlour maid to fetch and carry . . . and up in the shant plantations, the gangs are living like pigs.

There was another chap with Mr Purdon, a special constable chap from Manchester.

'Your name is Nicholas Farrer?' asked Purdon. They was sitting, I was standing.

'Yes, sir.'

He had a face like a butcher's arse, did Purdon, and the fella with him was little better.

'How old are you, Farrer?'

'Knocking twenty,' I lied.

'Where do you come from?' Purdon settled back in his leather armchair.

'Wales.'

'What part?'

'Pontypridd.'

'So you were working in Wales before you came to Woodhead?'

'That's right, sir.'

'Do you know the Bradford area – a place called High Doss?'

'Never been to Bradford, sir.'

The constable pondered this. 'Have you ever worked in wool, Farrer?'

I shook my head. 'No. Why?'

'Where are your parents?'

'Dead, sir.'

The constable looked at Purdon. 'That's true.' To me he asked, 'Where did they die?'

'In transportation.'

Purdon leaned forward. 'Transported? What for?'

'Don't know, Mr Purdon. I was only eight.'

'Have you heard of anyone named Nicholas Wortley?'

'No, sir.'

The constable got up. 'It was long odds, but we have to check when we get departmental inquiries. Let him go, he's clearly nothing to do with the Horseferry murder.'

Purdon rose, saying, 'That's all right, Farrer – just routine, nothing to bother you. But while you are here I'm bound to say that you're too young to take on Gaffer of Shant Five: it was all right for a time, but I'm replacing you.'

'And I've been doing it for over two years!'

'That's enough! You keep a diary, I understand.'

'Yes, sir.'

'Of what?' His small eyes roved over my face.

'Just bits and pieces.'

'Your Gaffer kept one, too, didn't he? That's why I sent you to him. A progressive account of the work of a butty gang, Constable,' he said over his shoulder. 'When this accursed tunnel is finished such a document could be valuable, don't you think?'

The constable grunted.

'Providing it contains no subversive elements. But you wouldn't be such a fool as to include controversial issues, would you, Farrer?' Purdon brought out a cigar and held it to his ear. 'Folklore, primitive beliefs – some of these people are really quite interesting.'

The policeman was bored.

'Farrer's marriage yesterday was an example. They jump over a broom, you know.'

I was tiring of him, and so was the constable.

'Right, Farrer, you can go.' I'd got to the door when he added, 'By the way, I wouldn't mind having a glance at that diary.'

'Any time, sir,' I said, and left them.

Something had happened. The Bradford police were still making inquiries into Horseferry's death, though it was three years since Joe had been hanged for the killing. Being so long ago, I had, until now, banished it from my mind.

Abby was sitting cross-legged on the edge of the cornfield by Grains Moss when I found her.

'What did Purdon want?' she asked, lying back.

'Och, nothin' much. But I'm losing the chance of permanent Gaffer. He's bringing somebody in.'

'You love me, Nick Farrer?'

'Aye.' My thoughts were elsewhere.

'How much?'

'Eight-and-fourpence.'

'God! There's not that much money in the world!'

'There is if we go from here.'

'On Shanks's pony? Are ye addled? We've only just got spliced.'

'You like it here. I don't.'

'Nor me – well, not Shant Five, I mean. I'd like to keep a cat, but that bloody monkey would eat it; and it's only one storey which means there'd be no brat-cage for the kids if I turn some out.'

'Are you in the family way, then Jesus, you didn't waste much time.'

'No, but when I do go broody, I don't want rag dolls for folks like Cat-Eater to pull to pieces. I'd rather deliver in the Glossop Grubber than that apology for a shant. Now Shant Fifteen over at Dunford was a shant and a half, and the fellas was tidy, with no scratching under the armpits at company. And that Tabor were a decent chap when you got to know him.'

'We've been married a day. Are you plotting on leaving me?'

She lay back with a straw in her mouth. 'Sure, I'm sorry in me heart for 'em, now I'm gone. The new skiv they've got is in the family way; she's smoking cheroots and drinking Guinness and they don't know if she'll have a gollywog or a smoked haddock.'

I turned to her. 'You've seen the Shant Fifteen mob this morning?'

She nodded. 'Tabor – he was on his way to Glossop.'

'Up here? This is miles off the road.' I gripped her arm and she shook me away. 'This time yesterday you were in bed with me. You keep away from Tabor!'

She got up, blazing Irish. 'Because I'm wed to you that's no wise I should duck me friends, and you'd best get used to it.'

I said, hauling her back to me, 'See Tabor again and I'll be down to Dunford and put him on the line!'

'You toe the line with Sven Tabor, mate, and you won't know which end up you are – he has boys for breakfast.' And then she lifted her arms and put them around my neck and kissed me on the mouth. 'Will ye make love to me, ye darlin' creature?'

'Where? Here? Don't be daft!'

'Aw, come on, give Abby a treat.'

'I made love to you last night.'

'That was the rehearsal!'

'You're mad, Abby Nothin!'

'Aye, and the lunatics have a better time than us. Ye sweet mooney thing, I'm mad for ye. Please . . .?'

So I made love to her in the five minutes left before I had to go back for the night shift.

The moon, I noticed, was round and full, always a sign that Abby was coming romantic, always a sign that you could never know what to expect of her. There was a call in her for Connemara gipsy fires when the moon was wearing his belly-band.

As I tied on me yorks and got my clumpers dubbined for the tunnel, she came to me and whispered in my ear:

'I didn't see Tabor today. Do ye really think I'd be flannelling around with a big gunk like him within a day of you making me your one and only?'

I sighed, holding her. 'How about that new woman he's

got in his shant. Was that moonshine, too?'

She went on tiptoe and kissed my lips. 'Moonshine every inch, but ye must admit, it made the most wonderful yarn.'

I held her away. 'Can I believe any damned thing you tell me?'

'No,' said Abby.

Chapter eighteen

The year passed and the winter came again with her freezes and sneezes, howling her gales over Longside Moss, blowing dew-drops in clusters around the huddled shants, and the whole shivering country from Penistone to Glossop lay frozen under her hammering fists.

Icicles as long as Kaffirs' spears hung from the ceiling of our hut; you could stand your soaked trews on their shins at night and jump straight into them in the mornings.

Never will I forget that bitch of a winter on Pikernaze; even God was blowing on his mittened fingers, and up at Woodhead reservoir, now known to us as Suicide Pond, folks were reluctant to take the plunge, while in spring or summer it was standing room only. A lot of navvies knocked themselves off in hope of a heaven elsewhere than at Woodhead, but the coroners put it down to a tumble while their back teeth were awash. Not so. When St Peter calls the roll, he'll be looking into the activities of Lord Wharncliffe and his shareholders, and if I'm down there first, Tom Ostler used to say, I'll shovel on a few more coals.

Byron, our deaf-mute of the club foot, slipped into the reservoir in January and did a breast stroke under the ice, for they found him half a mile from the weir where he'd left his clothes. The valve man saw him through a foot of ice, staring up at the sky; around his neck was a cord and on the cord was tied a note saying, 'I'm coming, Annie,' and nobody knew what it meant, poor sod.

Queer, come to think of it. I'd lived with him for years and never knew he could write, and being a deaf-mute he naturally didn't say a lot. Tatty cried a bit, I remember; he thought a lot of Byron.

About this time I was getting into Gibbon's *Decline and Fall of the Roman Empire*, which Ruth Brandt had told me to read, but since Abby was inclined to be demanding, I couldn't make much headway, though I did have more time to myself since Tom Ostler had taken over as gaffer.

Mr Purdon reckoned I was too young for the job, and he was probably right: people don't respect you if you're young, he said, and Tom Ostler was very old – about thirty. To be accurate, he was thirty on Christmas Day – and a fortnight later he had passed on to the Upper Palace where only good Catholics like her went, said Abby.

Woodhead, it appeared, had a particular liking for gaffers.

Our butty gang was now in full swing towards the Quarry shaft and beating all records; blasting and shovelling eastward on the magnetic needle of a mariner's compass. Myself, I preferred the two-plumb-bob system, sighting back to the entrance light and then working the line on candles.

Tom Ostler came up with Purdon – trouble always came when that bugger was around – and it was an Irish parliament then, with everybody talking and nobody listening. Then Jake O'Hara told Purdon to sod off and leave the butties alone. And that was the end of Jake O'Hara. He left Woodhead, went to Southampton and fell head first into a caisson of wet concrete they were mixing for a harbour dam: nobody missed him until the night shift ended and the fifty tons of concrete set overnight. Later, when they drilled for anchor bolts, they came across a baby's hand: it was Jake's (concrete contracts when setting). So the newspapers had a field day and called it 'Christ in concrete'.

No point in breaking Jake out, so they left him in the foundations where he could hear the ships going by. He'd like that, would Jake, being a nautical chap.

★

The second one we lost that week was our new gaffer, Tom Ostler.

It was getting bad in the tunnel now that we were well under the hill. The only light you had was from candles, and when you were working under the air shaft, these kept blowing out. Under the shaft, the wind froze you to the bone; once past it, the air became fetid and dank. The rock walls streamed water and you waded in a foot of filthy slush. When you blasted, and this was often through millstone grit, the air choked with gunpowder fumes.

The face was dangerous, too. Everytime you swung a pick, you risked a rock fall, and the rocks in Woodhead descended like knives, as bad as slates, an old quarryman told me; slates can amputate like surgeons when on the slide.

So it was handle low, swing and throw; stripped to the waist despite the cold; working in semi-darkness for hour after hour. Drill the borehole, ram in the powder, blow on the bugle and light the fuse – then walk, not run (if you run, you can trip and fall) to the nearest sheltering niche in the wall: and wait, mouth open, body turned, fingers in your ears.

Crash!

Jesus! The mountain didn't like it. And, not liking us blowing up her vitals, she tended to hit us back occasionally.

Pikernaze Moor hit back on January 8th, 1844.

January 9th, 1844: Yesterday Tom Ostler, our new gaffer, was killed with three men from the McNamara butty gang. It was a bucket accident; a premature shot-firing while the bucket with the lads in it were travelling up the shaft to the top. We picked up the lads in bits and pieces. To prevent such accidents needs serious investigation, for they will continue until a safe system of control is invented.

We were tunnelling within fifty feet of the lads coming in

from the Greystone Quarry air shaft, and were expecting to join up at any moment.

'Can you hear them?' asked Tom Ostler, and everyone in the gang stopped work to listen.

Life can concoct some marvellous excitements: like pulling on your trews of a summer morning or getting into the first daze of the homebrew old and mild; spending money, your first trip on a merry-go-round, or the girl when making love. But *nothing* can beat the comradeship when a tunnel tiger puts his fist through the hole and waves it about in search of a comrade's hand.

'They're coming,' whispered Tatty, who had ears that could hear brown grass growing.

'No it anna, it's behind us,' said Zeke.

'It's for'ard, I tells ye!'

'He's got a hole in his head,' said Zeke. 'It's behind you, mun.'

'Stop talking and listen,' commanded Tom Ostler.

'Will they blast?' asked Ifan.

'Dear God,' sighed Alf Posh.

'Will they blast, ye bloody idiot, with us five foot t'other side of rock?'

'Jesus, I'm dry!'

'Me, too. I could do wi' a quart of skull attack.'

'After we get up.'

'Ye know something? I think they're coming to the right of us . . .'

'Don't be daft!'

I looked around their sweat-blackened faces in the flickering light of the candles. All were stripped to the waist, despite the frost outside; all were with honour when it came to a fall.

I've never worked with better butties, though they were heathens; I've never trusted men more. It is strange how danger always compounds the latent friendship in men. They'll fiddle and short-change each other in pub sawdust; they'll scandalise like women in a four-ale tap; and they'll fight like savages in the sun for a shilling. But once they go underground they're at their best in manhood, when the chap next to you will hang on to your boot when the roof is coming down, and die with you when the air is running out.

Women don't understand the purity of male comradeship, and the dirty old world, always suspicious of something it doesn't understand, looks upon it as some perverted intimacy. But the dirty old world, as usual, is wrong. For the quickest way out of a navvy hut with a boot behind you is to act the fancy pants or put ashes of roses under the arms.

'I'll halve the skull of the first man through,' said Cat-Eater, lifting his shovel, and he was the nearest thing to an orangutan I've seen. 'This is our bloody tunnel, what's it to do with them?'

'Stand clear or I'll halve yours,' said Tom Ostler. 'The lads are coming through.'

And as he said it, the half of a pick came through the wall, first the pick and then a hand, a hand that waved in search of another, and Tom stepped over the muck, reached up and gripped it. And we heard on the other side of the broken rock a mad cheering, and we cheered, too. Next a voice cried:

'Stand clear, boys, we're coming through – the Quarry Butty gang!'

'Ay ay. Stand clear!'

Now a face appeared and it shouted: 'Are you the Tom Ostler butty?'

'Aye, mun!' yelled Tom. 'You'll have heard of us, for we were tunnelling while you sat on your arses. Come on through, lads. We've tapped the homebrew!'

The hole became bigger, and in the blackness of the tunnel beyond, I saw a sea of dancing candles.

Six-hundred-foot underground we had joined another tunnelling gang under Woodhead. Snap on – the point of a pin to the head of a pin, by an engineer's calculation, done on a drawing, achieved in the dark, by candles.

'Praise be to God,' cried Ezekiel, and down on his knees, he lifted his blue-veined hands up to the roof. 'Anointed, we are, with the oils of rejoicing!'

'Get up, ye silly old bugger,' said Tom. 'Atonement don't come in half pints, Zeke. It's penitence or nothing, and God ain't nothing' to do with it – we dug this tunnel.'

'For someone drinking so close to the Devil, you're taking a bloody chance,' and Alf Posh raised his tin mug high to the boys crawling through from the Quarry gang.

We sat in the candlelight, us and the Quarry men, and drank a cask we'd brought for this occasion. And Tom glanced at the roof.

'Best bring this lot down before it falls on us,' he said and rose.

It was the last words I heard him speak.

Tom and three of the Quarry gang drilled, rammed and tamped the charges, and everybody else left the tunnel. Tom ran the fuse and lit it close to the air shaft. But somebody had left an exploded charge in a borehole and the fuse ignited this as the bucket, with Tom and the three others in it, began to ascend the shaft. The explosion occurred when the bucket was halfway up. It travelled like a bullet out of a gun for 500 feet, then shot out fifty feet into the air, spraying its occupants out like small, red flowers.

Abby cried, but we didn't talk much about it in the shant.

Gone, weren't he?

And that's a bloody end to it.

Chapter nineteen

I knew Abby would leave The Hermitage at the next full moon, and she did.

They say you have to kill a hundred Welshmen to get a pound of brains, so I suppose I asked for it, taking on a Connemara gipsy.

I awoke that night to a rustling of scarecrow trees outside the window; stark black they were and ragged, talking about the last beautiful summer. And when I put a hand out to touch her, Abby had gone.

'*Daio!* Why worry, boyo?' cried Alf Posh, taking me off. 'She'll come back when Tabor's done wi' her. Besides . . .' and he crept up to me like a cat in cream, 'the cheese is that much sweeter when nibbled by another mouse.'

'I'm going to Dunford to get her,' said I.

'Are ye indeed!' replied Ezekiel on his praying mat. 'When a concubine plays the whore against you, you divide her bones and send her unto all the coasts of Israel. Leave her be.'

'Tabor will kill you, Welsh Taff,' added Cat-Eater. 'He's cock o' the line in Dunford.'

'He's not cock o' the line down here.'

Cried Educated Ifan, falsetto, 'I'll call for Shadows and Bones and they'll measure you for teak and brass handles.'

I felt empty without my girl.

My love for her was couched in an unusual obeisance; rejection always angered me and this was a wounding loss. So I sat for a while and brooded in the icy silence of my loneliness. I worked, yet did not work; slept yet did not sleep. Perhaps it was her piquant charms I missed the most, for one can still love faithfully even when the loved is as nutty as a spring squirrel.

Yet pride, not loss, sent me over the hill to Dunford three days after Abby had left me.

Cock o' the line, was he? Sven Tabor the Scandy Terror? We'll see about that.

Sven Tabor was large: at six-foot-five he could give me inches and he had a man's weight.

He was a lazy oaf, they said: slow, ponderous, drunk with strength; no kind of gaffer worth having, being content, when once he'd started his butties in the morning, to moon all day with his arse turned to the sun. Bright-haired and handsome, Abby reckoned he was a throwback to the Norsemen who had conquered Ireland in the 10th century AD. 'Around Cromwell's time . . .' said she.

Hooking out my woman from under me nose: I'd give him bloody Cromwell.

They must have had an Irish wake on the go in Shant Fifteen when I arrived, for the shant door was opened by a leprechaun with a bowler hat tipsy on his head, and he was celebrating for a hooley, said he.

'Can I be of assistance to ye, me lovely large fella?' asked he, polite, so I reached out, pitched him into the roadway behind me and slammed the door to warm its hinges.

An Irish hooley, did he call it: more like a debauch of 3rd-century Rome, with bodies lying about half dressed, bottles tipping up and ale filtering through beards without so much as a swallow.

I reckon they'd got the George Hall Casbar on the go, for the place was jammed with boozies and harlots, all showing garters and Grand Canyons, and there's never been an orgy like it since Cleopatra blew the candle out. The music and jabbering must have been raising the dear departed down in Glossop, and that was twelve miles off.

Then somebody saw me: one by one, they saw me, and a squeeze box drifted down to a minor key, and a set of Irish bagpipes went off the note.

Silence.

I walked through them to the middle of the room.

Dead silence.

'Where's Tabor?' I asked.

Hands on hips, a Scots woman breasted up. 'If you canna see him, mister, call yourself lucky.'

I stared into their hostile faces.

'Where is he?'

'I am here,' said Tabor, and I turned.

He came from the skiv's partition and I guessed he had Abby in there. Handsome bugger, give him credit.

Stripped to the waist he came, gently pushing people aside.

A foot taller than anyone but me, his head was a mass of bright curls, his fine body tanned with sun and wind. And standing in the doorway behind him was the outline of a woman in the glow of the lamps, and I knew it was Abby.

'Ye daft bugger, get off. He'll kill ye,' said she.

Tabor was beside me now, and his eyes, bright blue, burned in his square face. I saw above his heavy brows the old white scars of fighting.

'What you want, Welshman?'

'My woman.'

'Any woman here. Take pick.' He jerked his head at the room.

I jerked a thumb at Abby. 'That one.'

Tabor grinned wide and wiped his bristled chin with the back of a hand. 'You go, eh? Or you get trouble.'

'I take her with me or you're the one in trouble, Tabor.'

He sighed, as a man sighs when nails go through his hands, and said:

'Listen. You are a boy, eh? Tabor only fights with men.' He emptied big hands at me. 'Look, you go now, eh? When I have finished with her, I will send her back.'

A woman, older than the rest, pushed a path through a

clutch of people. 'I seen it all, son. Too big, too young. He'll kill ye. Leave it go.'

I looked around the faces of the men. Some I knew were there; Moonraker the Wiltshire man I saw, and he winked; Mountain Pecker, who came from Yorkshire. There was Primrose, a squat, wide-shouldered ape of a fellow, and Fatarse, a walking skeleton; Lock whose name was Key, and Slenderman who was a roly-poly pudding. Few were with grace; most would steal from their grans. But all were with honour when it came to Toe the Line.

I asked, 'Is it clean in here?'

'Like a new pin,' said Slenderman.

I made a fist and hit Tabor's shoulder. The gentry, they tell me, smack a face with a glove.

'Toe the Line,' I said. 'I lose, she stays; I win, I take her.'

'Is that a fact!' cried Abby, pushing into the room. 'What about me?'

'You don't come into it.'

Tabor made a lad's face, like a boy soprano who'd hit the wrong note, then opened his shoulders and shoved at the people for room.

They shrank away, leaving us a circle; the little leprechaun skittled in between us and chalked on the boards two white lines a foot apart.

I unbuttoned my coat and let it fall down behind me; flung my arms up through my vest and let it dangle. Leprechaun put a penny on his thumb and flipped it up; Tabor, being challenged, had right of call.

'Heads.'

The crowd craned forward.

'Heads it is,' I said, 'you first,' and I spread my feet wide on the line, the easier to be knocked off balance.

This is when fools make mistakes. Take a boxing stance and you're a gonner, Gaffer used to say. With eyes wide open, watch every move, take the punch and let it bowl you over. And only cowards duck, remember.

'You done this before, eh, Welshman?' asked Tabor.

I thought I discerned anxiety in him as he copied my stance on the second chalked line, but I could have been mistaken.

This was not a boxing contest. It was hit and be hit, fall and come back upright. The man who was standing at the end of it won; you lost when you couldn't toe the line.

True, the most brutal injuries could be inflicted – broken noses and cauliflower ears were scars of courage and exposed with pride – but few fatal injuries occurred despite the primitive confrontation. This was because the feet were parallel to the line and the contestants were off-balance, yet you could still end up with only half a face.

But move even slightly to the coming punch, deflect it or duck it, and by navvy law that was a coward's way out. You lost in disgrace.

Gripping my hands behind me, I waited. Tabor took a deep breath as he drew back a fist. I saw the fist coming and closed my eyes to reject the automatic attempt at evasion. The fist landed, a wild right swing with all Tabor's weight and strength behind it, on my temple. It bowled me over sideways like a cartwheel into the arms of waiting men. Instantly obliterated, the lamps on the ceiling slowly emerged from my haze of pain: flat on my back I lay. The men made no attempt to assist me. Ten seconds was the limit. Shaking my head I was on my knees at six and on my feet at nine as the leprechaun, kneeling beside me, shouted the seconds.

'Twenty seconds rest now, mind,' cried Slenderman, who came from the Rhondda.

Tabor waited until, still delicate, I regained the line. His mouth was trembling, but not with fear. I knew the reason when he put his hands behind him: his striking hand was broken. And I saw his face as a dancing shade before me, his features withering and shrinking into strange distorted shapes, and I heard Abby shout:

'Providence and mercy spare us!' Her voice was shrill. 'Is any woman worth it, you useless pair o' gunks?'

125

I struck, feeling the impact of the blow jarring through my body, and Tabor went backwards into the arms of the people, his boots waving farewell. At first he lay there so still and silent that I thought he was dead, and then, on all fours, he scrambled up as the tolling seconds reached ten. Coming up to the scratch, he toed it and his bloodstained face swayed before me as he launched his second punch. I heard my cheekbone crack under the force of it, and sank to my knees.

Blood dripped, splashing in little scarlet stains at my knees. And, even as I knelt there I heard through the mist of pain a sobbing like an animal trapped, and it was Tabor.

The crowd moaned bassly, like bulls at an empty manger.

· 'His mitts are gone, Welshman,' said someone.

Somebody helped me to my feet, I forget who it was, then Slenderman, the roly-poly said, 'Jesus Christ, mun, your head's like nutty slack – ye must be from the Rhondda. He's broke his hands.'

I straightened. Tabor was bowed before me; with one eye shut tight and coming up like a balloon, he had his broken fingers clamped beneath his arms, moaning.

'This time I break my hands,' said he. 'Very often I break my hands at this.' He jerked his head in Abby's direction. 'Take her.'

Abby backed away as I approached her, her arms up defensively.

'Goin' with you, am I? I'll say not – back to that dump ye call a home? I'd rather be kicked in the head by a horse.'

Gripping her wrist, I yanked her after me with her boots skidding protestingly on the floor, and she shrieked, while the people clapped approvingly.

'Ye squintin' fool, will ye take your hands off me? I want to stay wi' Tabor,' and Tabor said at the door:

'Take her, and welcome. The Devil himself stitches her garters. She is trouble and I am finished with her – take her!'

And he held the door open for us as I towed Abby Nothin

after me, and the moon was round and full, sitting on the shanty roofs and enjoying every minute as I pulled her, shrieking and crying for a pig-sticking all the way back to The Hermitage.

Once there, I flung her on the bed.

'Right, you,' I said.

Slamming the door behind me, I unbuttoned my belt.

'*Arrah!* This is marvellous!' cried Abby.

Round about dawn, Abby awoke and, seeing me out of bed and looking in the cracked glass she called a mirror, came to me with a sweet soprano noise, and said, 'Aw, ye poor darlin' thing, what has he done to ye?'

'He's handed me a cauliflower ear,' I said, and Tabor had, for me right lug was swelling up like a balloon, red and purple.

She held me and, weeping, said, 'By me erring ways I've disfigured you for life, mun. Just look at your bloody ear, you poor wee soul.'

'You're making too much of it.'

'Sure to God, I'll never forgive myself, Nick. Will it have to come off?' Abby peered, on tiptoe, in the dawn. She held me, with real salt tears flooding her eyes, and said, broken:

'God forgive me for mixing you up with me, Nick Farrer, for I don't deserve ye, indeed I don't. That big oaf Sven Tabor do fancy himself with the women, and he got me when I was in a minor key, or I'd never have left ye – I swear to Jesus on me dying soul.'

'Have you seen an ear like this in a month of Sundays?' I asked her, prodding it.

'I'll make it up to you, Nick, and strike me dead if I vary away from you again. It breaks my heart to see your suffering, all for a wayward bitch like me.'

'Ach, don't bother yourself!'

'So if I'm not humbuggin' you too much, I'll surely stay.'

'That's right,' I said, taking her off. 'For if you leave me flat again, I'll kill you!'

'Ach, you're a wonderful fella, so you are,' and she kissed me. 'For without your love, I'm as naked as an ash tree in the month o' May. If I stay on without goin', will ye love me to everlasting, Nick?'

'For ever and ever. Now get back to bed.'

She had her arms around my neck now and I was trying to lever her off, and she whispered, 'I'll rear a pig at me breast before I'll leave you again, me foine big chap.'

'So I'm gathering. Meanwhile, lay off because I want some sleep.'

'Sleep? What the hell? I can do that up Dunford wi' Tabor. Aw Nick, come on!'

'Away with you, woman!' I said. 'It's an hour to yo ho! and you've had me up all night.'

'Don't ye want me, then?'

'Hell, I've just had you!'

'Don't ye love me, then?' She sat on the bed and put her hands over her face and wept. 'Holy Grail, you're that huffy, so ye are, I never know where I am from minute to minute with you, Nick Farrer. There's me staying decent for you and you hating the sight of me. What kind of a marriage is that?'

'Go to sleep!'

'Then will you just hold me and whisper in me ear?'

So I heaved her over into the warmth of me and held her until the dawn came up like a scimitar in a sky of blood-stained accidents, and the shant was bathed in a warm, roseate light.

'Gee whiz,' whispered Abby, 'that Tabor fella's got a face like a navvy's armpit. What did I see in him when I could have conspired with you?'

And she loosened her tears into a flood, soaking me, and in the vacuum drift between sleep and wakefulness, I held her.

'Never will I leave ye again, Nick Farrer – *never!*'

I made a mental note to put another bolt on the door.

Chapter twenty

As will have been gathered, we navvies were very peaceable subjects, with 'God Bless the Queen' every ten seconds.

If ever we were tempted to violence, this was usually the result of foreign interference. For instance, if you were an Irish navvy, you tried to keep clear of the Scots, for the Scots were given to praying and drinking on a Sunday, and it needed only a few toss-pots to send every McGregor in kilts mad daft – more so if he stumbled over an Irishman.

Likewise, since the Irish reckoned the Sabbath was a holiday, they fell into the habit of tracking down stray Englishmen to give them a going over in the name of Oliver Cromwell.

Nor were the English blameless: seven days a week they roughed up the Irish because they were Roman Catholic, and the Scots because they were Presbyterian.

It was different, of course, when we were working, for work involved the dignity of labour, and at threepence an hour, one couldn't afford the time to fight, which was a pity. But every eight weeks' pay day provided an opportunity for a randy and to entertain foreigners to another civil war.

Like two years ago in Dunfermline when the Scots put up posters:

All Irish buggars north of Fife Share must be away and owt o' the countey by Monday next or els with a pick handel we wil bloody put 'em orf.
Your most humbel servants,
Schots Men

Immediate compliance was demanded or all hell would come loose in Dunfermline.

All things considered, therefore, our working gangs at Dunford and Woodhead got on reasonably well.

'I heard as how they cropped the ears of a Welshman up on the Chester-to-Holyhead, though,' mentioned Cat-Eater. 'I'm all for that.'

Jimmy Webb, a Derbyshire navvy-ticket man, had been drinking his pot in The Mason's Arms up in Bangor when somebody made the suggestion, in Welsh, that this English bugger might look better without his ears. In fact, the Welsh, who since Owain Glyndwr had always resented English interference, then suggested that they should crop the ears of every Englishman in sight to distinguish them from the Irish. It went further when local Welsh navvies, angered at the number of Irishmen employed, put every son of Erin to flight with sticks, bottles and stones, public order being restored by the arrival of the Durham Light Infantry.

'They should be cropping English ears here, as well as in Bangor,' said Abby, and gave Cat-Eating Scan a look to kill.

She'd never been partial to Cat-Eater since he'd consumed her Persian.

'They tell me they've got water lavatories over in Glossop,' said Iron Man Cass, a new chap just in.

Zeke, who was dozing on the truckle beside him, said, 'I met a navvy called Moleskin Jim once. He knew a holy Father in Donegal who had a water closet, and the village folk thought it were a bosh for storing holy water; the priest were blessing it while sitting on it, they said.'

'They're backward in Donegal, an' no mistake,' said Abby.

Zeke continued, 'And the priest sold Moleskin Jim to a farmer for five shillings a week and pig-swill to keep him. He were only six year old. He was a good old navvy man, was Moleskin, but he died in the mud in the clay pug mills down Shiretown.'

Iron Man Cass said, lighting his clay, 'I had a mate who

was sold like that. His name was Dan Sullivan, and they hanged him for kicking a woman to death – mind, I'd 'ave kicked her, too, if she'd belonged to me.'

Tatty said, 'Back in 'forty, I saw Doolan and Reddie hanged for knockin' off an English ganger. One had hit him with a ratchet bar, another jumped on him, poor sod. There was a third chap, too, but he got transported.'

'Some of those English gangers are first-rate bastards,' said Abby.

'It were summer,' said Tatty, reflectively. 'A young soldier fainted, I remember, when he heard their spines crack. They hanged 'em side by side along the Edinburgh-to-Glasgow, on a signal – same place as they'd killed the ganger.'

Iron Man Cass added, puffing smoke, 'Mind you, Dan Sullivan never did it. Afterwards they found it was the woman's uncle who knocked her off. Do you reckon the innocents go straight to Heaven?'

'Doubtful,' said Zeke.

'Doubtful? You're a Bible Joe – don't you know?'

'If there *is* a Heaven,' added Zeke.

'I anna goin' there, any road,' said Cat-Eater, moodily. 'They say they've got bugles at five o'clock in the mornin'.'

'That Angel Gabriel, I expect,' said Abby.

We didn't pursue the subject further because Hairy Ambler came in.

Hairy, so named because he hadn't a hair on his body, was on the tramping-ticket. When he was a lad down London Wall, he owned a parrot called Pablo who shouted, 'Back, back, back!' and backed a horse and cart over the Embankment and into the Thames: then he did another, then another and folks heard him at it, so poor Hairy got booted off the job, plus Pablo. Later, he did the tramp regular on what we called the 'Navvy Newspaper', picking up bits of news on his travels and relating it to gangs on sites all over Britain.

'We're sort of like the Israelites,' Hairy used to say. 'We pitch our tents anywhere, get the navvy bob, and go our way,' and this he had done for over forty years.

Some navvy ticket trampers did well out of it, for every site visited guaranteed a bob, and that was enough to take a man into the Grubber Workhouse for a week, with a meal of soup or porridge. In isolated sites like Woodhead, where we saw no newspapers, this was how we kept in touch with life.

'How do?' said Hairy, being Lancashire, and he sat at our table while Abby fetched him cheese and bread, and this he washed down with a quart of Allsops, kicking off his boots while he fed, and his feet were as skinned as shaved apes, red-raw.

'Dear God,' said Abby, and bathed them while he ate.

I watched. There was beauty in it, save that she didn't dry his feet with her hair.

'Can I swear in front o' the woman?' asked Hairy.

'If there's words ye don't know, ask me,' said Abby.

'Because I caught a tartar down at Hackney Spike; I thought she were a shant skiv, but she were one o' the new missionaries, and she battered me cruel for a couple of "fooks". You got missionaries here?'

'Not yet,' said Abby.

'They'll come. I got a note on me scandal sheet here,' and he unfolded a soiled newssheeet. 'Walker's got 'em down at London Wall, God bless him, and he's payin' over the odds, lads.'

'How much?' asked Zeke.

Hairy blew on his soup and licked bits of stewed rabbit off his hairless lips. 'He's even paying a penny over for his Fragments, and two of those – night watchmen – 'ave only two arms and a leg betwen them.'

I lazed back on the truckle, and listened. Hairy was speaking of men like Walker and Firbank, the latter saying that no navvy on his sites need fear grey hairs.

Later, it was said that more money passed through the hands of contractors like Peto and Brassey (which is why we call money 'brass') than saw the treasuries of Europe's capitals, and the names of both stand high today as men respected. But the name of Firbank meant something more to the hearts of the toughest of the banditti, which is what the public called us. We, the outcasts of society, despised and isolated, were looked upon by Firbank as his possessions.

Joe Firbank began work at seven years old, with a chain between his legs down Durham's pits, hauling coal trams into otherwise inaccessible stalls, where the roof was eighteen inches high. The idea here was to get 'em young so their bones would grow horizontal; then they could use the cripples on the deepest, shallowest galleries.

By candlelight little Joe had taught himself to read and write, left coal's muck-holes and became a navvy on Weardale. There he was a nipper lad crashing the bumpsticks, like I had, but escaped the fate of hundreds of lads of his age – bumped and bleeding under the wheels – and travelled the country with pick and shovel. Educating himself on the road, cramming himself with knowledge, he had landed over at Dunford on the Woodhead, again like me, and had taken up sub-contracting.

Now, as an instantly successful employer of navvy labour, he shared his compassion with his fellows, later becoming, like Walker, an employer of what he called 'Fragments' – the crippled and maimed. When the tales of navvying are told to future generations, Walker and Firbank will be remembered.

The talk went on into the night, and soon Hairy Ambler had an audience.

Rainbow, a tar-brush fellow, came in off shift, I remember, and if I recall correctly, Gorger, a roly-poly who never stopped eating was there, and Black-and-Tan, who only drank lemonade, and Wingy, who had a wooden leg painted in brilliant colours. He was a gipsy chap who lost his leg when a nipper at Stockton, and kept it at home under his bed, pickled in whisky, till his wife complained to the lodger.

They all came in together, because the shift in the tunnel was ending, and soon I'd be down in the bucket with Cat-Eater and Tatty. And all were plastered with black, stinking mud, for the going was dirty.

'Come on, missus, show a leg!' for Abby had been sleeping.

'Where's me fookin' dinner, woman? Come on, come on!'

'Yell like that and ye'll get no bloody dinner,' said Abby.

They bantered with her, they slapped her rump, threatened her with a kicking and held her off while they tasted the broth, for Abby was a cook, give her credit – the smell coming up from that bubbling bucket would have brought spit to Satan.

'Where's me hare, Abby?'

'And me baby bunny, Fan?'

'Touch my cockerel and I'll have your arms off, Rainbow!'

'Jesus!' cried Black-and-Tan. 'Not old Hairy again!'

'You leave Hairy be,' shouted Abby, and brought up her broom, threatening them away from the bucket, and they sat at table in their stained and clay state while she ladled the stew on to their buckled tin plates; slapped down cottage loaves held in her apron, then lifted up the strings.

They ate like savages, snatching at the little carcasses of hare, rabbit, pheasants, and chickens, tearing at them with their strong, white teeth, wiping their bearded mouths with the backs of their hands in gasps and grunts.

And while they were eating, Abby fetched their ale; unlocking the steal-bar that kept the barrel safe and carrying the foaming jugs in a jangle of keys.

While Abby served them, they beset her with their vulgar buffoonery, an astonishing stream of witticism and drollness that belied their graceless manners. Their appearance, caked with mud as they were, their inelegance, their squalid lumpishness did not serve their jaunty, often brilliant sense of comedy. They were defaced as humans, and they knew it; they accepted their lot of the picaresque and defiled; they were at the bottom of the human heap, a blemish on the face of an unforgiving society; yet they were decent when it came to the majesty of comradeship.

Lying on my truckle, I watched them, and listened. And I think I realised that night, as I saw their ruffian antics, heard their bawdy talk and filthy epithets, that there existed within them the epitome of goodness, because they were men with souls.

These, whom the accepted social order called banditti, performed their gluttony at table, leaving to the bankers the exploitation of true grossness. These were the men who made things, who were raising dirt monuments to Britain's flourishing wealth.

Such as these received no government compensation for the ending of a disgusting slave trade, whose owners went down on their knees in church in search of higher profits. No, they were the whipped, not the whippers. These, I thought, were the children of the Industrial Revolution, part of the ragged army upon whose misery the wealth of the counting-houses was based. Royalty, the glories of Victoriana and Britain's snob aristocracy prospered on the strength of these who, like half-a-million factory children, toiled and died to beget Britain's private fortunes.

'Hey up, Gorger, leave my plate alone.'

'Shadows and Bones'll 'ave you, mate!'

'Who the hell's Shadows and Bones?' asked a new man.

'Like I told the ganger down Wealdstone way, I'll dig you down six feet, you bastard!' said Hairy.

'Will you bathe me now you've done him, missus?' cried Wingy. 'Purdon docked me half for wet working, 'cause I've only got one leg.'

'You'm lucky to get anything off that sod,' said Black-and-Tan.

'Who called the cook a bitch?'

'Who called the bitch a cook?'

'I'll 'ave you for that, Black-and-Tan!' cried Abby.

'How come you got no hair on you, old Hairy?' asked Rainbow. 'Did a woman pull it off?'

'Don't you matter me private business,' replied Hairy, but I knew.

He was aged fourteen and down Dumper's Pit in the Cynon Valley, he once told me. 'And the pit was chock full o' gas, you understand?'

'Yes,' I said.

'Now, if you was a pit boy bent on a fortune, you could volunteer for gas-flashin' – you know what that is?' asked Hairy.

'No idea,' said I, though I had.

His gnarled old hands told the tale and his eyes were dull, like the glazed eyes of the burned – opaque and filmed – and Hairy said:

'You got a sixpence for gas-flashin', see? And if you ain't eaten for a couple o' days, sixpence comes important. So down I goes in the bucket with a soaked sack on me back and another over me head. And the foreman's dug a hole at the bottom just to fit a lad – understand?'

'Yes.'

'Then I lights me candle in a holder – like the kind you takes up to bed – ties a bit o' string on it under the air shaft, pays out the string, don't I? and gets into me little hole. There I sits with the wet sacks over me and slowly pulls on the string, drawing the candlestick holder towards me and the gas, got it?

'Mind you, I did this all over the Welsh coalfields, for the colliers struck – they wouldn't go down – canaries were dying like flies those days. But this time, down Dumper's Pit the gas was coarse. And it didn't ignite until it was on top o' me. There were a flash like Kingdom Come. And it flashed and flashed again and set me sacks on fire. So I sort o' roasted in that little hole, didn't I? And when the foreman comes down eventual, he says to me, "Who's that cookin'? There's a smell of roast boy down here."

' "It's me," I said. 'Get me out, Foreman," and he did; he was a regular nice fella.' Hairy sighed. 'So that's why I got no hair on me today. I stopped gas-flashin' after that – it's a bit dangerous, ain't it? Instead I went on the tramping ticket, and I ain't never looked back.'

'You'll do, Hairy,' I said, and left him.

Chapter twenty-one

Abby left me again when the moon was full, as usual, without a word; but she did leave a note on the bed:

'Goodbye'

So I'm leaving this place for good.

I'm leaving Woodhead long before the tunnel is finished, and some might say I am walking out on the job. By the way things are going in this slaughterhouse – the accident rate, the sickness, the hard lying and sweated labour – they'll be a couple of years before the thing is finished, and this doesn't account for the wrangling of the railway shareholders, the changes of engineering staff, the temper of the managers.

In any case, I wouldn't have stayed to the end and the official opening; without Abby beside me to split her sides at the antics of the company directors and the battalions of hangers on – steaming through the tunnel with bunting and booze aboard – I just couldn't stand the hypocrisy. Too many of my mates have died; too many good men have been maimed; I couldn't accept the celebrations. Aye, and far too many hearts have been broken on a shilling a week benefit and no compensation; we won't have built a tunnel under the Pennines, we'll have constructed a charnel house complete with bones. And the engineers and company directors should be behind bars – Wharncliffe right up front – for the crime of genocide.

But more . . . now that Abby's gone, and I think for good, there's simply nothing left to keep me in the God-forsaken place.

Earlier, while the hut was sleeping, I made my last entry in Gaffer's diary, thus fulfilling my promise to him that I would keep the diary until the tunnel was finished.

June 11th 1843: Tomorrow is my birthday, I'll be nineteen, and I am leaving Woodhead tonight. Too many good men have died here to look upon this as a job well done; it is not a time of celibration.

In my time as unofficial Union representative I have organised Sick Benefit payments; sixpence a head per month isn't much, Mr Doherty, but it is a beginning, and I have deposoted £186 and odd money with the manager of the new Co-operative Bank in Manchester, and hold an official receipt, so mind he don't steal the money. Before I go, I will leave this diary in the hands of the bankers, too, that you may glean from it what you will. My intention, like our Gaffer's was to record the conditions of work demanded, the long hours involved, and the heavy and dangerous nature of tunnelling requirements. Woodhead will be typical of future tunnels, but it will stand on its own as a human slaughterhouse; here we have manufactured corpses.

Perhaps things will improve when we get a hold over these vicious employers; they who deny us a Union yet allow their own to flourish. Perhaps our hope lies with the newly formed Miners' Association (To whom please send our money), to which navvy branches like this may one day be affiliated. I speak for the lads who are dead and gone so this railway could run from Sheffield to Manchester.

Please contact the Miners' Association for me, Mr Doherty. Good luck in all you are trying to achieve, to you and Mr Robert Owen and good men like you. The bank manager will write to you on my behalf.

Yours truly,
Nicholas Farrer

After I had written this, I lay down on the big four-poster where I used to make love to Abby.

She had been gone a fortnight now – right off the job – no,

she wasn't over with Tabor at Dunford, that's the first place I looked.

Perhaps it is my mood tonight, but everything suddenly seems to be dying. First I'd lost Gaffer, then Little Bert, then Tom Ostler and Byron. Jake O'Hara had died, then Dandy Dick and Alf Posh – they both lost legs or arms underneath a runaway. The only people left in The Hermitage who were here when I first came to Woodhead were Cat-Eater, Zeke and Tatty, none of whom was really worth having. And a lot of the new men come in were surly buggers: it isn't the same when your real mates are gone.

As I closed the diary, Zeke came ambling in.

'There's a fella down at the station askin' for ye, Taff,' said he.

I looked up. 'Did he say his name?'

'Didn't ask it. A big chap, knocking twenty; speaks all tonic sol-fa, like you.'

'Welsh?'

'Don't ask me. I don't understand the lingo.'

So I got up and looked at the moon, which was waning fast now Abby had gone. On the night she had left, he had been sitting over Pikernaze like a grinning pumpkin. She always went spare in the attic when the moon was full.

Dai Bando from High Doss, it was down at the station; sitting with his arms around his knees on a navvy's red handkerchief, the sign that he was available on the tramp.

'Jesus,' I ejaculated. 'What brings you?'

Dai got up; life had stretched vertically: a sunflower head on a builder's lath, with haricot beans for eyes still and a spotty complexion. Aye, life had changed him from the bright-faced boy in High Doss; only his mother could love him now.

He said, 'I began on platelaying with the Taff Vale, for I got out of High Doss soon after you left, Nick Wortley. I heard as how you changed your name to Farrer.'

'Did you now?' I eyed him. 'What's on?'

'Come for a job, haven't I?'

'Here, at Woodhead?'

'Why not? You're here, ain't you?'

'What does that mean?'

He was after something, and I didn't know what. The Bandos were simple-minded but not simpletons. And now I wondered if this one knew anything about the police tip-off to the Glossop Special Constables.

You couldn't trust a Bando. Dai's father used to knock off a pig, hang it in the cemetery vaults near High Doss, then cut slices off it and sell it at double price to his missus for his dinner.

But he had nothing on Dai's uncle, Bobo Bando, who had his chin clipped off at the Battle of Waterloo. Bobo and some of his muckos had been detailed as pall bearers for Nelson's funeral. And when they'd heard that England's hero had been pickled in alcohol, they tapped the pickling for a randy. Talk had it that Bobo, who couldn't swallow properly, poured the concoction straight down a speaking trumpet into his stomach, and they didn't see Bobo for days. Which, according to Dai is how they got the term 'half Nelson'.

Now Dai said, 'It don't mean nothing, boyo. Who cares what ye call yourself? But a lot of people cared about you when you did the bunk from High Doss. The police, for instance.'

'The police?'

'I need money, and I need it bad,' said Dai Bando, and he looked at me. 'Not just for eating; folks don't have to eat if it comes to the push. Opium.'

'What?'

'Opium,' said Dai, and then I remembered Uncle Bobo and the poppy drug he had brought back from his sailing days.

Dai Bando stood before me and I saw his emaciated face, his rags fluttering in the hot wind, his broken boots.

'I've got no money, Dai,' I said.

'Perhaps no, but Ruth Brandt has.'

'Ruth Brandt? I don't even know where she is!'

'I do. Listen, Wortley, I reckon you owe me. Do ye know they hanged my pa? Joe Wortley fizzled and gave every name he thought of; he named Rolly Hill and Benno Oldroyd; he gave poor old Tim O'Shea, young Bridget's feyther, and he weren't even in on it, he even signed for you, his adopted son.'

'Me? I wasn't on the Horseferry business!'

'You weren't, till they broke his fingers and then he gabbed to the Devil. They hanged 'em dead, my pa included.'

'God help him.'

'God help Joe Wortley? God help *you*, ye means. Don't you read the newspapers? The name o' Nicholas Wortley were all over the pages.' Dai drew himself up and smiled. 'And only me and Patsy knowed where you'd got to.'

'Patsy?'

And I saw, looking past him, a woman standing out of the sun. Raising a hand, Dai clicked his fingers and Patsy O'Hearne, with her hands behind her back, sauntered towards us.

Life had changed Patsy in five years from the harlot of High Doss to the beggar of Woodhead. Yet, despite her tattered clothes, the matted black hair that straggled her face and neck, she still possessed her strange feline beauty.

'We got to have money, Nick Wortley,' she said, joining us.

'Go to hell!'

'Jesus, would ye cut the throats o' the walkin' dead? God save you kindly. In the memory of your sweet mother, give us bread?'

Despite the horror of the meeting, humour touched me, a mental phenomenon I have known all my life. Looking at poor Patsy, a rhyme came to me, and I smiled at my own thoughts: 'Here lies the body of Patsy Jones; a thousand hands have caressed her bones. They had her standing, they had her lying; in the end they had her flying.'

'What you laughing at, Nick Wortley?'

'Nothing!'

'Ye'll laugh on the other side of your face when we've done with you,' said Dai. 'We want money and you can get it off that Brandt piece. Patsy was looking through the window of the Big House and saw her give you some.'

'She got married and went down south,' said Patsy.

'Then she'll have changed her name. Look, I can't give you money, but I can get you a job – at least you'll eat.'

'Doin' what?' asked Patsy.

Dai said, ignoring her, 'Old Sam Brandt married her off to some old fella building railways, I heard tell.'

'Where?'

'Search me. Wherever there's new railways.'

Their stomachs were rumbling; I could hear them yards away, and I pitied them.

'Come with me,' I said. 'Eat first, and we'll talk later.'

It was a mistake, and I paid for it later.

'Ay ay,' said Patsy, 'we'll talk about money, Nick Wortley. And even if you slope off, we'll come after you. We'll come after you, Old Nick, and see to you proper if you slope, and find you wherever you may be.'

Now, down at The Hermitage I introduced them to the shant men. Lounging off shift, many of them strangers to me for they had just joined us, they looked up at Dai and Patsy with surly disregard.

'Well, I never did!' exclaimed Patsy. 'Twelve of 'em! And all big fellas.'

'She'll need a wash, mind,' said Zeke.

That same night I got up well before the dawn, and with a bundle on my back I left Woodhead Tunnel and took to the road, and the sun was cutting the throat of the sky in blood redness that could have been an omen.

There was nothing else I could do. Now that they had found me, I had to slope off.

It was June the 12th, 1843: I didn't know where I was going, I had twelve shillings in my pocket; Abby had walked out on me and I had no prospects; only hope, perhaps, was to scarper off abroad somewhere.

Some birthday!

Book two

Chapter twenty-two
1848

I tell you this on a baby's life, there's no place in the world like Wales in summer. Nothing to compare with the gorgeous decorated parade that Nature spreads so bountifully. Of north and south, the country or the people, you can take your pick of beauty.

In North Wales the people are private and contained – 'Would you like to come in for a cup of tea?' they say; while in South Wales the folks are ebullient: 'Come in and 'ave a cup o' tea, love.'

Because they fought the Romans in their rock fortresses with tooth and claw, they look at you twice north of Rhayader, to see if you've got a Roman nose. Down south they don't care if you haven't got a nose; you can be French, a Spaniard, a Japanese or an Eskimo, so long as you behave yourself, which means adopting south-Welsh ways. Two nations? No! People are people – the same in the soul wherever you go, though the habitation comes different.

As Abby once said, 'We all come from caves, but we had pictures in ours.'

Five years I'd been away in France first employed on the extension to the Paris-Rouen north to Le Havre Line, and had now come off a ship in Cardiff. Having cleansed myself of the mutilations of Woodhead and put Dai Bando and Patsy off the scent, I was now back in the Welsh valleys in the same economic state as I had left them when I was eight years old. And as I entered the little town of Rhymney on that hot July evening, I felt as one with my country and my people.

There was a gaggle of girls squatting on their hunkers outside the Farmer's Arms as I came in off the railway, and I

147

knew for certain they'd take the mick, but if you want a bed you're in the hands of the locals.

'Hey up!' I said, resting my bundle.

'*Jawch*, listen, girls, he must be English.'

'Welsh,' I said, 'so a little less old tongue. Can you tell me of a bed for the night?'

'We can lean ye on a rope in the Grubber at a penny a throw.'

'Come on, come on!'

'How about Meg Beynon's place?' They connived and giggled.

'*Diawl*, no! Her old man kills the bloody lodgers.'

'Or Aggie Evans?'

'She'd starve the bugger.'

One got up. She looked like a brickfield maiden, more ragged than her companions, her arms were bandaged and stained with blood. She asked:

'You mind the English?'

'I'll take a Chinee, if she can cook.'

'You know Clarence Row?'

One whispered, making big eyes, 'Mind, he do look a proper Charlie, don't he!' but I ignored it.

The first girl smiled. Behind its caked dirt, her face held a strange aesthetic beauty, and she said, 'Look, follow the railway till you hit the Carno Old Houses – anyone'll tell you, for that's too far. There's a pub on the corner of Clarence and Landstone. Ask for Mavis Tommer in Number Three.'

'But don't mention the name of Poll Plenty!' shouted another.

They crowed and cackled like hags of the French Revolution. Off-work-dirty, aye, but solid gold, and I'd not have changed them for London debutantes. And then one shrieked, cupping her hands to her mouth:

'Hey, Da Point-Five! Come over by 'ere!'

Out of the pub clattered half a man. With his legs off to the thigh, he was strapped to a little trolley on pram wheels,

148

and he shot towards us with amazing speed. Reaching us, he wheeled about, his impish face wreathed in happiness.

'What you want, my lovelies?'

'Mave Tommer. You been up to the overman today?'

Said he, 'I'm on me way there now.'

'Then will ye take this gent, for he's after lodgings.'

He grinned up at me and I tossed him a penny, but he snatched it in mid-air and tossed it back. 'Ain't beggin', mister, and for old Sam Tommer I do things free – give me a tow?'

I took his trolley lead and swung up my bundle, winked at the girl with the fine sensitive face and we towed each other up to No. 3 Clarence Row, Da Point-Five and me.

'Stranger, you're about to enter a palace o' saints,' said he.

A palace of saints the Tommer household might have been, but it was set in a sea of desolation. Not for nothing was Rhymney called the 'Black Patch', even by those who owned it. For my money it compared with surrounding industrial areas of the time, including Dowlais, of whom a visitor said:

Before some cottages fetid pools stand about; the cinders are flung from the doors and other refuse is cast among them which taints and ferments the air. I saw here what I had seen but once before in Liverpool – humanity that had actually become putrescent; offensive to the sight and smell – an apathy of proprietorship such as is rarely seen in any town or village or city of the Kingdom.

The ironmasters of Rhymney, for all the tame historians' efforts to canonise them as benefactors of the poor, were as guilty as Lady Charlotte Guest of Dowlais for the social degradation they heaped upon their workers.

The Guests, like the Crawshays of Merthyr, Bailey of Nantyglo and the unholy Fothergill – Rev. Monkhouse partnership of Tredegar, actually built fortifications to protect them from their employees, and few voices were raised in protest at the blatant exploitation. One lonely curate in Dowlais refused Lady Charlotte Guest the Holy Sacrament, but the Rhymney Iron Company was getting away with social murder by the time I got there. The Merthyr-Dowlais cholera, which at this moment was claiming hundreds of lives, was a direct outcome of those towns' putrescence, and since Rhymney was but a few miles from Dowlais Top, it was only a question of time before the disease got a hold amid all this dirt and filth.

Its mineral wealth attracting speculators around the turn of the century, Rhymney of the sylvan glades and mountains was doomed.

The Crawshays, who despoiled everything they touched, formed a company with Benjamin Hall, Watkin George and others. In 1817 Hall's son (who later gave his name to 'Big Ben') took over the ironworks and the process of Rhymney's defilement was systematic from that date.

Consideration for immigrant workers – many from the famines of Ireland – was tossed overboard in the rush for quick profits. Even the industrial designs of the Bute Ironworks of 1825 were copied in architecture from the ruins of Dendra in Egypt; an establishment which paralleled Pharaoh in terms of slave labour. To complete the eruptive exploitation, one, Andrew Buchan, opened a company shop that charged his famished workers – who were forced to buy from it with company tokens in lieu of coinage – 40 per cent over the prices in competitive shops – shades of Mrs Meltz.

By 1835, over thirty coal pits and levels existed in one small area of Rhymney. In these laboured children below the age of seven. Women were delivered of babies here, and sleeves and trousers were emptied, eyes put out. And the reign of terror quickened as new immigrants swarmed in. The companies seized them and harnessed them in droves for the wealth of City financiers, most of whom had never seen the sky over Rhymney.

I tell of this only to make a point: cruelty to the labouring poor in the name of greed could be found not only in an isolated case like Woodhead, which represented, for me, the attitude of industrial adventurers of the time; it also spread its tentacles of lust for profit to every corner of Victorian England.

I had left Woodhead in hope of a cleaner existence. I found in Rhymney an equal crime on the body of humanity.

Mrs Mavis Tommer was a big, raw-boned Lancashire piece with her hair in curlers and a face for chopping firewood. But she was all gentleness when she opened the door.

'I'll fetch my Sam straight off, Da,' said she to the little man, and disappeared into her tidy hall. Here gleamed brass and trinkets and I smelled a kitchen fire and roasting meat. Lumbering up to the door came her husband; a belt-and-braces man, and I knew at a glance he was hot-pot Lancashire.

'Evening, Da,' said he to the half-a-man.

'Evening, Sam Tommer. Is it well with ye?' asked Da.

'Well enough!'

'Thanks very much, Sam Tommer,' said Da from his trolley.

'Think nothing of it. I'd 'ave done it for anyone.'

The little man bowed. Sam Tommer bowed back.

'Good night to you, Mr Tommer.'

'Good night,' said Sam, and was about to shut the door when he set eyes on me. 'What can I do for ye?'

'Lodgings,' I said.

'Hold on. I'll get me missus,' and he left me standing while Da Point-Five paddled away.

'What did I tell you?' he shouted over his shoulder. 'It's a palace o' saints – saints, the pair of 'em.'

You could have shaved using Mave Tommer's door knocker. Talk had it that she used to polish old Sam's head with furniture cream, that clean and proud was she. She even treated words with thrift, as if she counted them before delivery.

'Your name?'

'Nick Jones,' I lied.

'English?'

'Welsh.'

'Single?'

'Aye.'

Her angular face threatened to chop mine in half.

'Chapel?'

'Church.'

Mavis Tommer sighed. 'Oh well, can't 'ave everything, for we've got a jumper in our pulpit in Ebenezer and 'is words do sparkle like the crowns of princes.'

'Aye,' said Sam, double bass. 'His words do sparkle, true, but there ain't a lot o' oil in ' is lamp, you ask me.'

'I ain't asking you, Sam Tommer,' said Mave.

But there was no disputing the dinner she gave me that night – *cawl môch*. If Gorger had seen it back in Woodhead, he'd have looped the loop. And while I ate, Sam smoked his clay and read the *Clarion* and Mave raised her great dark eyes over her flashing needles, for she was knitting a jersey to fit an ox – Sam Tommer.

'No followers, son.'

I gave her a nod, a grin and a wink, thinking of the ragged girl with the bandaged arms and small, aesthetic face.

'I said no followers!' The knitting came down.

'Yes, missus,' and Sam said at his newspaper, then to me, 'We got to live by bread alone in this establishment – no followers, get it?'

'Yes, Mr Tommer.'

Lighting his pipe, Sam stared at it in the dying light. 'You got a job, Mr Jones?'

'No.'

'What you doin' about it?' He turned in his chair and one of his braces caught in the top of the chair and tightened his shirt, exposing a broad expanse of muscled, hairy chest.

152

'Start looking tomorrow, Mr Tommer.'

'Fancy coal? I'm assistant overman at Lefel Glai. The drift runs under Clarence Row – listen . . .' and I lowered my spoon. The little rank-on-rank house trembled as to a subterranean fist.

'That'll be the eight o'clock journey,' said Mave. She glanced at the mantel clock. 'He's late.'

'Tell the time by them, we do,' said Sam, and spat in the fire.

He turned, and I saw on his broad coal-cut face the strength of features hewn from rock which I knew well from Woodhead: the tell-tale tattoos above his eyes, the riven cheeks.

'I asked ye if you wanted a job.'

'Count me in.'

'With shoulders like your'n you'd get your own stall. You dug anything before?'

'Tunnel tiger on the Paris–Rouen,' I said, and his expression changed from astonishment to delight, and he whispered while Mave was out in the scullery:

'Fookin' hell, can ye beat it? And I thought you was an office pansy! When she ain't lookin', I'll buy ye a pint.'

Mave came back with a kettle and he added in chosen words, 'Ah well, young man, give it some consideration, eh?'

'Considerin' what?' asked Mave, sharp as a Cardie needle.

'Him coming underground on a stall.'

She pointed a bony finger at me. 'You keep from underground, Nicholas Jones. As God's me judge, one's enough in the house. Ye go down Lefel Glai without my permission, look what happened to Da Point-Five.'

'Ay ay, what happened to him, then?' I asked.

Sam grunted saying, 'You've heard of the millstone plug – droppers, we call 'em up in Durham – ye must get those in tunnels.'

Mave said, her eyes going big, 'They'm heavy old plugs that drop down through the earth . . .'

'He knows, missus, he's been a tunnel tiger . . .' and Sam continued, 'Well, little Da got caught by one, see? It dropped in his stall while he were undercutting; knocked him down and pinned his legs to the thigh.'

'Poor little soul,' said Mave, and wrung her hands like a Calcutta beggar.

'It pinned him proper,' said Sam. 'Up I comes with a fireman's axe, and says to Da, "Look, my son, the roof'll be down next and it'll take half an hour to dig ye out – you got no legs now, any road. Do ye want to live, or do ye want to die?"

' "Chop me out, Gaffer," said Da, so I give him a rag to chew on, didn't I? And I chopped his bloody legs off. And do you know some'ut? He never raised a sigh.' Sam puffed at his pipe. 'So now he comes every day to thank me for being alive.'

I gave a thought to Little Toby Atkinson.

'Every day since – six years now – rain or shine, summer or winter.' Mave flung me a meaningful look. 'So don't you heed my Sam, for I reckon it's a-written in the stars – all wrote down, see? One day Lefel Glai's a'goin' to get you, Sam Tommer.'

'Dear me, hark at her. She do go mooney on the stars an' suchlike, don't ye, Mave?'

'No more mooney 'n you, Sam Tommer, since the Devil affronted me.'

'Who?' I asked.

'Never you mind,' said Mave.

'Old Nick took leave of her without her permission – that's what you reckon, ain't it, Mave?'

'Never you mind,' repeated Mave, 'but I've got me suspicions.'

'But if he do come again you're going to give him a hard time, ain't you?'

'He'll 'ave more than he bargained for,' said Mave, and Sam got up in creaks and groans, saying:

'Ah well, I think I'm going to stretch me legs. You like to come, Nick Jones?'

'Ay ay.' I rose from the table.

'And don't you go leading him astray, Sam Tommer,' said Mave. 'There's some long gullets hanging in the Farmer's taproom, remember!'

'Aw, come on, missus! You knows I only drinks sarsaparilla!'

'Best you do – for you anna sleepin' with me, you come back here stinkin', remember.'

'God,' I whispered on the way out. 'She's a tartar, ain't she?'

'She's one o' the seven virgins,' said Sam. 'Our Mave's the worst thing to have 'appened since original sin. Take it from me, my son, marriages are made in Hell. What about a pint?'

Later, he said, as he lifted his second quart in the Farmer's, 'This Lefel Glai – Da Point-Five'll tell ye – any collier within miles'll tell ye – is the safest old drift we've ever had in Rhymney, ain't that right, landlord?' And he clapped the man on the shoulder.

'No. You're mad,' said the landlord. 'Who's this, then, another sixpenn'orth o' accidents?'

'Give him a quart and stop your gaff,' said Sam, and we drank deep together.

It could have been the start of a wonderful friendship, but it wasn't.

Anyway, I started down Lefel Glai with Sam Tommer, assistant overman, and he shared his stall with me, which was a three-foot seam running down to eighteen inches, and at times I didn't know if I was on my arse or my elbow.

Worse, I had to compete with Sam, for he could kill a rat, pack the gob and bring down the undercut all in one movement, singing 'Rule Brittania' spare time. And it was clear to me, the moment I was underground with him, that he knew his way around.

Our tram towers were women, and one was the Welsh girl with the aesthetic features. Her name was Blod.

The Mining Act passed by Parliament in 1842, which prohibited women or child labour working underground, had not yet been enforced, certainly not in Wales; this was proved by the Commissioners' Reports of 1847 which discovered children of under six years still down in the pits. As with the Althorp's Act of 1833, which laid down that no child under nine years should work at all – the employers laughed at it.

'Ay ay!' cried Blod on that first morning.

She looked smaller underground, as if the pressure of Mother Earth had compressed her beauty into that of a child. On all fours she came down the turnout to Three Stall where Sam and I were getting it out. With her long black hair tied back like a horse's mane, she came shod: leather pads on her hands, two more on her knees, and iron-toothed scrapers strapped to her toes to give the mare a grip when hauling.

With a chain between her legs she came, grunting and straining up the pitch, for the rise to our stall was one-in-twenty. Her dress she had swept up into a train like a lady's gown, and this she had rolled up and piled across her back and shoulders, to cushion the roof falls, so her knees and thighs were bare. A phenomenon of movement was Blod when she approached, though you could hear her grunts a hundred yards off – a white face, two bare arms, two bare knees and thighs, moving against the blackness, a human disembodied.

I'd thought she was a brickworks girl, but I was wrong; her arms were cut and bleeding from the squeeze in narrow places.

156

'Where the hell you been, woman?' cried Sam, straightening.

'Jesus, you anna human!' cried Blod. 'They're ganging down at the turnout three deep. What do ye want from me?'

'Now, that would be tellin', ye marvellous creature,' said Sam. 'You got a treat for Overman?'

'Ay ay, come by 'ere and I'll spit in your eye.' She laughed gaily. 'Mornin', Clarence!' she cried to me.

'I'll give you bloody Clarence,' I said, turning over.

About ten months after I first arrived at the Tommers', I arose one morning in late spring to wash outside in the tub. The dew was sparkling on every leaf, with the old gold crumpet brimming fire after his long winter sleep.

Looking back, I reckon that the time I spent with Sam Tommer and Mave was about the happiest of my life: no fears assailed me, no hopes were unfulfilled; the memories of Woodhead's massacres were painted out in the sylvan beauty of the mountains and the neighbourliness of the people of the Black Patch called Rhymney.

As creatures of our time, we did not question the injustices, the gap between the lazy rich and the labouring poor.

In the Potteries, the killers were asthma and tuberculosis: lads in their teens and younger died like flies, the *Patriot* told us; even the *Cambrian* railed against the practice of uncaring employers whose lads ran backwards and forwards from the cold-wet air of the pottery wheels into oven temperatures of 130 degrees. They died, too, from dipping the artifacts of gentry taste into a solution containing carbonate of lead.

'You could take this child's chin and shove it into his mouth,' said a witness before the Royal Commission investigating the match trade when describing the effect of 'phossy jaw' – a condition caused by splashes of the heated phosphorus used on match-heads. But if the report on the

157

'Condition of Factory Children' had been washed overboard by the employers who opposed it, the fight of the embryonic unions went apace.

Shaftesbury's descriptive brilliance – he referred to the workers as 'like a mass of crooked alphabets, so bent and twisted are they by their deformities' – had produced but a small echo in the crippled hearts of our national politicians.

Things in Wales were as bad, perhaps worse, than conditions in Yorkshire, where fathers still beat their children for falling asleep, to save them from a worse beating by the factory overmen. And the heroes of Chartism – John Frost, Zephaniah Williams, William Jones and a thousand other intellectuals – were safely in Botany Bay. Here the flower of a self-educated lower class laboured under the whip in transportation, or died under the brutal prison conditions of Norfolk Island.

The cream of labour's leadership, men who had led the hopes of the under-fed millions, had been extracted from the radical organisations by armies of government spies under such men as Melbourne, he who selected the innocent Dic Penderyn for judicial example – death by hanging – and perpetuated Victoria's filthy sentence of hanging, drawing and quartering.

I tell of these things as an act of conscience. I was aware that I should continue the fight for social justice which old Gaffer had sown within me. But safe houses make cowards of us all; my new world was in a reasonable condition and I accepted the easiest line. Like Chartism, which once burned a bright flame in the hearts of every Welshman, the fire within me was slowly being extinguished by ease and comfort.

It was a very gay bachelor's life: women were plentiful; memories of Abby Nothin faded into the old reflective dream of Ruth. The haunting outcasts of Woodhead, with their lust for revenge, were erased in the beauty of another April morning in Rhymney.

★

Down in the Old Furnace area, columns of yellow, sulphuretted smoke were pouring out, dulling the sun. The beating day-shift steam hammers of the new Union Ironworks pulsated like Vulcan's heart. The ground trembled beneath my feet as I plunged my hands into the garden tub. Sing and dance, shout with the scald of the cold, stripped to the waist; tuft up the hair with soap, puff it under the arms.

'*Jawch!*'

Old Mave Tommer now, halfway out of the window upstairs, waving her dishcloth at me. Young Mrs O'Sullivan, the Irish piece next door, big-beamed and fat-bosomed, pulling out her mangle for the Tuesday wash: 'Me mam called yesterday, Mr Jones. Mornin', Mrs Tommer. It do put you out, girl, don't it! You can 'ave a few bits in my copper, if you like. Ach, dear me, what a lovely spring morning! No conscience in the weather lately, is there? Your man on early shift, is he? I'll tell my Annie to play respectable if he's sleepin'.'

Now Mave, from the kitchen, 'You still out there, Nick?'

'Coming now just!'

'Your bacon's goin' to a cinder. Sam Tommer!' she bawls up the stairs. 'Next time I calls it'll be with boots!'

Next door but six, there's a palaver, for Grandma's got the wrong bloody teeth again and Alfie, aged six, is swinging on the door of Kingdom Hall and Grandpa's still on the seat. Next door but three, one of our Tommy's suits is being cut down for our Dick, and hold him steady, for Gawd's sake, while I do 'im under the crutch. Pigs and piglets are snuffling, somebody's done it in Aunty Gertie's boots; dogs barking, cats being booted, children being belted for wetting the beds.

Wizened harridans play hell with sobbing daughters-in-law, boozy old uncles are still on their backs, their sheet-tight stomachs rising and falling in a choir of snores.

And the colliers are coming down from the cottages near the Beaufort. All women inside please, lest it brings bad luck in't pit. Commands are being shrieked from the parade ground up by Barrack Road where squads of drooping English fatigue drills wilt in the morning sunlight, and I'll give 'em bloody soldiers if they happen round here, says Mrs Bridget McNamee, who comes from Cork. Kids are playing hoopla now, babies screaming to drown the hooters. You've never heard such a racket since they found the curate in bed with a redhead from Abergavenny, said Sam.

Peace now in Mave Tommer's prim little kitchen – peace in the smell of bacon and the tick-tock of her new emporium clock.

'Last night,' said Mave, 'I 'ad an intercession with a spirit.'

'You 'ad what?' asked Sam.

I'd heard it all before. In her flowerbox outside the window, the sky was dulling over; even the daffies looked as if they'd been out all night, and so did Mave.

She said, 'A lot o' funny old things do happen in Rhymney, mind. They've found bones and old cans in the new excavations, you heard?'

'I know one thing,' said Sam, munching. 'It must have sent the pastry flat. Even old Croats and Slocombe get better apple tart than me – that last lot dropped out of a horse.'

'He do come about midnight, most nights now,' said Mave at nothing. 'Ever since we 'ad that conjurer under the bed, remember, Sam?'

'Jesus,' said Sam, as I got into my tea.

'Atonement he do come after, I do think,' said Mave.

Sam shot me a droopy look, took Mave's hands and said, 'Don't start all that again, Mave, my love . . .'

'God will strike a match,' said she at the daffies, 'and the tinder of me soul will be in torment for ever.'

Sam whispered, 'Look, girl, that's all me eye – your sins beside the powers of redemption is like hitchin' our po to

160

the stern of a British man o' war. You anna done nothin' wrong, don't fret, Mave.'

She turned to me. 'I ain't given to bad language, as you know, Nick Jones, but the bugger's after me, sure as fate.' She took my hand. 'I shouldn't 'ave done it, should I, really speakin'?'

'Done what, Mave?'

'Never you mind,' said Sam.

Later, underground in the stall, with the horse-way going like Hamlet and the coal tubs crawling like ants in the hive, old Sam pulled his lamp over and turned his sweat-stained face to mine.

'Tommy time, son?'

'Aye, bait,' I said, and we sat together on the gob, throwing coal at the rats who knew bait time to a second; a pair of them crawled out to stand on their hind legs to clean their whiskers.

'Every so often she do get these geniflexions,' said Sam.

'Gets what? Mave, you mean?'

He pushed in a cheese sandwich. 'Ay ay, sort of nautical collaterals. She 'ad one last night – reckons Old Nick's in bed wi' her.'

I rubbed my face with the back of my hand.

'She reckons it's . . . it's, well, out of the ordinary, if you know what I mean.'

I said I didn't.

'Now, come on, ye wasn't born yesterday – come on!'

'Oh, that,' said I.

'My Mave do reckon it's wrong see. But it ain't a thing ye can talk to the vicar about, is it?'

'Why not?'

I thought he was contemplating this, then he said, 'I could kill that kid next door, ye know.'

'What's he got to do with it?'

'Well, a couple o' years ago me and Mave were as happy as two larks – a marriage of nobility and grace, the vicar

161

called it. Then that kid next door starts kicking his balloon about and loses it, and we thought it 'ad gone up our chimney.'

I wondered where this was leading.

'So that night, around midnight, our Mave gets out of bed to use the chamber – mind, I'd been down to the Beaufort and was back teeth awash, but I was up like a bolt when Mave shrieked and shot back into bed with her nightie up.

' "What's up, Mave?" ' I asked her.

' "Somebody interfered with me rear," ' said Mave.

' "Ach, don't be daft!"

' "He did, *he did*. Somebody put his hand on my bum – I tell ye, Sam Tommer, there's a conjurer under the bed," and she sat there squealin' and cryin', so I tucked up my nightshirt and climbed out and pushed the lighted candlestick under the bed for a look, and there was the most almighty bloody bang that blew me back into the bed again.'

' "Christ, he's got a gun!" shouted Mave, and pulled the sheets over her head, and there was me trying to hold her down, for she was yelling to raise the neighbourhood, with doors comin' open and windows goin' up and what the hell's happening to Mave Tommer, her old man must be killin' her, and then I remembered that kid an' his bloody balloon – I'd just exploded it, and blown the candle out.

' "Quiet, quiet, woman!" I shouted, and held her, and she was shivering like a jelly.

' "It's the Devil under the bed. It's Beelzebub!"

' "It's nothin' of the sort," said I. "It was that kid's balloon," and this settled her wonderful.

' "Well, I never!" said she. "Of course, Sam, just fancy me thinkin' a thing like that!" and she leaned over and reached down for the chamber-pot, got hold of the candle instead of the handle, and I reckon she rose ten feet.

' "It's him, I tell ye!" she shouts. "I've got his John

162

Thomas!" and she was out of that bed, down the stairs, along Clarence, and I didn't catch her till she got to Capel Ebenezer.'

We sat in silence save for the squealing of the rats as they packed the gob in the next stall down.

'And our martial relations anna been the same since,' said Sam.

It was just before the end of the shift that the mare Blod came up with her tram for a last haul. She came with Crid Olwen, her mate who took in lodgers in Bryn Seion Street, and Crid had her little lad with her, aged five, sitting in her tram; as pale and skinny as death, was he.

Old Sam loved little lads and he lifted the lad out and cradled and cooed, and Crid said he was called Ifor Bach after his dada who was killed down Meredith last autumn, after getting drunk at Waun Fair. Meredith Pit that later was the grave of a girl whose lover threw her down its shaft.

And now Old Sam looked into the child's eyes and stroked his face upward with gnarled fingers, and I saw his tears in the flickering light of the candle. Crid said, shoving him:

'Aw, come on, Sam Tommer! Your Mave'll give ye one like him if ye play soft wi' her, like.'

Hollows for eyes had she, for she saved her food for her son ('I mean, folks like us can't expect to eat regular, can they, Nick Jones . . .?') and her hair, coal-grimed, was like tangled seaweed as she took the boy from Sam and fed him at her breast.

'It's the milk he do go short of, sorry. I'll be feedin' him through the school railings at this rate, won't I? – when we get a school?'

'Mind, your fella would 'ave gone for him,' said Sam. 'He were right keen on little lads, weren't he?'

I watched. The little boy suckled gentler than a baby.

In growing anger, I watched, remembering that gentry

fillies handed their brats to wet-nurses lest they spoiled the shape of their breasts, while Crid Olwen, widow, fed her son in coal dust 500 feet underground.

Overman's whistle went for the end of the shift just then, and Blod and Crid hauled off on all fours with their trams, but Blod stopped and called over her shoulder, 'Oh, Sam, there's a Pontypridd lad up on Fourteen Stall askin' if you take in lodgers.'

'Tell him we got one,' bawled Sam, packing tools.

'Says he'll share a bed wi' the one you got. Says he's a friend of yours, Nick Jones.'

I looked up, lifting my candle. 'A friend of mine? Did he say his name?'

'Dai Bando,' said Blod, and hauled off.

'It'll be you he's after then,' said Sam.

Caught up with me already. I'll have to go from here, I thought.

Which was a pity, for I'd begun to love the people of the Black Patch called Rhymney. And more than anyone I'd miss old Sam Tommer and Mave who was fancied by the Devil.

Later, I heard they'd up and gone over to a place called Resolven in the Vale of Neath, taking with them Da Point-Five.

God speed them.

I tell you something else, on a baby's life – I've never come across such people.

Chapter twenty-three

So I left Rhymney Valley, and was sad.

What is there that catches at the heart when you leave a well-loved place and loving people? Price Street, Church Street, Bryn Seion and Brewery Row. Clarence Row where Mave Tommer's washing flapped on the line, and the trams of Lefel Glai telling the time by rumbling underneath the kitchen – when Sam was due home, when to put the joint in, when to start for chapel.

Now the old engine house at the side of Clarendon Row, always puffing steam, and the house they took down – Mrs Evan Evans' place – where the ropes ran through to the drift. Black-faced colliers coming and going. Smells of aniseed balls and rhubarb tart and crusty brown loaves in the ovens at the bottoms of the gardens.

Oh, this beloved land that ensnares the heart!

Camphor balls in funeral suits; black manes of horses in the window of Zachariah Put-You-Down; and the fiery denunciations of Joseph ap Pringle-Jones echoing down the street of Carno from Capel Ebenezer on Sunday evening, and the lovely-ap-lovely singing of the tonic sol-fa sopranos and the tuning-fork contraltos ringing down from Lower Cross.

And now I was on my way again with my bundle, making for Pontypridd where certain delectable inhabitants, bless them, are always prepared to give away little bits of themselves to others less fortunate.

For instance, in Mr Adam Top-Note's Sunday School, from which I'd graduated, aged seven (aged forty, he was still a boy soprano, having hurt himself on a bicycle), you could always get a dunk of Nellie Williams's sherbet dab or a lick of Jasmine Certainty's toffee-apple when they weren't looking. And if you stood howling on a brewer's grille and claimed you'd lost a ha'penny down it, you could bank on landing a penny from the first English idiot.

Clothes on a washing-line will always give you a hint as to the character of a town, so I studied these intently as I went over the Old Bridge into Taff Street, Ponty.

Although it was market day, the wives had been at it with their tin baths and washing-boards since early morning, scrubbing their fingers to the bone. Down on the Taff shore as I went over, they were there in gaggles, sweating like colliers as they hit the buttons off their old chaps' shirts on the rocks, singing and jabbering; giving everybody a going-over from Queen Victoria to the Mayor of Newport.

Women make a town, not the men: they husband the seed and bring it forth while the planter looks on; they generate the perfumes of romance and kitchens. With their little lace pretties or two-acre bloomers on a washing-line, the delicate chemises or two-gallon hold-'em-ups ballooning in the wind, the whole of woman's history can be read in the coloured washing of a little Welsh town.

The sun had his sleeping bonnet on and its tassel well down as I pushed my way that evening through the market crowds, the market being the beating heart of Pontypridd.

Anything from a pin to a shroud can be bought in the market; things like battleships needing advance orders.

As usual, it was like an Irish parliament, with everybody talking and nobody listening, for the Welsh, especially valley folk, are given to solemnity, sanctity and are silent by nature.

Hawkers were bawling their wares; market farmers slapping up the little cold carcasses of poultry, with porkers, alive and dead, well to the fore. Trinkets of twenty-carat gold were being flogged for next to nothing; haberdashers rolling out bales of cloth from Flannel Street, Abergavenny; teeth being extracted to the music of a brass band, hair being cut, feet butchered by qualified chiropodists.

Special dispensations were offered on coffins – sixpence a foot for white pine, love, twopence a foot more for mahogany and brass handles – with potential customers trying them for size: cut price for females over six-foot-six and males under four-foot-four, with free lilies of the valley for the dear departed.

You could have opened a human sardine factory on the evening I returned to Ponty, for the people were packed twenty deep around the stalls, arguing with the packmen from Cardiff, and the women pulling out the materials, saying, 'Oh, ain't it lovely, Blod?' and others shoulder to shoulder in the eating-shops, putting down bowls of granny's broth and faggots and peas.

Tar-brushed mandarins were shouting their wares: 'All the way from India, girls – stolen from a maharajah's palace,' with kids playing Touch Me Last around the women's skirts, sticking themselves up with aniseed balls and cough drops.

Wizened grandmas were pinned on sticks, arming tottering grandfers too old to die. Hags and crones, bright-eyed girls and boys with longing eyes – this was Ponty on the day I came back.

The place was going full blast, giving out a great orchestral sound on the still mountain air, and you've never heard such a racket since a hypnotist in black took pink garters off the Bishop at Michaelmas Fair.

Mind you, what I like best about my people is their inborn docility, but like most nationalities they can be the victims of provocation, like Mrs Billa Jam Tart when an Indian fakir fiddled her over a painting of 'A thrush dying on Sunday morning'. Normally generous to incoming strangers, she hit him a Merthyr dork that turned up his hobnails and rammed the dying thrush down over his ears.

But such actions are the exception rather than the rule.

And one thing was sure, there was a welcome for me in the Tredegar Arms where the customers were putting it down like lift-and-force pumps.

The Allsops called to me after the dust of the road, and I shouldered my way through the boozies, slammed down a florin on the bar . . . and looked straight into the lovely face of Jasmine Certainty, once the love of my life and now surely passed on from a surfeit of affection.

'*Diawch!*' exclaimed Jasmine. 'Look what the dog's brought in,' which, for Pontypridd, is a truly ecstatic welcome. 'What you doin' round these parts, my lovely?'

'Looking for you.'

She was called away by clients then, and two old girls I remembered from my past were giving the sorrows of Baal a going-over. Sodom and Gomorrah they were called, and Sodom said:

'His relations don't write to him no more – he got the grandfather clock, ye know? So I write him birthday cards and forge their signatures, bless him,' and Gomorrah replied:

'Aye, poor old bugger. Never mind, my duck, he'll soon be dead.'

Jasmine came back then; her mascara eyes drifted over me and she said in a Handel contralto: 'Well, well, 'ave you grown some! I could spend some time fallin' over you in the dark, sonny. What's your name?'

'Nick Davies.'

'That weren't your name in the past, was it?'

'The past is a long time dead.'

Jasmine pouted red lips and looked like Delilah did before the roof fell in. 'Dear me, with a body like yours, I expect you've got a lot to hide.'

I nodded. 'Paternity orders, mostly.'

Now she lifted a bottle of lemonade and looked at the label. Give these valley pieces half a chance and they extract the water.

'What's your pleasure, sonny?'

'You,' I answered, 'when you're finished here tonight.'

'You'd be lucky!'

She leaned towards me and the shadows were deep in her breast, and she whispered, 'Tell ye what, boyo, drop a penny down by 'ere and your pint'll turn into a quart, for the landlord's an old sod and I'm saving up for Christmas.' She added, patting herself, 'The one on the right is old and mild, the one on the left is Guinness, and the one in the middle ain't that bitter.'

'I'll take a lease on it. Threepence a week?'

The clients were bunching at the bar, giving us queer old looks and sighs, and while Jasmine was pouring the pewters, I looked around the bar and listened to the sounds of home.

'No need to get nasty now, Blod,' said one.

'If virginity means virtue, girl, I'm bloody perfect . . .'

'Dogs are terrible snobs, ye know . . .'

'Aye, she's a handsome wench and ought to milk well . . .'

'Gets right up my nose, he do . . .'

'Yes, I know, and he's a bit skinny up in the attic an' all . . .'

'She do never iron the flap of her chap's shirt, ye know, but she always does the lodger's.'

'The doctor says I've got an antiquarian in me passage.'

'No, love, no – an antiquated passage. I've got one, too.'

'Oh, that's nice – 'ave you, Sal?'

These were my people; this was my country; Ponty was my town. They can be as grave as the tomb, as religious as tribal monks and fussier than two hens' arses, but you couldn't buy them for gold.

Now they pressed about me, for they were piling in at the door of the public in smells of jellied eels, Woodbines, boot polish and saveloys, and there was one I noticed immediately, for he was topping six-foot-six, a mountain of a man. The moment he entered I smelled him for gunpowder, which was the smell of Woodhead. Beside him, two old scholars were engaged in an argument concerning the theory of Marlowe putting it over Shakespeare.

'You been around,' ain't ye!' said Jasmine, coming back from the clients. 'Where did you pick up that cauliflower ear?'

'Playing tennis.'

'Oh, dear me!' Hand on hip now. 'Would ye like to play tennis with me?' And she went coy and made no eyes to mention. 'I've got a spare room if you're looking for a bed.'

'You wouldn't lose by it.'

'Nor gain a lot. Remember, Nick Watchercall-it, when we was five years old? "I'll show ye mine if you show me yours"?'

'Behind the woodshed!'

'Good days, weren't they, lad!'

'No,' I said. 'Perhaps good for you, Jasmine. My people went to transportation, remember?'

'I didn't know about that,' said she, and left me again.

When she returned, I asked, 'Are there any jobs going around here?'

She thought a bit, then jerked her head to the big man in a corner, saying, 'If there is, Rees Evans will know about it. He's a striker in Brown Lenox. I'll whistle him over,' and the man turned as she did so, two fingers in her mouth like a collier.

'I'll do a good turn for you, one day,' I said.

Rees Evans came over, gently handling people aside, and I sensed the power in him. He had the look of a mountain fighter, with a nose that had been into somebody else's business, and white-scarred cheeks and ears like little bits of his brain battered out of his skull. Now he stood back and weighed me for size, nodding.

'He could make a striker.'

'I'd be obliged to you, mister,' I said.

'Me, too,' said Jasmine.

Rees Evans said, looking past me:

'Don't be obliging back, sonny. She's me brother's. All

170

right? Eight o'clock tomorrow morning – Brown Lenox. I anna promising anything, but I'll speak to Foreman.' He swung about to face Jasmine. 'What about a bed?'

She was pouring a client's quart, and said over her shoulder:

'Try Mrs Ezra, the Jew. Good cook, clean as a pin. She dusted out her cottage on the day she was evicted. Davies Terrace, Number Three – happy little soul, like most fat women.'

With the stalls coming down in Market Street and the packmen getting on their way, the final assault on the ale houses was made.

They came hulla-ballooing into the Tredegar Arms shouting their orders and pushing for room, and a dear little fella called Tommy No Hands flapped his empty sleeves at the bar, climbed up on Jasmine's counter and, to wild applause, began to sing:

Near Ponty town we dwell, me and me old jam tart.
On Market Day we decided on a treat,
Saying we'd meet in the middle of the street,
But some wicked fella got her at midday
And stole her clean away!

Everybody was clapping now while Tommy No Hands whirled his sleeves like catherine wheels and did a sort of hopscotch on the counter, with mouth-organs going *oompa! oompa! oompa!* and out hopped the two old girls, Sodom and Gomorrah, and began a Highland fling in the sawdust, kicking up their high-laced boots and shrieking for Sioux Indians, and Tommy yelled:

Then I searched everywhere,
Merthyr, Dowlais, Aberdare,
Trying to find the thief.
Over the mountain top I went,

Scoured the towns all over Gwent,
And thought I'd die of grief.

And the customers bawled in chorus, 'He thought he'd die of grief, poor soul, he thought he'd die of grief!'

Then over to Rhymney and Beaufort flew,
Having heard she'd been seen there with a Jew
And a couple of Chinamen bound for Crewe,
And I thought she'd end in Timbucktoo
For love, love, love.

And now the chorus: 'He thought she'd end in Timbucktoo, for love, love, love.'

So imagine my surprise;
I could scarce believe me eyes.
For just when I began to sing this ditty
There was me old jam tart.
Three sheets in the wind, while I mourned her loss,
Sitting on the knee of a colliery boss,
Knocking back gins, so pretty,
Boozing in the Old White Hart!

Chorus:

Boozing in the Old White Hart,
Sitting on the knee of a colliery boss.
There was his old jam tart!

Shouting 'Good night!' I shouldered my way to the door, kissed Jasmine in my mind and walked out into the soft evening air.

The light was russet brown, I remember, like the breast of an ageing robin; swallows and darkness were swooping over the land.

Half an hour later, I was knocking on the door of No. 3 Davies Terrace near the chain works, which was thundering and baying on the clouds in brilliant, scintillating colours. Mrs Ezra, widow, was four-foot-ten, she told me: 'Rub me own footprints out, my love, but girls with duck's disease are very good cooks, you know.' Her breast and stomach were manufactured in one piece beneath a snow-white apron, and the face of Mrs Ezra was a bunch of laughs. 'After all, ye've got to laugh, haven't ye – life is so ridiculous, ain't it?' said she.

And now: 'Hallo, my charmer. Ain't you a fine big fella! Lodgings, is it? Jasmine sent ye, did she? Come you in, son, and make yourself at home.'

A starched white cloth, a quart of ale and a plate of steak and kidney pudding; seven bob a week, all found, including sheets.

No wonder God divided the sea off Barry to let the Israelites proceed.

'*Darro!*'

Landed on my feet.

Chapter twenty-four

Brown Lenox Limited, then called the Newbridge Works, was the beating heart of Pontypridd. I could remember, even as a child in Pwllgwaun, lying in bed in No. 16, sucking my thumb and watching red light playing on the window of my bedroom: when the Big Works hammered the Cyfarthfa iron, you could read a newspaper on the Old Bridge at midnight.

Indeed, my little town might never have come about had it not been for Samuel Brown, an officer who retired from Nelson's navy to invent and produce wrought-iron chain, replacing the hempen rope used for ships' anchors. But that was way back in 1806, and since then, the firm had mushroomed so that almost every other man in Ponty was employed there – that is, until the advent of coal.

This began with little private shafts in 1800 – like Boyo Glyn's Pit and bigger drifts like Fforest Fach, which was sunk in 1838. And now, with the sinking of the big Coedcae shaft about to begin, the commercial value of coal was realised. Later came the famous Dan's Muck-hole.

Originally, coal was transported over the mountains to distant towns by pack mules – their drovers, the outcast roughnuts of the iron industry, fighting like animals for right of way on the narrow, precipitous valley tracks. Then came the famous Stockton to Darlington railway in 1825, followed by the Taff Vale railway in the 'hungry 'forties', built by a navvy contractor called Wythes using the mechanical genius of another – Mr Abraham Jowell – more of whom later.

Tram roads to start them off were followed by the Glamorganshire canal that flowed to Cardiff. Meanwhile, Brown Lenox had grown from a specialist ironworks into one of the most important engineering outputs in the world.

Sam Brown, former lieutenant in the Royal Navy, had by his inventive genius turned the village of Newbridge into a flourishing Pontypridd.

'Name?' asked the foreman.

'Nicholas Davies,' I answered.

Another official change of surname would be diplomatic, I thought.

I saw Rees Evans drift back to his forge. Stripped, he looked even bigger, an Atlas swinging a ten-pound hammer.

Big men were necessary, of course. The man at the desk before me was built like a bull, yet his voice, when he addressed me, was strangely gentle.

'What you done, Mr Davies?'

I didn't mention Woodhead; tunnelling wasn't my business now I was pledged to engineering. I replied, 'Clockwork shovels on the Paris–Rouen railway; later under Brassey and Locke. Mackenzie, too – he worked a mechanical shovel on the Paris-to-Le Havre.'

He lowered his pencil. 'You worked the shovels under Tom Brassey? What the hell you doin' here?'

'Travelling, mainly.'

'You could do well in Ponty. Isn't it time you settled?' He was a Johnny North, I could tell by the song in him.

I replied, 'No steam shovels in this country yet, Foreman. I'm come in off the road – got to take what I can get. Striking, like Rees Evans?'

'You're not ambitious, yeh?'

'Not particularly.'

The foreman rose. 'Steamers are coming; men like you are at a premium. You worked them – truly?'

'American steamers.'

'Maintained them?'

'Black gang working, I've done it all. Ay ay, the clockwork diggers are coming, right enough. Carne had muck-shifters sixty years back on the Hereford-and-Gloucester, and Tom Brassey dug the London sewers on steam cranes – drags, mainly. Aye, they're coming.'

The foreman jerked his head. 'I'm not putting you swinging, you'll do a good man out of a job. Follow me,' and I did so.

'I know one fella's got two steamers coming,' said he.

As I followed the foreman through the great sheds the floor was overflowing with activity.

This was a firm and a half, and I'd have liked to work there.

Here, in a Crawshay's Yard, in a scintillation of sparks and fire, molten iron was being poured from cauldrons, and stripped and sweating, giant puddlers stirred the bubbling, incandescent vats. It was controlled incendiarism by pygmy men: a gang of firing-irons here, red-faced ash-men raking out fires, many wearing the tell-tale cancerous cheek burns caused by heat, which they would carry to their graves.

On we went, the foreman leading: on to the chain-welding shops where chains of 4-inch-square links, each link weighing four hundredweight, were being made to replace 28-inch-circumference hempen ropes. Twenty such links formed a chain tested to 300 tons for use on the new ironclads. Here would be forged the biggest anchor chains in the world, including those for Brunel's *Great Eastern*.

And all about us, as we threaded a path through the forges, there arose a tumultuous shout of labour. The skilled men sat in groups. Some, it being break-time, were bathing their eyes with cold tea, the tannic acid reducing the redness and risk of cataracts brought by furnace glare. Others were tipping up bottles of weak ale and water, guzzling it down to replace sweat lost by the gallon. Steam hammers were crashing down. Huge protuberances of red iron flamed out of steam-enveloped rollers, moulded into shape to last 1000 years – buoy pendants for the shipping lanes, cables for the Royal Navy and Maritime Service.

It was a fizz-gig of activity and excitement, and I'd have given my soul to work for Brown Lenox by the time we reached a door marked PRIVATE. The foreman tapped on the glass and we entered.

'We got a steam shovel man here, Mr Lenox.'

Half an hour later I was on my way out of Brown Lenox with a letter in my pocket addressed to:

A. Jowell, Esq.
Penycoedcae Villa
Pontypridd
Glamorgan

Private to Bearer

The morning was brilliant with sun. The old gobspit spiders, anticipating autumn, had been at it all night, weaving dew-laden patterns on the hedgerows as I crossed the canal on my way back to Davies Terrace. And Mrs Ezra was down on her knees on her doorstep, I recall, scrubbing into a world of molten fire.

Smoke was rolling out of the casting sheds, dulling the sun. Canal barges, loaded to their gunwales, began their horse-drawn, sleepy journey down to Cardiff and the ports of the world. Marvellous place was Mrs Ezra's: you could reach out from her scullery and put your finger on the pulse of Ponty.

As I reached her house, the Crawshay furnace went into blast with a roar, sending a single valedictory flame shooting into the sky, lighting up a world of topsy-turvy roofs as the phosphorescent impurities were torn from the ore.

Mrs Ezra sat back on her heels and brushed stray hairs from her face. 'You're back early, son? No luck with the job?' so I showed her the envelope.

She got up, wiping her hands on her sack apron, ejaculating, 'Abraham Jowell! You've got an introduction to Abe Jowell?'

'Who is he?'

'Didn't they bother to tell you?' and the sun was on her face. 'He's the biggest thing to happen since old Sam Brown started up in Newbridge.' And she held me at arms' length, beaming.

'Dear me, and in my house, too? Jowell the Jew, is it? My, my, Nick Davies, you must be a very particular person!'

I didn't pursue it. Her face suddenly showed that she was not to be tampered with, and she knelt again and got on with her scrubbing.

Chapter twenty-five

There was a scent of burning pine needles in the night air as I crossed the river by the Malsters and took myself up the long steep hill to the Jowell villa called Penycoedcae, which, loosely translated, means the 'house of the highest trees on the hill'. It was a diadem of a night, one of besoms and witches whistling around chimney-pots; stoats were slinking and little things screeching.

Moonlight is the sunlight of the dead: this moon Jesus must have seen before the kiss of Judas.

Unaccountably, on that journey into another life I was followed in my mind by visions of Dai Bando, and Patsy's threatening wrath.

I've seen some dull old places in my time, but never one like this, with its coat of arms on the drive pillars and the wall surrounding the place. Gabled and gaunt, its top windows overlooked distant Ogmore and Porthcawl.

Houses, I reckon, are like people. You can have a blowsy matron of a house with broken windows and nothing in its larder, yet fat with mother comeliness, merry smiles and children's laughter. But this Penycoedcae was a skinny virgin of a place: gloved, imprisoned in stays and smelling of cold tea. They said that it was once a smugglers' haunt with wines from Brittany in its cellars and folks on rope neckties dancing down the well of the stairs, and I can well believe it.

No reply when I hammered on the back-door knocker, so I went round the front, had a look down the front garden wishing-well and pulled a bell-chain. A distant jangle sounded like a toll of doom, the door swung slowly open with the creak of a coffin lid and an old chap peered out; he had the face of a starved ghost, a wig to match and hands for embalming corpses. But his voice, when he spoke, came from a rent in the shroud of his soul.

'Mr Jowell is expecting you,' said he, his nose up. 'Please step this way.'

As he closed the door behind me and locked and barred it, I saw above my head an inscription:

JUDGE YE NOT A MAN'S CONDITION
UNTIL YE BE IN HIS POSITION.

I remember reflecting that I wouldn't mind being in Abraham Jowell's position about then – builder of railways and said to be one of the richest men in the county.

But I'll say one thing for little Abe: he fed me.

Taller sitting down than standing up, the old Jew regarded me with suspicious eyes from the other end of a long refectory table in a room of gilt, gold and tiger's eye.

Standing pilasters topped with metopes and egg-and-tongue guarded us in a room as cold as charity and twice as chilly. It was a mausoleum ablaze with artificial tinsel: a red-toothed grate and gold-plated chandeliers. Abe Jowell, I remember thinking, must be very lonely to be as rich as this.

With his bewigged servant in attendance, a gangling maid and a fat cook in a shroud of white apron hovering near, he sat, the Ponty Jew, as the locals called him, within his threadbare poverty.

'This is your home town, you say?' His bald head gleamed in the distance.

'Yes, sir.'

His mouth, red as a vampire's, opened to snap at his fork. 'How old are you?'

'Twenty-five.'

'Married?'

'Single.'

'I understand you've just come in from France?' he asked next, and I explained in detail.

'And you've worked steam shovels over there?'

I nodded. 'The new Americans.'

Later, drinking port, he said with a red-faced grace, for his starched collar was killing him, 'I'm mechanising, Davies. I've got two steam diggers coming into Cardiff from Kansas – on the canal. They'll dock at Brown Lenox.

'Years back I sub-contracted under George Wythes on the Taff Vale railway; after that I went on my own with the Hirwaun-and-Ponty – station construction, mainly. I've tendered for the new viaduct at Pontlottyn and I'm building the Pontypool-to-Hereford spurs at the moment. Plenty in. But the pick-and-shovel navvies are on their way out: steam and coal is the new thing . . . You're quiet, aren't you?'

'I'm listening, sir.'

He sipped his port. 'God knows how I came to this place – perhaps I made the mistake of marrying a Jew with a Welsh outlook. I've got works up in Doncaster and as far south as Southampton docks, but she wanted to live in the land of our fathers. It won't be for ever, thank God – I hate this place.'

I thought him vulgar and disloyal, and disliked him.

'But you've done well out of it,' I said.

'True, true – a quarter-millionaire in ten years – even Peto can't compete with that. Your turn now. Tell me about steam shovels.'

I began, 'They cost two thousand pounds apiece . . .' and he snapped an interjection:

'Don't bother yourself with finance yet. I want the technicalities.' To emphasise the point, he stamped with a stick on the floor.

I answered, 'One clockwork needs an engineman and seven labourers to work it – the black gang.'

'So many?' He sucked his teeth.

'One is his assistant, the other seven lift and carry.'

'Performance?' He began to light a cigar.

'A steam navvy can fill two-hundred-and-forty wagons in a day – that's about a thousand cubic yards.'

'A day of how long?'

'Ten hours, the normal pick-and-shovel shift.'

He lazed back, smoothing his brewer's goitre with slow ponderous hands. I've seen some stomachs on taproom barristers but never like the one in Abe Jowell's lap.

'Fuel?' he asked.

'A pound a day.'

'Wrong. I can work my Kansas pair on thirty shillings.'

'If you know, why ask me?'

He fixed me with small, bright eyes. I had judged his age to be sixty, but now he looked older, probably because we had mentioned money.

'Because I wanted to see if you knew. Did you like working for Brassey?'

'Better than I did for most.'

'Then why did you leave him?'

'Ponty isn't your home, Mr Jowell, but it's mine.'

'*Hiraeth*, they call it, or some bloody thing?' He showed big teeth.

'You don't know about that unless you're Welsh.'

'Tend to speak your mind, do you?'

'I haven't a lot to lose.'

'Don't you want to work for me?'

'If the money's right, I'll work for anyone.'

I looked past him. The old Brown Lenox night shift was rougeing up the cheeks of the harvest moon, who was sitting on the tops of the pine trees and grinning down at me. I thought: bloody fool, Nick, messing around with this one when you could be swinging the hammer with Rees in the Brown Lenox forging house.

There was in this man an endemic wickedness; it was an

182

evil I sensed, but never understood. He was watching me again when he said, tonelessly:

'I've just got the Hengoed-to-Walnut Tree junction, including the viaduct. I want to build it with steam shovel and End-on – hasn't been tried before. How much?'

'How much what?' I was tiring of him.

'I want a resident engineer – a ganger man. The first job is sinking a new pit – the Coedcae, a mile down the road. Seven days a week, which means Sunday working. Sink the Coedcae and we'll take it from there. Have you sunk a pit before?'

'Tunnel air shafts – hundreds of feet.'

He grunted. 'How much, then?'

I thought of a figure and remembered Old George Wythes who tendered £10,000 for a contract, told his wife about it who said he should double it, then they slept on it and they doubled it again when they awoke in the morning – in the end, they rounded it off to £50,000 on a woman's intuition; he got the contract and made £40,000 out of it. I thought of £3 a week and said:

'Fifteen pounds a month.'

'Jesus, man, you'll break me.'

Suddenly gulping at his port, Jowell rose and crossed the room. Moving aside a portrait of the hero Nelson, he produced a key from his waistcoat pocket and swung back the door of a little wall-safe, saying over his shoulder, 'You have money?'

'Not much.'

'Abe Jowell pays in advance: a small amount always hooks the fish. Five sovereigns?'

'Thank you.'

Somewhere in the big house a piano was being played – Chopin, I think. It appeared strangely out of relationship with financial bargaining, and then, with the Jew's curt nod of acceptance, the playing stopped. It was like the drop of a curtain at the end of a drama, but it wasn't: it was merely the end of Act One, the preliminary to an unfolding sequence of my life.

Soon Act Two would begin, with all its promise and terror, but this I only knew later.

Jowell said, 'I've got a fishing lodge with living accommodation down on the river near the site of the Coedcae. You can rent it. I'll get one of the gangers to knock you up an office. With a cook in daily, you'd be right on the job . . .'

While he was speaking, a woman had entered, so I scarcely heard him. Because the woman was in shadow I couldn't see her distinctly, but she was dressed in white and moved with regal dignity, and Jowell cried, getting up:

'Ah, you've come, my dear! I want you to meet Mr Davies, our new engineer for the Coedcae contract . . .'

The woman moved into the light of the chandelier above us.

It was Ruth.

Chapter twenty-six

Mrs Ezra had the disconcerting habit of sitting on the other side of the kitchen table and beaming at me while I ate my egg and bacon.

'Now I'd like that, I really would,' said she.

'Have some?' I indicated my plate.

'Me working for you down at the lodge and you working for Abe Jowell. Mind, only his mother could love him, but his wife's a little darling. Not very strong she is herself, neither – got a weak ticker, so they say.'

She added, 'It was her who paid my rent arrears. Always thinkin' of others, she is. It were my Solly's fault, largely speaking – never been in debt in me life. "To me beloved wife and comrade, I leave the back rent," he said in his will. He were an anarchist, ye know.'

She humbled a tear and dashed it away. 'Jews get three chances, see – my Solly had four. Dear little soul!'

'Mrs Jowell paid your back rent, did she?'

'Else I'd 'ave been evicted. When do you want me to start?'

'As soon as I move into the lodge.'

At the door, holding my empty plate, she said, 'Don't trust Abe Jowell, will ye, son?'

'Why not?'

'Ain't my position to say no more 'n that, Nick Davies – just don't trust him.' She turned away as the letter box clattered in the hall, and returned with an envelope.

'A letter for you, it seems – my, my, ain't you becoming important!'

It was from Ruth.

The proposed Coedcae, later the Lewis Merthyr pit site, was just outside Ponty, and the fishing lodge was just beyond that. I didn't leave Davies Terrace to go there until the moon was high.

There was in the night air a magical odour of sweet-scented pines and wisps of gipsy fires, for the Petineros, come in for the horse fair, were camping on the other side of the river. The river was chuckling obscenely as I walked its bank, taking advantage of the night's perfidious expectation, for the world seemed to be holding its breath.

She, the ancient Rhondda, who had soaked the sandalled feet of Rome, had seen all this before, including the early autumn nightingale who sang to me now, his beak upturned against the opal moon. I stopped momentarily to listen and watch; saliva bubbles from his throat were drifting up against the stars.

I thought, as I crossed New Bridge and went up to Merlin, of the secret assignations this harridan stream had shared: Roman centurion and Briton bond-maid, Welsh Tudor and barbarous English. Here on this same ground, I thought, robes were ripped and chainmail stained with blood.

Upriver, the fishing lodge was stark black, a bullfrog crouched for the spring. I approached expectantly: something rustled in the undergrowth beneath a gable, the lodge door opened and Ruth came out. She stood there for a moment, dressed in a black riding-habit, then came down the steps towards me.

I saw her against the quicksilver gleam of the Rhondda river, and a sudden wind ruffled the composure of the scarecrow trees about us, sweeping away the barrier of our parting.

She looked smaller, somehow, and certainly older, the coming matron of her years touching her face with uncertain fingers, but then she smiled, and she was Ruth.

'*Nicholas!*'

I stood with my suit on sideways and my boots on backwards, and had I worn a cap, I'd have snatched it off and screwed it. Ruth, as always, was my superior.

'You got my letter?' she asked.

All the plans I had accomplished in dreams melted away in her nearness; I was a trembling boy again.

I had known other women. A Spanish girl in a field outside Toledo; her hair was auburn. A French girl with hair like rings of gold: sunlight on a table covered with chintz, pink curtains framing a sea of tipsy Paris chimneys; her name was Chantelle and she was seventeen. We lived together for eighteen months until her chap came home from the French Foreign Legion.

Then, of course, there was Abby. Did one make love to Ruth as one made love to Abby? I wondered. Or to Chantelle, or to Marija, the auburn-haired one with hayseed on her breast? Anyway, what was this talk of making love? The one before me now was not to be snatched at and taken: this was Ruth.

To this day I do not know how she came to be in my arms; what began as a kiss of greeting ended in gasping breath.

'Oh God . . . Nicholas!' she said, and I held her.

Dry-mouthed at the possession of her, I held her, even when she tried to force herself away.

I said, 'We'll get caught, you know.'

'Quite probably.'

'You don't care?'

Her face was pale in the scudding moonlight – the wraith of lost dreams. I kissed her again, and Ruth said, 'No, I don't care. You're ten years younger than me and it's mad, but I don't. Now you are with me, nothing else matters.'

She drew away from me and we stood apart and the wind ironed the quicksilver ripples of the river into a smooth, satin sheen.

'Come, I'll show you your future home,' and she took my hand. 'Think of the irony. Abe himself suggested I should show you around.'

It hinted of deceit.

Her horse, Tom, wandered out of the bushes, munching grass, then raised his head in mute surprise at seeing me.

Within the little lodge, Ruth lit a lamp; golden light flooded the river.

I said, 'Suppose your husband arrives?'

She emptied her hands at me. 'I am doing what he asked. Besides, he's up in Doncaster.'

Ruth appeared to have changed; no longer the feckless girl of High Doss.

Later, we made tea on a little oil stove and sat facing each other within the bond of friendship.

Later still, I asked, 'When did you marry Abe Jowell?'

'What you really want to know is why.'

'All right, why?'

Now that I could see her more clearly in the better light, I noted her physical change. The cygnet of the High Doss classroom had grown into a swan. Her age now touched her with a new symmetry and grace, and the old desires assailed me.

We sat apart, but her eyes were of such translucence that they seemed to mirror my soul; the air moved within the little room, and it was perfumed. She said:

'Soon after you left High Doss, the Owenite reforms flattened the wool markets and my father lost money badly. About this time I fell in love with the son of another Jewish family, and he lived in Gloucester. We were to have been married the following year, but he was drowned when the Aust–Beachley ferry went down. I thought I'd never smile again.

'Father became ill – this was soon after the police inquiries into the murder of Mr Horseferry, for which Joe Wortley was hanged in York. As well as your adopted father, others died because he named them – those two men, Hill and Oldroyd, who often visited High Doss, remember? Two more hanged as well – Tim O'Shea, young Bridget's father – remember Bridget O'Shea? And poor old Mr Bando, Dai's father, who was nowhere near Shipley on the night Mr Horseferry was killed. Joe Wortley even named you.'

'And Dai Bando's been looking for me ever since.'

'Also the police. Is that why you changed your name?'

'Wortley, Farrer, Jones and now I'm Davies,' I said. 'But enough about me. Your fiancé died?'

Ruth nodded. 'It happened at the same time as Samuel Brandt Wool Manufacture Limited collapsed and Papa formed a partnership with Abe Jowell. I was essentially within the bargain. My father made it clear that the future of the family lay in my hands.'

'So you married the old reprobate. For God's sake!'

She replied with empty resignation. 'It was all to no avail. Within six months of my marriage, Papa died, and what assets were left passed to Little Abe.'

A faint sense of disgust beset me – that any woman could find it possible to give herself to Abraham Jowell and an old man's pitiful sexuality . . . Ruth went on:

'Actually, he's a lot kinder than he appears and he demands nothing of me. Look deeper, and you'll find we're worth each other.'

'That's a bitter thing to say.'

'Reality sometimes is.'

We sat in silence; the night put cold hands between us. Then she said:

'Abe's god is money, of course – and status. That's why he "bought" me, someone about half his age. At the moment he's enjoying a truly benevolent streak. Charitable institutions – formally acknowledged, of course – have just benefited to the tune of twenty thousand pounds; he's after a knighthood. And at a time when the poverty around here has to be seen to be believed.'

'It was always so.'

'Have you heard of the Abe Jowell Foundation?'

'No.'

'That's us. The trick, you see, is to bequeath the money

through a trust; then nobody can accuse the powers-that-be of nepotism and knavery. The whole thing's a venal fraud.'

'He knows where he's going, doesn't he!'

She laughed softly. 'There's no flies on Abe. The House of Lords, that's his aim.'

'Rascality is the sign of the times,' I said, and a silence came between us, until Ruth said:

'They burned down High Doss, did you know?'

I stared at her. 'But the people!'

'Turned out lock, stock and barrel, though I did my best to prevent it. Papa was dead by then, of course, but Abe wouldn't tolerate a co-operative in competition with the wool trade. He used the excuse of the Horseferry murder, and the militia came in, turned everybody out and burned it to the ground.'

I gripped my hands. Ruth added, 'It was actually dangerous living in Big House after that, and a relief to get away. Abe wanted to live up in Doncaster, but I insisted on South Wales, where he'd built the Taff Vale railway.'

'But why Pontypridd?'

'Because I hoped that one day you might come back here.'

'You mean that?'

Her eyes were shining with a strange light.

'It was the one choice Abe gave me – I could have lived anywhere.'

All this, I thought, was the chandelier and tinsel of their shabby palaces. At a certain level, one bargained away one's morality, rather like colliers in Rhymney, who, afraid of fairies, left food for them out of their bait-boxes, virtue being an elusive substance in a world of fear.

'You're thoughtful,' said Ruth.

We were unspeaking now; leading the horse, Tom, between us, we crossed the fields up to Penycoedcae. It was a night of wind and lanterned stars, with the moon so round and full, sitting on the rim of the mountains, that you could have reached up and touched him with a finger; the little brooks were shouting and losing their tempers in the darkness of the beech plantation, and here we stopped, leaving Tom to wander. Taking Ruth in my arms, I leaned back against a tree.

'I love you,' I said.

'I must go,' whispered Ruth.

'Oh no, please stay!'

'No, I am uncertain now; it is far too soon.'

'Too soon? It's nearly too late.' I began to unbutton the top of her blouse and she turned her head away as if in dissociation, and when I tried to touch her breast she stiffened, pushing my hand away.

'What's wrong?'

She said, gasping, 'Please don't touch me!'

'But I love you. Why not?'

'Oh God, you'd never understand, would you? Just don't do it, that's all!'

'Dear me, you are prim.'

'All right, so I'm old-fashioned!'

'I didn't say that. I called you prim – there's a difference.'

She straightened herself with business-like authority and smiled into my face. 'I . . . I really must go, Nick.'

'If you do I shall never see you again.'

'Don't be ridiculous!'

'Perhaps I'll see you, but you'll never belong to me, and I thought you loved me.'

'I do, I do!' She kissed my face and I hooked my arm about her, pulling her against me now, kissing her lips and face and hair.

'Ruth, I want you, I need you. Please stay . . .' I caught a glimpse of her eyes, large and startled and I knew she was seeking escape. I said, softly, 'Is . . . is it possible for me to make love to you?' and she looked momentarily perplexed, then said:

'Yes, of course.'

'Then why not? God, we've waited so long!'

Entrapped by youthful dreams, I kissed her again with an almost primitive longing, turning her against the tree, and momentarily she responded, caressing my face; she was in a rare old state now, me too, for her hat came off and her hair came down and a nightbird, disturbed above us, clattered away as if the Devil was after him – and no wonder, for another few moments of this and we were sinking down to the ground. And then her bloody nag came up, thinking I was killing her, I suppose, for he nuzzled and slobbered all over the back of my neck, and I looked over my shoulder and thought it was Beelzebub with his rolling eyes and two-inch teeth. This put Ruth double, holding her stomach, for as fast as I elbowed the old sod away he came back, and when he got me by the collar and hauled me off, Ruth was nearly paralytic. Pulling herself upright, she fought to cover herself, for I'd practically got the top of her off and she was holding together the neck of her petticoat now and shrieking laughter. For as fast as I elbowed the thing away he came at me again. And Ruth's laughter echoed over the lawn and doors started slamming and lights began to come on. Then I got a boot to Tom and he scampered away, and there grew between us as we stood there a new and vital understanding.

'Soon?' I asked her.

'Move into the west wing, Nick . . .'

'What about Abe?'

'Oh, to the devil with Abe!'

It astonished me and I stared at her. 'But I thought this was the trouble . . .'

And she looked at me as if I were a simpleton child, and said, 'You might have moved around, Nick, but you've got a lot to learn about women. Give me time – don't rush me.'

'When?'

'Soon, darling,' and she kissed my lips, 'soon . . .' The last I saw of her was running to catch Tom, who was grazing on the lawn: snatching his rein, she turned once to wave, then ran with him down the gravel drive to the stables.

I didn't stop for more but, whistling to have my teeth out and up to my elbows in my trews, I struck out for the bank of the river, stepping so light in my boots that I scarcely touched the grass.

The going was hard but promising; this, after all, was no Abby Nothin.

Women, men said, were queer cattle; each had to be treated in her own particular manner. I decided to give this deep consideration.

And as I walked the years slipped away in distant visions: moonlight again shafted the dreadnought sleepers of High Doss; alighting on the blue-whiskered chins of Old Soak, Little Darby the Fuller and Plum-Belly. And my adolescence beckoned within the conjured pictures of youth's defilement.

Behind the high-boned beauty of Ruth's Hebrew face I saw again the scarred pattern of my pillow in High Doss. And the plate-broken moon, now as then, touched her golden mouth.

Chapter twenty-seven

Life is a contemplation of the absurd and the sublime. If you can't laugh at it, like Mrs Ezra, you are lost. For instance, the quickest way to shift every barmaid in Ponty was to send Tommy No Hands in during slack time when the colliers were changing shift.

Talk had it that Tommy lost his hands in the hammer and press at Brown Lenox, but I doubt the story. Of one fact alone was I certain – he was the best pit sinker Wales had ever possessed, and I was lucky to get him under me when digging the shafts of the Coedcae for my new employer.

Public sympathy is bestowed on a man with a disability, and rumour had it that Tommy No Hands caught Jasmine first in the Tredegar Arms, where I first met him. Into the pub went Tommy, lined up three pints of nose-varnish on the bar, drank them one by one with his teeth while Jasmine clapped appreciatively, but then suddenly announced, crossing his legs:

'Oh dear me, *I gotta go!*'

'*What!*'

'I've got to go, *now!*'

'But what do you usually do?' cried Jasmine, pale.

'I gets one of me mates to give me a hand,' and he looked around the empty bar and started hopping.

'*Jawch!*' cried Jasmine. 'Oh, *no.*'

Had she glanced up, she'd have seen his butties peeping through the windows.

Then he enticed Charity of The White Hart, the Wednesday after Easter. Prim and shy was Primrose, but thereafter ravished by erotic dreams. Then he went over to The Old Merlin and put it over Cushy Cuddlecome's sister, but since Tommy No Hands was still alive and kicking after this event, I didn't put a lot of believing into this. Jasmine, however, was totally embarrassed, she being a highly refined person, as was widely appreciated.

'I'm not being caught twice, though,' she announced. 'Next time he tries it, I'll chop off his bloody waterworks,' which was why Tommy was never again seen in the Tredegar Arms.

He was a most remarkable fellow, this Tommy No Hands. In between affronting Ponty barmaids and sinking pits all over South Wales, he used to study Egyptology, and could quote yards of Omar Khayyám and the history of the Medes and Persians. Tommy reckoned that Darius the Great, who got shipwrecked on the coast of Macedonia in 492 BC, had no hands, either, and used to obtain assistance from a local virgin, the only one officially recorded in Babylon about then.

I said to Tommy now, 'Listen! My gaffer, Abe Jowell, is sub-contracting for this Coedcae job. I'm Jowell's engineer and you're my ganger, understand? You don't bother me, boyo, and I won't bother you,' and Tommy folded his elbows on his chest and asked:

'How many shafts?'

'Two,' I replied. 'An elliptical downcast of sixteen by eleven and an upcast nine foot square.'

'Depth?'

'Until you find coal. But the upcast no more than four hundred feet and the downcast fifty yards deeper – with a sump, of course.'

'When?'

'Completion date? Day before yesterday.'

'It'll be done before that,' said Tommy, and put back his head and bawled at his ragged contingent of sinkers, navvies, carpenters, masons and revetters in the field around him – and they looked like the Retreat from Moscow – 'Now come on, me lucky fellas, I want coal, and quickly.

Coal, *coal*, understand? And the first man slacking is down the road. I got no hands, but I got boots. Right, can ye hear me at the back?'

'They can hear ye up in bloody Mardy, Gaffer!'

Sinkers loved and respected Tommy No Hands, just like Jasmine did, and Charity and Cushy Cuddlecome's sister.

'Right, into it!' shouted Tommy.

And that's how I built the Coedcae; later men called it the Lewis Merthyr.

But all we found in the first three months of digging was water, and the pumps were at it day and night.

'What did I tell ye?' cried Tommy. 'You digs pit shafts beside a river, of course you'll get water. And the same bloody thing'll happen when they dig Ty Mawr.'

I often wonder in quiet moments if the coming generation will give us credit in the nineteenth century.

Hundred of thousands of us in my generation sweated our guts out. The sinkers dug the pits, raking around in the bowels of the earth, and got no credit; I could name a thousand pits and fill ten pages; each foot of digging soaked with blood.

I could fill another score of pages with the names of the men who died for coal; coal for the fires of the world; coal for the coke ovens and iron furnaces from Blaenafon to Hirwaun.

Men died in roof falls – one or two daily for years; were entombed, as in Dinas Pit in 1844. A hundred and fourteen men and boys were killed in Cymer Colliery eight years after this: nearly three hundred were burned to death in the Albion later – a pit called 'the Widow Maker'. And long after my time, 439 were killed at the Universal in Senghennydd, which was a butcher's shop for Wales, but good profit for Lord Merthyr. Colliers at a penny a pound.

How many died unrecorded, it is impossible to tell.

They died singly, in groups or in scores; burned to a

cinder or just fried and left to die; asphyxiated, drowned or maimed, with no pension. And, as I travel over the ravaged land of my fathers I see the ghosts of those walled up a thousand feet below; I see the shattered outcrops where my generation fought to win coal; and I think, as I pass over the caverns of darkness where my people died, of the flash of the gas around the face and the scattering hail of death. I think of the skeletons of seven-year-olds, crippled and awry in blackened places within the tortured earth: the shattered bones of a two-year-old's hand . . . taken down by his father to earn another tram; the groups expired within a circle around the dead candle, strangled by firedamp.

Likewise, when I travel by train along the Taff Vale railway, who wonders, as I do, at the monumental industry of those who made the gigantic cuttings, embankments, culverts and fences?

Who built the viaducts, whose enormity straddles the countryside valleys? Who built the stations and the doors marked 'Gentlemen' and 'Ladies' – the waiting-rooms, the locomotive sheds, the marshalling yards of Crewe? How many fingers were smashed under the stone copings of the platforms and magnificent stone façades of hotels marked with pride: GREAT WESTERN RAILWAY?

Who manufactured the freight wagons? Who extruded the steel of ninety-pounds-a-yard run, bull-head and flat bottom, amid the fumes, copper and sulphuric? Who hears the screams of men with firebox burns?

Aye, who gives a damn for the graves that stand on the hill and crouch in the valleys? Not the lady in her broad-brimmed summer hat within the first-class carriage, frilled and powdered on her way to Ascot. Not the sun-filled child on a Sunday outing to the sea, or the pin-striped businessman going up to the City for another day of financial chicanery. *Rat-a-tat-tat.* This is the song of the permanent way; the four-foot eight-and-a-half built in Victoria's 'Age of Heroism', when men could be had for twopence an hour. Who gives twopence for the lifter and packer, the ballaster, the signalman or driver on a slave wage with a thousand lives in his pocket?

Nobody. Not even I who have done these things: not you, who lack imagination.

We are all guilty of ignoring another's suffering: you have to see a leg being sawn off before you can visualise it.

Financiers and kings, palaces and finery; these are the subjects pleasing to imagination. We reject the agony of those who gave their bodies to build our heritage.

Yes, they are waist deep in water down the Coedcae tonight. Earlier, Tommy No Hands was lowered down on a seat to inspect the depth, but the rope holding him broke and Rees Evan went down after him to bring him up; both were drowned in the sump.

How many visitors will give these two a thought, I wonder, when they crowd into the famous Lewis Merthyr Pit – once called Coedcae – in a century's time?

It was Jasmine who wept for Tommy No Hands, although he put one over her; she wept, did Jasmine Certainty; barmaids being a tribe to whom the gods have given the power of understanding.

Chapter twenty-eight

Winter came blustering into the Rhondda and the land was thumped into ice by Atlantic gales, torturing the trees of the river into crippledom.

Over in starling woods the rooks, bad-tempered with cold, were passing judgment on wrong-doers; later, if they found them guilty, they'd peck them to death. Humans and rooks have much in common, said Mrs Ezra.

'Mind, it's goin' to be a harsh old winter this year,' she added as she dusted the lodge. 'It always do when the birds are short-tempered. Where you off to this morning, Mr Davies?'

'Walnut Tree Junction, the new end-on,' I answered.

'Ain't it frizzed up there? Even the sheep at Walnut Gap are coughing rheumatic.'

I was tiring of Mrs Ezra. Time was when I found her Jewish nuances attractive – they lent a fragile spice to her lovely Welshness – but lately I was wishing her to the devil. Her insistence that I belonged to her personally and that my business was hers was paramount. It was a housekeeper I needed, not a possessive aunt. I longed for a few moments of *cantabile*, not Mrs Ezra's eternal cantata.

'Now keep yourself well wrapped up, *cariad*.' She sighed maternally. 'Ridiculous weather, this – no shape to it, but it do help a bit, mind, when it comes to my hot flushes. I'm on the change, ye know. All right are we, my lovely?'

'For God's sake, Mrs Ezra!'

'I've brought old Ned round the front for ye, but he anna himself this mornin' – a bit delicate with the wind he is, like me, poor soul.'

Ned, my horse, was one of the Penycoedcae hacks, appointed by Abe to carry me on my journeys. We had disliked each other on sight; he'd have my hand off as soon as look at me. Also, I'd never heard a horse fart like him, which he reserved for my moments of tryst with Ruth; at such romantic times his behaviour was disconcerting.

The Coedcae sinking was going badly. At a depth of eighty feet, Glyn Moses, the new gaffer, had struck river floodwaters, as Tommy No Hands had predicted; so I brought in one of the steam shovels to drive a second lift-and-force. I'd collected the two steamers off Brown Lenox's canal pond when they came by barge up from Cardiff. The second shovel I dragged by horse-team up the road to Hengoed.

I hadn't seen a lot of Ruth lately, hadn't the chance with Abe away all the time, which kept me busy. This time he was down in Southampton – for a man in his late sixties, he certainly got around. I was surprised to meet Ruth riding that morning.

'You off again, Nick?'

'Somebody's got to do it – Abe's never here.'

The early sun was upon her face and she looked pert and beautiful in her riding-habit: if you belonged to me, I thought, I wouldn't be up so early in the morning. But over the past four months, Ruth had proved as unattainable as when I'd known her in High Doss. It was impossible for her to entertain me in the house and difficult for us to meet in my lodge where Mrs Ezra held court. Eyes are everywhere when you're in the public eye.

'When will Abe be back?' I asked.

She shrugged. 'If I didn't know him better I'd think he had a woman down south; he spends enough time there.'

She turned in the saddle as a groom came running to us with a letter.

'From Southampton,' said Ruth, taking it. 'This might tell us something,' and she read it, continuing: 'Yes, it does. And this has been delayed. He's due back here tonight . . .

no, wait, there's more. He wants to see you urgently when he gets in – will you come to dinner? he says.'

'What time?'

She flashed a smile. 'Make it early, darling, and we can have a little while together.'

There was about her a skittishness that was almost an affront; a woman saying one thing and meaning another. Fear could not be her reason for keeping me at a distance, but I did not know for sure; nor why she now resisted my advances. I said, bitterly:

'If we are together, it'll be the first for a very long time.'

Her eyes changed. 'Be patient, dearest.'

Ned lifted a rear hoof and performed stridently; it was now a three-cornered conversation, and I cursed him.

'Patient! We'll be in our second childhood before I get you into a bed.'

Tom circled, fighting the bridle, and she yanked him back.

'Is that all you want me for?'

'God, of course not!'

She touched my hand. 'The old chap can't last for ever, Nick.'

'He creaks, but he's still hanging, isn't he!'

'Old gates do this, but not for much longer. Meanwhile, it may mean little to you, but I've got virtuous views on marriage, and I'm prepared to wait. Oh darling, do try to look less frosty!'

'I want you, Ruth.'

Ned performed again, with astonishing timing.

'Meanwhile, while you're waiting, there's always Jasmine, isn't there? Isn't that what you males get up to?'

I didn't reply to this, wondering how much she knew, but galloped Ned away. And when out of sight I gave him something to go on with.

These rides up to Hengoed taxed me in the depth of winter. Ice seemed to form between the brain and the skull, and long before I'd cleared Ponty this time I was frozen.

Up in Hengoed, some 300 Welsh navvies had arrived under a Mr Merry, Abe's sub-contractor: Abe had got the Hengoed main contract on a shoestring, and so had Merry, and between them they were skinning the economics to make ends meet. When I arrived at the site of the end-on, the men were huddled about in shivering apathy, their heads turned against the blustering wind. Vaguely, I remembered that first morning on the top of Pikernaze before we got under cover like moles in the ground.

Mr Merry came up: he was built like a farmer, big and beefy, polished knee boots, a purple waistcoat and bags under his eyes like the fleshpots of Jerusalem.

'I want this lot in huts,' he announced. 'There's three hundred here now and another two hundred coming up from Swansea this afternoon. Leave 'em out freezing and I'll have a sick list as long as me arm.'

His accent was Lancashire black puddings.

'Then get them under cover.'

'That's your responsibility!' he snapped.

'Oh no, it isn't! The contract's clear – sinker huts, minimum accommodation, labour and materials: Jowell and I are nothing to do with it.' It was snowing now, little flurries blowing up between us.

Having failed with his attack, Merry became defensive, saying: 'The bank's foreclosed; give me a hand, Mr Davies. I need this job or I'll be bankrupt. The men are frozen.'

I said, 'Look. You undercut good contractors to get this job; you've got it, and you'll not renege. Abe Jowell isn't a benevolent institution.'

He interjected: 'Some advance money, then?'

'An advance? Jesus, man, you haven't even started!'

He put his hands together as I remounted the horse, and said: 'For God's sake! If not for me, Mr Davies, for the sake of the men?'

A sea of blue faces stared up at me.

202

The serf, I recalled, wore his hair bobbed so that his face remained downcast when he addressed his master. The thought stirred uneasily in me as I rode through the small army of navvies leaning on their shovels. A man on horseback asserts a fine authority and they appeared aware of it. I opened my mouth then to suggest that I would help by providing some tented accommodation on a temporary basis. Instead, I heard myself say:

'You've made your bed, Merry – you lie on it. And if you don't like it you can take this lot down the road, for navvies these days are threepence an hour and I can have another five hundred like them up here in the morning.'

Merry stared up, his face filled with anger. 'My God, Little Abe's got himself a right bastard this time, hasn't he!'

'Try me harder and you'll discover what kind of a bastard I can be.'

As I rode away in the scurrying snow I glanced back and saw the sub-contractor's navvies standing like frosted statues around the stopped end-on. And I remembered the early days of winter on the top of Pikernaze, when you could leave your trews upright overnight and slide your legs into them, ice-hard, in the frosty mornings.

I had no time for these men. Compassion, I suppose, has a limit: it is as expendable as thread that weaves a garment: in terms of economics, much depends upon which side you're on, I was discovering. So Judas, believing the betrayal complete, rode down into the valley.

On the long ride home I became aware, for the first time in my life, of the oppressive responsibility that assails a man in authority, for the graph of profit these days was assailing me like a nightmare dream, and all who threatened that profit became enemies.

Merry, for a start, was careless, obdurate and, withal, a fool. He had landed himself in a financial mess and tried to off-load his responsibilities on to me. And the fury he had distilled in me somehow transferred itself to the men themselves, since they were the tools of his attack upon me.

I saw them no longer as Woodhead heroes who upheld the dignity of labour in the face of exploitation, but as jackanape idiots who stood around in abject self-pity, unable or unwilling to help themselves.

Wealth and responsibility, I was finding, change a man's ethics overnight; a financier is to a financier what a tiger is to a tiger; both have claws and prey upon the weak.

With Pontypridd now in sight among the snow-clad hills, I found nothing in my heart but pity for the freezing navvies who stood in misery while the wind howled about them, and I learned something more that day; while power corrupts, absolute power corrupts absolutely – great men are almost always bad men; this explained the greed of men like Crawshay, Guest and a host of other masters of the day.

In an infinitely smaller but similar way, it also had begun to explain *me*.

I knew a self-loathing that I have never been able to understand in the light of my behaviour.

Ruth was dressed in white, as usual; it suited her, enhancing her slim figure without revealing too much of the intimacies. She was now as I remember her – a spectre on tiptoe between the beds of High Doss.

The table was beautifully set for dinner. Ghosts of servility, preceded by trays, swept in and out with frightening efficacy: Clive the butler, Grace the parlourmaid and others whose names I didn't know.

I said, giving my cape and hat to Clive:

'Has Mr Jowell arrived?'

'He has not,' replied Ruth, 'and I'm worried. It's impossible that he could be so late.'

I sat down and took the offered port. 'He's probably called in at Leadenhall Street to give a jolt to the City,' but it didn't compose her; inner emotion was evident in the twisting of her fingers.

'He's been late before. What's so wrong?'

She raised her strained face to mine. 'Premonition.'

'Oh, come on!'

'No, Nick, no . . . I've got the most terrible dread . . .'

'Don't be silly!'

She was pacing about now. 'Do you know something? I think he's dead!'

I snapped, 'If anything had happened to him, you'd have heard about it. You're getting yourself into a rare old state over nothing – drink your port.'

We were still sitting at the dining table three hours later when the front doorbell jangled. Ruth looked as rigid as an iced nun. A maid appeared.

'A gentleman to see you, ma'am.'

It was the police superintendent from Pontypridd.

'How did it happen?' asked Ruth flatly.

The policeman was tall. His heavy coat was stained with travel; about him pervaded the faint, musty smell of tobacco and damp clothes.

'Difficult to explain, really speakin', ma'am. It seems that the gentleman got off the train at Aberceynon for some reason, instead of coming on to Pontypridd. Here he took a coach – that would be about five o'clock this morning – presumably with the intention of coming on by road. But the coach never reached here; it went off the road near Grovers Corner. Among the killed – three of them – was Mr Jowell; I got his possessions here, ma'am.'

'Oh God!'

'The driver were goin' at a rare old rate, it seems. Reckon the horses must have bolted.'

'Where . . . where's my husband now?'

'We've got him in Pontypridd now, ma'am.' The policeman hesitated. 'We . . . we'll need an official identification, lady,' and I got up.

'I'll come too, Superintendent.'

It was Abe Jowell all right, and I was astonished that such injuries could be caused by a simple coach crash: the back of his head was completely crushed.

Ruth, who insisted upon identifying him, stood stock still, staring down at his battered face.

I saw the purple waistcoat with its mother of pearl buttons, soaked with blood; the savaged throat where the cravat had been torn away. And one eye, bulbous and bloodshot, stared defiantly through the mutilation.

Respectfully, a constable covered Abe's face.

Another man, in plain clothes, came from a side door; he was tall, possessed of an educated authority, and said:

'Would you like to sit down, ma'am?' He added, 'I'm a police investigator, sent from Cardiff.'

Now, in a nearby office, the inspector asked, 'Do you feel able to answer one or two immediate questions, Mrs Jowell?'

'If I can.' Ruth bowed her head.

'You have been at home all day?'

'Yes.'

'And this gentleman, Mr Davies?'

Her reply was curt. 'Mr Davies is a trusted servant of the company, and my husband's friend.'

'He has been with you all today?'

I replied, 'No. I returned from Hengoed for a dinner appointment at Penycoedcae Villa . . .' and Ruth interjected:

'I have this letter,' and she gave it to him. 'My husband especially wished to talk with Mr Davies tonight – indeed, he invited him to dinner. We were awaiting Abe's return when this awful news arrived.'

The man turned to me. 'Then you were out all day, Mr Davies?'

206

'Yes.'

'Where?'

'I left my home – the lodge down at the river – just after eight o'clock this morning and I went by horse to Walnut Tree Junction.'

'The one Mr Merry, the contractor, is building?'

'Under my supervision. That's why I was there.'

'And you met and talked with Mr Merry.'

'In the presence of a few hundred others.'

'When did you leave the Junction?'

'Probably about midday,' and Ruth said, 'Mr Davies arrived at the house at five o'clock. What are you inferring?'

The man said, with patient charm, 'Clearly, Mr Davies could never have got to Grovers Corner and back after the time your poor husband was murdered, Mrs Jowell, I am merely establishing the immediate facts . . .'

'Murdered!'

He nodded. 'In my opinion, though this has yet to be officially established, his wounds were caused by a weapon.' Opening a drawer, he withdrew a small bag. 'These are your husband's effects – the contents of his pockets. His wallet, as you see, is empty. Did he carry much money?'

'Never less than fifty guineas.'

'Not a penny was found upon him.'

'He also wore a ring, a signet.'

'No jewellery was found. Robbery could have occurred after the coach crash.'

There was a silence. The man said, 'I suggest you take Mrs Jowell home, Mr Davies. Clearly no suspicion falls upon you, but these inquiries have to be made.'

'Of course.'

I handed Ruth into the trap and was about to rein away when the investigator delayed me. Smiling up at Ruth he said:

'It is excellent to have friends about you at a time like this, Mrs Jowell. But you will not fail to call me if I can be of help.'

'Thank you,' said Ruth.

'You have known Mr Davies long?'

'For over twelve years.'

'A valued relationship; now is the time you need him most.'

We drove away.

At the end of the road I looked back.

The man was still there.

Chapter twenty-nine

Rather like the saintly James Richard of Treforest, who took into his home the famine people and became a Welsh apostle to the Irish, so Mrs Eliza Ezra, Israelite, took unto herself a vagabond Welshman and succoured him.

For only a little while I had her, and then one night, coming back from Crumlin, I was surprised to find the lodge window open and the curtain blowing out.

And Mrs Ezra lying dead on the floor.

I reported the open window to the police, but the doctor who signed the death certificate put her death down to 'natural causes' and the police took little notice of me, although they said there wasn't a mark upon her body.

The winter had come and gone. Spring came flourishing over the mountains on the morning we took Mrs Ezra up to Glyntaff where Jews slept before entering the Kingdom. I was a little disturbed that Ruth put her beside old Abe, who was surely destined for different regions.

The sun came up raging that day, I remember, painting up the snowdrops, ripening the buttercups. Dormice blinked from winter sleep, asking what time it was; bad-tempered hedgehogs stretched, yawned and quarrelled with their wives; swifts started their antics over the Rhondda's brooks and streams. Big-stomached and burly, ready for anything, the old sun boasted about the beauty of the country, and the corn around Penycoedcae, as seen by passing crows, glowed like flung sovereigns. Barn owls shrieked, ring doves cried themselves to sleep; cattle were long-shadowed sentinels of dusk in a bun-eared, bob-tailed April.

I got up from Mrs Ezra's grave, leaving part of me behind

with the flowers I had laid there: a gift to the mother I had found to replace the one I could scarcely remember.

Ruth pressed my hand.

The day was glorious; the sun blazed upon her frilly dress; Ruth always looked delightful under a parasol – wearing white, said she, to please the uncomplying Liza Ezra.

'Poor old girl,' she said. 'I suppose she'll be another ghost to lay, bless her,' and she looked as if she'd said nothing out of the ordinary. I asked:

'What on earth do you mean by that?'

'Well – Grace, Cook and Clive – you know.'

I said I didn't.

'The funny things that go bump in the night, remember? Now they're saying they are seeing things.'

'Seeing what?'

'Abe's ghost.'

'You're not serious!'

'Of course not, but they are, so it's important. Poor Grace reckons she's been having midnight visitations.'

'Visitations?'

Ruth was pert. 'Must you echo everything I say? Yes, Abe's ghost – the master rising from the grave, and all that nonsense . . .' and she paused and turned to me. 'When you stop to think of it, we've given him pretty good reason . . .'

'No reason at all! What do you mean by that?'

'Well – husband scarcely cold in his tomb and widow consorting with the company agent, and all that.'

'That's the last thing we've been doing!'

'Perhaps, but you must admit that Abe's scarcely been missed; no long trails of weeds, no official mourning. Every time I see the pastor he looks at me twice.'

'Abe's dead and gone. What would he want, an illumined address? It happens to us all, and the pastor, whoever he might be, can mind his own bloody business.'

210

'The village doesn't like it, either, and please don't swear.'

'Villagers never do. They'd prefer to see us apart and pledged to eternal misery; people are always sanctimoniously virtuous when it comes to death.'

We walked on. The sun burned down; birds were darting in winged rushes above us. Ruth said softly, 'Abe was good to you, you know. He gave you a start. A little more gratitude might improve your behaviour, don't you think?'

'The only thing Abe did was keep us apart.'

'In what way?'

I replied bitterly, 'And he's doing a damned sight better job of it dead than when he was alive!'

She smiled as if I were a wayward boy. 'Nick, Nick, what a child you are at times! Just give it a little more time – don't be so impatient – everything will come right in the end, you'll see.'

She was patronising now. Women come in a hundred different varieties; some specialise, I'm told, in teasing. I was beginning to suspect Ruth of dangling me on a string that I could never haul in. To loose myself I concentrated upon another scene – the gravestones of Glyntaff cemetery; they looked like the Pontypridd Cricket Eleven in white flannels on a Saturday afternoon; the sight actually broke the monotony of my hatred for Abe Jowell, and my growing resentment of Ruth. I said, 'So what are you going to do about it?'

'About what?' Ruth was equally cool.

'The Penycoedcae apparitions.'

'What can I do? If it continues the servants will leave.'

I said lightly, 'Don't worry. Abe won't haunt for long once he finds there's no money in it.'

'Don't be indelicate.' Her tone softened. 'They tell us not to canonise the dead, but we don't really miss people until they're gone.'

'You miss Abe?'

'In some respects.'

I said flatly, 'Meanwhile you're not doing much for his competitor's success.'

Her hand was upon my arm, and she turned to me, and I saw her face under its wide-brimmed straw hat patterned with the gold of the day; bee-hum I heard and the drowsy sounds of the early spring. 'In fact, my love,' she said, 'I was about to ask if you'd like to move into the house today.'

'Penycoedcae? A bit early now, isn't it?' I was surprised.

'Not at all. If you confined yourself to the west wing you . . . well, you'd be a sort of paying guest, wouldn't you? We could even dine together in my place. Even the most ardent scandalmongers would scarcely call that cohabiting.'

It was flippant, and I didn't like it. Why is it, I wonder, that so many women interpret a man's need as an inherent male weakness?

Other women were physically available, and I'd had a few in my time: strangely now though, physical love with anybody but Ruth appeared impossible; I had tried this and failed.

Pedestrian love is lust and is degraded by desire, which is divine between true lovers: nothing can circumvent a love that is spiritual.

By the joining together of bodies through love we are cleansed of animal defilement.

True love between men and women cannot exist in dreams, or defy celibacy; its demands must be met or it will die. Had Ruth, by affectionate word or touch, told of her love for me, this in some measure might have sufficed, but of this she was afraid. And so, consumed by my physical need of her, I could have none to replace her.

Her marriage to Abe Jowell and her misplaced virtue was isolating us both, and I hungered. If Ruth, for her part, had the smallest need of me, she expressed it in neither word nor act, so I eventually turned to another.

Jasmine Certainty expressed her views in no uncertain terms: 'What's wrong wi' you, Nick Davies? You need to see a bloody doctor.'

As I took Ruth back to Penycoedcae one day in the trap, she said, 'I'm changing the name of the firm, Nick. I have a free hand under the terms of Abe's will and I'm giving you a half share in everything. Farrer Enterprises. How does that suit you!'

We swayed on the seats along the rutted lane; the little cob, loving it, beating a rhythmic music with her hooves, like an echo of the early summer. These were days that had forgotten the seasons, of late snowdrops, with the banks still decorated with daffies and harebells.

Ruth was talking business again, and I glanced at her. Sometimes these days she looked pale; it was a transparent pallor that enhanced her frail beauty, and I wondered if Mrs Ezra had been right about her having a weak heart.

The sun beat down; the afternoon was warm, with quick flushes of meadow wind. I thought: half of the Jowell business! *Half!* God knows how much that would be in terms of money and prospects. It was a far cry from the penniless boy who was dumped into High Doss out of a travelling workhouse cart . . . Ruth invaded my thoughts:

'Move in when you like, Nick. Take the business over. I've had a look at it, and it's all quite beyond me. Make yourself an office in the west wing, take all the decisions. You know what I feel about big business; I'm out of my depth and don't even want to be involved. Incidentally, I've made a new will. In the event of my death, everything comes to you: somebody has to handle it.'

When I reined in outside the house, I said, 'All right, if that's how you want it. But what about you and me?'

She smiled beautifully. 'One step at a time, darling.'

'God, you make it sound like a business statistic!'

'Nick, somebody has to be practical – you're such an incurable romantic.'

She turned away, infuriating me; these days she lectured rather than informed.

'Yes, well it so happens that I love you. I love you and I want you. For God's sake, woman, I'm living with you in every other respect. Can't you see that it's driving me mad?'

'There's more important things in life than a bed.'

'But there's nothing more important than owning, physically, the one you love. What the hell's wrong with you? Are you ill, or something?'

She was standing at the window now, staring out at the trees, and it turned her.

'Listen, and understand this once and for all, I love you as much as you love me; perhaps that is why I find less attraction in the physical aspect. My love for you needs nothing to bolster its sincerity, no fevered nights, no pillows; it exists, often unspokenly. And if I loved you less I'd probably be pestering for the bed and making you as miserable as you are making me!'

I had never heard her speak so much on the subject; her vehemence and sincerity chastened me.

I said softly. 'You say you want me. Is that true?'

She lowered her face. 'I long for you. Do you know this pain? Men make such passionate claims upon it, but with what accuracy and truth? It aches and aches; sometimes I think it will drive me mad.'

'Then my love . . .' and I went to her and took her in my arms, but she forced herself away. 'Why not? Is it marriage you want?'

'No, you are too young!' She began to cry, her fingers forming a cage over her mouth, smothering the indignity.

'Oh, *Ruth* . . .'

Turning, she fled.

At this rate of delinquency, I thought, I'd end up in the Soprano Glee Club.

In expectation of a quick sinking of the Coedcae pit, I had

built a rank of terraced houses called Nyth Bran, just south of the farm of that name. In them I had housed Tommy No Hands's sinkers, but now work on the pit had stopped through flood water and the sinkers had been turned into colliers, working mainly down the Old Hafod. True, they paid me a rent of three shillings a week, but they were working for David and Jones, not me, and I wanted them to vacate. The firm was trying to buy me out of the Hafod area, but coal was there on the north bank of the Rhondda, and I wanted to retain a foothold.

'Both Hafod and Coedcae have pumping problems,' said Ruth. 'We've got the Walnut Tree thing under contract, and you'll be tendering for the viaduct at Pontlottyn, you say. With mechanical shovels on site, aren't two viaducts enough to be going on with?'

'It's the principle!'

'Are you sure it isn't pig-headedness?'

'Business-headedness, if you like,' I replied. 'Of course there's water trouble at Hafod and Coedcae; of course it will cost money. But I want to keep an influence over there. The railway mania's over; coal is the new thing and the Rhondda's jammed full of it. There's a fortune for the man prepared to speculate.'

We were having breakfast; sitting side by side at one end of the long refectory table, thank God. At Abe's meals I had been seated so far away that I could hardly see her.

'What does it entail?' asked Ruth. She ate with delicate precision, examining minutely each piece of toast and marmalade.

'Evicting the sinkers from Nyth Bran – they're not our people, anyway.'

'It won't do much for your image with the working class.'
She could be chiding.

'Perhaps not, but we've got to be practical.'

Ruth smiled at the window sun, again aloof. 'You're changing, Nick, aren't you!'

'Everybody changes. That's life.'

'A year ago you'd have bitten my head off at the thought of evicting people.'

'A year ago I wasn't an owner.'

'Of course. Abe took the same line.'

'He had no alternative.'

'One law for the rich, another for the poor?' and I replied:

'It isn't that, and you know it! Three-shillings-a-week rent doesn't even cover the maintenance. God, it isn't as if it's the depths of winter! They're tradesmen, all of them – pits are being sunk all over the Rhondda, and I don't know why you think we should subsidise our competitors.'

'Does the summer have such a distinct advantage?' She was watching me over the rim of her cup.

'What do you mean?'

'Only that I seem to remember you refusing help to poor old Merry who went bankrupt, remember? Hundreds of navvies living in holes in the ground? That was nearer Christmas.'

I got up from the table, throwing down my serviette. 'It's what Abe would have done.'

'Yes. He even tried to put Mrs Ezra out on to the street. God, what people you are, you captains of industry!'

There were times when I felt Ruth was slipping away from me. But I turned the sinkers out of Nyth Bran and put my own people in just the same, and that was an end to it.

After all, I reason, if Ruth was but a sleeping partner, I was entitled to the last word when it came to policy: further, with my share of the capital realising more than £100,000, I could presumably do what I liked with my share of the investment.

Strangely, however – and Ruth knew this – I never considered a penny of this to be mine. Money, for its own sake, never appealed to me: I'd often travel around the sites without a sovereign in my pocket.

It's profits and long pockets that matter, as Abe, who taught me, used to say.

I moved from the lodge into the west wing of Penycoedcae villa during that summer.

Amazingly, although Ruth and I were now under the same roof, my threadbare loneliness was worse for this reunion: together, we were yet farther apart; nothing seemed to bridge the growing gap between us.

Chapter thirty

There were now only three servants in Penycoedcae: Cook, a parlourmaid and old Clive of the tombstone countenance.

When Ruth had first married Abe Jowell, there had been a retinue of ten, apparently – from liveried footmen to stable lads – but Abe, for matters of economy, had reduced this to a minimum. Laundry, for instance, was taken down to the central wash-house near Merlin Bridge, and what horses were now stabled at the villa were maintained by a visiting ostler and farrier.

Grace, the maid, a sickly, adenoidal girl of gangling proportions, was given to emotional outbursts: with this in mind I treated what followed next with less importance than the occasion warranted.

I had now been living in the west wing of Penycoedcae for over a month: there I had a suite of rooms and an office, and my existence was one of seclusion and monk-like celibacy. Ruth being, as I have told, a firm adherent to marital fidelity, she appeared to believe that it should exist beyond the grave; a very different situation from that in which she had led me to believe. Coming to bed with me now seemed to be out of the question, and I had come to terms with it.

At dinner that night I put a poem into an envelope and laid it at Ruth's place at table: what ensued will stay for ever in my mind. She opened the envelope, waved a hovering Grace away, and read aloud:

Were you to leave me, I would not die,
Or make grief a trumpet to shatter the sky.
I would not ask for anything more
Than to walk according to natural law,

One foot behind, the other before.
I would rise at morning, sleep at night,
And tell unfailingly black from white.
I would use my brain to earn my bread,
Snarl when hungry, sigh when fed.
But I would not live, I would be dead.

Ruth lowered the poem, closed her eyes momentarily, and said:

'You finished it at last! Nick, it's beautiful!'

'It's the way I feel, and always have done.'

In my bedroom at a time approaching midnight, I was dozing in the vacuum of reality and dreams when a woman's shriek brought me upright. Leaping out of bed, I snatched at my dressing-gown and fought my way into it as I ran down the musty corridors leading to the servants' quarters. Here on their landing I collided in the dark with Grace, who opened her mouth for another shriek, but I silenced her.

'Oh, *Gawd!*' she gasped.

'For heaven's sake, what's wrong?' I demanded.

Clive, the old butler, appeared like a ghost of Valhalla, preceded by a lighted candle, his sleeping-cap awry. He said, while I was shaking the maid for sense:

'Something's in the house, sir. Cook saw it and fainted clean off.'

'Cook's always fainting – what did she see?'

'The ghost of Mr Jowell, she says.'

The girl in my arms was shivering, her eyes rolling with fright. I asked, 'You saw it, too?'

'Clear as daylight, sir! Saw 'im plain! Abe Jowell certain sure, beggin' your pardon. Wi' a stick and his coat all torn and 'is face covered wi' blood. Oh, Gawd!' She had a voice like a cinder under a door.

'Where was this?'

'Top o' the cellar steps, sir.'

'Cook saw it, you say?'

'Plain as me eye, sir, and she flowsied right off.'

I turned to old Clive. 'And you?'

'I did not see it, but . . .'

'But what?'

His face, grotesque with shadow in the light of his candle, had turned him into a motivated corpse, and Grace's eyes were wide and shining in the flickering light. Clive said in his undertaker's voice, 'Lately, mind, funny things've been happenin', sir.'

'Like what?'

'Well, comin's and goin's. Bumps an' that in the night, and bare feet sort o' slitherin' about on the boards. It fair do give me the willies, maister.'

'You're imagining it, the pair of you. There's always an explanation for these things . . .' and Grace whimpered:

'I tell ye, I saw 'im. Stampin' with his stick on the floor, he were, his one eye gone and the other open and starin'. Blood all over his poor face, sir, down his front an' soaking 'is cravat!'

Another candle came flickering towards us and Ruth appeared like an acolyte in white; all white was she, as I had seen her in dreams, her hair down and lying on her shoulders.

She said calmly, 'I heard Grace call and hurried to the kitchen. Cook's all right now, but she's very upset . . .'

Grace ejaculated: 'Good Jesus! She saw 'im full, see? He were sitting at the kitchen table and eatin' large as life!'

Ruth gave me a queer look and a sigh, and patted Grace consolingly, 'Yes, I know, Grace, but ghosts eat manna usually, not bread and cheese.'

'Mind, I can't stay here with the old master roamin' the house,' Grace pleaded, her hands together as if in prayer. 'I'll 'ave to go back to me auntie in Quakers Yard . . .'

Ruth led her away, Clive following like a sexton at a wake. I heard Ruth say, 'I do assure you, Grace, there's many more ghosts in Quakers Yard than here. Now, take

Cook back to bed. It's all a dreadful mistake and I want you to try to forget it.'

She was handling it with her usual competent authority, so I awaited her return with the candle. And as we went back to her room, she said, 'Something very strange is going on here, Nick, you realise that?'

'God! Don't you start!'

'I'm only saying that something's happening in this house that ought to be investigated.'

'Strange that we never see these midnight visitations!'

'The servants seem to.'

'Who's heard of a ghost eating bread and cheese!'

She turned, holding the candlestick higher. 'Do you realise that Grace's description fits Abe's appearance when we identified him?'

It stilled me.

'More, if you want to know, I've heard funny things in this house myself lately: voices, people whispering . . .'

'Carry on like that and you'll have us worse than Grace.'

'Don't be flippant.' Her tone was admonishing, and she turned her back upon me. I followed her along the corridor to her bedroom.

At the door, Ruth turned.

'Don't go, Nick. Don't leave me . . .'

I put my arms about her and drew her against me: the touch of her body was like a scald. She added:

'We . . . we're going to lose the servants, you know. Anything savouring of bewitchery absolutely terrifies them . . .'

'You're frightened, too?'

'I'm . . . I'm not entirely at ease . . .'

I could see by her pallor that it was a massive understatement, and said, 'You're not seeing things, too, are you?'

She began to tremble and the trembling, which began in her hands, moved to her arms and she gripped them in a vain attempt at control. I said, 'Darling, what's wrong?'

She raised her face to mine, and said quietly, 'I've just seen Abe.'

'What? Oh God, don't you start!'

'I tell you, I've seen him. I was asleep and heard breathing and opened my eyes. He was bending over the bed, looking down at me.'

I took her into my arms; she was shivering beneath her dressing-gown; the nearness of her was having the most desirable effect upon me, and she knew this, suddenly clinging to me. I said with an effort, 'It's imagination, you realise that, don't you? For every ghostly visitation there's a perfectly acceptable explanation.'

And she replied like a woman in a dream, 'You remember how he was when we identified him after the accident? That's how his face was tonight.'

'You've had a nightmare.'

'Perhaps, but don't leave me, please don't leave me!'

I said from the dryness of my throat, 'You know what will happen if I go back with you to your room.'

She said, with her arms about me, 'I don't care, I love you and I want you, too – somehow I must get Abe Jowell out of my life. Help me, please help me!'

Something was wrong, yet I could not define it: Ruth's whole being seemed tuned to mine in an elemental need, and I could not understand the sudden change in her. It was a bitter irony, I reflected, that while Abe's memory had been keeping us apart, it needed his apparent ghost to bring us together. And then I saw something that astonished me.

The neck of her nightdress was spotted with scarlet. I held the candle higher.

Yes, it was blood.

Seeing me hesitate, Ruth asked, 'What's wrong?' and looked about her in the candle's wavering light. 'Yes, I thought I heard something, too . . .'

'Nothing,' I replied, taking her hand, but the spots of scarlet staining her nightdress held me with rooted force, and then I saw something more; a smear of blood on her shoulder.

But the effect of having her near was greater than a thousand ghosts, and I swept her up into my arms and carried her to her room, which was bathed in the yellow glow of a bedside lamp, the curtains partly aside to let in the moon.

Let spirits, blithe or evil, walk abroad seven nights a week, if all my nights bring such reward.

I said, as I set Ruth down, 'All my life I've dreamed of this. No more nightmares, now I'm with you. And for God's sake, no more talk of Abe.'

Reaching up from the bed, she stroked my face and then raised her head and kissed my lips, and spoke . . . so quietly that I scarcely heard her:

'You . . . you will make it beautiful, won't you, Nick?'

'Of course!'

'Go gently, darling? I . . . I've never been used before.'

I bent closer in disbelief. 'But, you've been married to Abe Jowell for years . . .'

Ruth shook her head, 'It . . . it was never consummated. I didn't mind. In one way I was relieved. And after all, it wasn't his fault. It was mine for allowing myself to be pushed into such a marriage. But . . .' I held her, and she continued, 'But . . . oh, it was horrible! . . . the things he used to do!'

'What did he do?'

She turned away her face. 'Oh God, *no!*'

'You'll feel better if you tell me.'

She drew me closer. 'This is the mistake of thinking all men might be the same – devoid of sensitivity, and respect for a woman. Strangely, now that I am so afraid, the spell seems to have broken . . .'

I gave her a smile. 'Good old Nick – any port in the storm!'

This she ignored, saying, 'Just pretend that I am your wife. And . . .'

'And what?'
'And treat me with respect?'
'That will be easy,' I replied, 'because I love you.'

No Jasmine Certainty, this one; no capricious Abby Nothin of the crab-apple knees. This was a woman: until this moment all I'd known were girls.

And this was the poem I wrote after I had lost her.

Even then within my strength, I held you;
saw you by the shaming light, my friend so
wearied with expectation. We slept and
wakened, do you remember? And I claimed
you from sleep.

Ruth!

Girl of my bloom, my citron-breasted fair
one, I will paint your dreams. I hold you. Beneath the tangle of the
stars, I hold you; the night is whispering beyond our lattice
window. You are the wine-press of my mouth; your body is musk,
your waist sways like oleander.

Ruth!

Remember in the stanzas of our kisses I told you – that your brow
is cypress-curved, your arms dark stains upon my shoulders – for
you are burned to cinnamon by old Beersheba suns. Even the
flowers of your breasts are honey, your throat is wet with kisses.

Ruth!

Small daughter of my earlier years who had no breasts! Will your
womanhood wait for me, that I may be born of you? The dew of
your mouth falls upon me as the citrus sheds to sate the suckling
bee; your arms embrace me in the sweet disorder of your bodice.

Ruth!

Thy neck is a tower of ivory, thy bosom is of gold, thy shadows
blacker than midnight, thy smile fairer than the sunrise. You are

224

more beautiful than the temples of Lebanon and Zijar; your touch upon me is as the southern wind. Now we have discarded matron age and found your youth, found it pinioned under sea-sick bucking stars; so alien swords will write of us in blood, telling how painless is my love's archery.

Gogoniant i fywyd, i gariad, i wreigiaeth, i Ruth, gyda mi' Un!

Chapter thirty-one

The winter came and passed us by without a murmur of apology, though shivering bare-legged crows still protested to the moon.

Spring came tumbling up the mountains, painting up the Rhondda in gorgeous colours, laughing in the brooks and streams.

Over rich patterns of streaming bindweed and water flowers, the kingfishers swooped their flashing blue, and in the evenings newborn gnat-flies did their spiral minuets to entice upturned fishy eyes to sumptuous banquets.

And then came summer, big in the belly and bountiful. Even the beggars of Ponty market began stitching up their tatters. The sun and chattering Ponty wives beamed benevolently over the land, and the wheat was so high around the walls of Penycoedcae that I had to get at it with a billhook.

It was a bee-hum, cow-spatter summer with the knees of the old girls plastered with gold dross, and the wind smelling of cream.

Dragonflies wing-burred blue over the lilies of the park; carp strolled in the untainted ponds of Mardy. And at times I would slip down to the Tredegar Arms in my riding breeches and bowler; tap on the counter with my crop, look into the sloe eyes of Jasmine Certainty and realise that I was missing nothing.

'Dear God,' said she. 'You tell me who's fallen on his feet!'

'Double whisky and a little less cheek.'

'In love with her, aren't you! Settled you at last, has she?'

I drank, watching her.

'Sad about Rees Evan, weren't it?'

'Rees Evan?'

Somebody called to me then, so we never finished the conversation.

Ruth said, 'You know, darling, there's something very rewarding in having no servants at one's beck and call. I prefer being a housewife to a lady of leisure.'

Grace and Cook had been gone for months; ill-health had retired old Clive, and we had put him in the lodge and pensioned him off. Initially, when the talk got around of strange happenings in Penycoedcae, we couldn't get a servant at double the money, so Ruth locked up the west wing and we contracted into the kitchen where she did her own cooking. We had a downstairs drawing-room and an upstairs double bedroom.

Even the house, with the servants gone, seemed at peace with itself: no ghostly footsteps, no apparitions, Abe Jowell rested comfortably in the Jewish plot at the top of Glyntaff Cemetery. Ruth and I, in love, lived the halcyon months of that year in security.

With a workforce of over 600 navvies, I was completing the Hengoed spurs and the building of local station platforms.

The two national railway manias were long finished, but for a small contractor – and I had considerably reduced the Farrer Enterprises' capacity – there were still rich pickings to be had on local contracts.

I had sold off the Doncaster and Southampton interests at a small profit and was settling down to financial consolidation. The future looked impressive, and there was more money in the bank than ever.

Wealth, I was finding, is a mysterious commodity: man digs it out of the earth, fights wars for it, causes endless misery over its possession, then puts it into bank vaults and back into the earth again.

Money is fraught with a senseless carnivorism, I was discovering. Although I usually had none of it in my pocket, its increase had become totally necessary to my happiness.

227

If whoever spends my fortune after I'm gone gets the same pleasure that I had out of making it, he'll be the happiest of men. Also, there is tremendous satisfaction in knowing that wills are published, if only to infuriate one's friends and embitter one's enemies. I had already consulted a London solicitor to ensure that mine appeared in the *News of the World* and *The Times*.

Ruth's demise, not mine, came sooner than expected.

The summer was dying. We had decided to leave Penycoedcae for something smaller. We might even have taken over the fishing lodge had Clive not been occupying it. The rambling old mansion had originally been designed for family occupation, and there was little prospect of Ruth having children.

Earlier we had discussed a move.

'Somewhere nearer Cardiff, perhaps?' asked Ruth at breakfast.

Unfolding the morning paper, I replied:

'There's always plenty going on at the docks. That's where the real money lies – with the Marquis of Bute.'

'I thought you didn't want expansion?'

'Expansion within reasonable limits. If you don't expand at all, you stagnate. Let's wait until I know if we've got the Crumlin viaduct contract. By the way, that reminds me, I've got some papers for you to sign,' and I went to the wall-safe and took them out, watching while Ruth signed where necessary in her small, precise hand.

'Would that mean Pontypool?' she asked, handing back the papers.

'Probably, if we do get Crumlin. There's some really beautiful estates around the Abergavenny area. Places like Glanusk.'

'Joseph Bailey's estate? Nick, that's a citadel!'

'It might help a bit with the knighthood.'

She smiled wryly. 'God, you men! Look, if you really want a knighthood, all you do is send twenty thousand pounds to the Distressed Gentlefolk Association via the Clerk to the Parliamentary Committee, or something – the address is in the bureau. He'll pay it straight into Conservative Party funds and then you sit back and wait for the Honours List.'

'You can be a cynic, too, can't you!'

'And a realist. Also it might help if you joined the Freemasons. Abe did.'

I said evenly, 'Don't you want to be Lady Ruth?'

She smiled beautifully at me from the other end of the table.

'Lady Ruth Farrer-Davies – how about that?' I suggested.

She put her head on one side and regarded me as one does a mischievous child. 'Nick, Nick! What babies you men are! Look, we're happy – certainly I'm happy for the first time in my life. Let's stay that way – just you and me – buy something smaller and settle down into the rut of pleasant middle age.'

'Old age, you mean.'

She emptied her hands at me. 'And why not? The aim is to grow old, but not disgracefully. Nicholas, we're rich. We simply don't need any more than we've got, and a bought title isn't going to make us any happier.'

She didn't understand; it was of no use explaining to her.

Ruth's basic fault was her inability to realise that life must never be limited in its aims and ambitions. A man has to progress right to the end, or face moral and physical decay. The navvying business was flourishing; everything I touched seemed to be turning to minor Midas gold. Much more would come. And my ambition didn't limit itself to a knighthood; I was thinking more in terms of the House of Lords.

It could be done.

Sam Peto became a baronet. Tom Brassey's son became an earl. Certainly a little ermine would be acceptable in the Farrer family.

But a title, and no son?

Life, however, is mistress to fortune, and there was always the possibility that, since Ruth was ten years my senior, I could yet have a son and heir by a younger woman.

I despised myself and constantly rejected the thought, but it persisted, for a man without a son is like a meteor flashing across the sky. Yes, the possibility existed, and if the opportunity ever presented itself, I would do it properly. Was I restricted to my own class? The aristocracy, especially the impoverished variety, appeared to present some very eligible daughters.

It was the end of September and the year was dying. The beech plantation around the house, piled with the golden refuse of past autumns, awaited with pent breath the onslaught of wailing winter, and the cold came early.

Hens sat grumpily on eggs gone cold, or barged each other about on the perches, gossiping about the cockerel. Wild duck flew away with the swallows, coots started slipping on their backsides on the ice of Beech Hill pond.

Ruth came in after riding, her cheeks bitten red with frost. We still had no servants; rumour dies hard in small communities, but the house didn't appear to bother Ruth; indeed, she was in her element – cooking, cleaning, swiping the dust from one place to another, as women do.

Many couples would have called the situation idyllic.

There were nights of blustering wind and log fires, a rich and satisfying togetherness. Yet, haunted by the possibility that it would relegate the years into carpet slippers and a fireside, and steal my youth away, I couldn't come to terms with the threat. In this life you only have to hold your breath and you're seventy.

'But that is what it's all about, darling! That's living!' cried Ruth.

'It isn't. It's dying.'

I had come in from Crumlin – on another Ned, a fine

young stallion I kept especially at Pontypridd station for the gallop home, old Farting Ned having long since gone to the knacker's yard where he belonged.

Later, after dining uneventfully with Ruth (she had gone early to bed), I put on a smoking jacket, filled my pipe and settled to read: it was Plato's *Republic*, I remember. With my feet up and the book in my lap, I later dozed.

Within the emptiness of approaching sleep I heard a scream, and awoke.

Ruth screamed again.

Racing up the stairs three at a time, I swung back our bedroom door and barged inside. The twin casements of one window were open; the heavy curtains had been pulled back and the lace drapes were wafting gently into the room. I swung back to the bed.

'*Ruth!*'

Ruth was lying upon her back like a woman in deep slumber, and I saw her face in profile only by the light from the window – a crescent moon. The bedclothes were undisturbed; Ruth's hair, neatly braided and tied with ribbons, was lying upon her breast.

With a thumping heart, I approached her; sickness rose to my throat, and I swallowed it down.

'Ruth!' I called her name, bending over her. '*Ruth!*'

With shaking hands I found the bedside candle and matches; the match flared, banishing shadows; the room settled into the candle's warm glow and I saw Ruth's face more clearly.

There was upon her features an expression of utter astonishment.

Automatically, I ran to the window. The yellow drive lay below me as dark as a witch's cape; the wishing-well stood as a silent sentinel, a witness that could not speak. A little wind was blustering in secret places.

Running downstairs I ran out on to the drive as if coming out of a nightmare dream.

There was no sign of an intruder, but then I looked up to the bedroom window and realised for the first time how closely it was positioned above the portico entrance. Below were the flowerbeds, but when I searched them later, I found not even a suspicious footprint.

Now, back in the bedroom, I gathered Ruth against me, and sobbed.

I did not immediately send for a doctor. I had seen too much of death not to recognise it instantly.

With Ruth cradled in my arms I watched the dawn come up, but still I held her, and could not let her go.

Afterwards, I knew, would come the conscience suffering.

Book three

Chapter thirty-two
1852

The wise ones tell us that after a bereavement one should not make up one's mind on anything too soon; that the best course is to stay put for a few months in the same environment as the lost one, until you come to terms with the grief.

Had I done this, what followed next might have been averted.

I left Penycoedcae almost immediately after Ruth's funeral, packing a bag and taking a train to Bristol. There I boarded a cargo-bummer bound for Brittany, which I had loved since my time in France on the Paris–Rouen with Brassey.

Lost, I wandered for months, seeking Ruth in Parisian cafés and wayside *estaminets*. During one period practically penniless (as usual, I had forgotten the necessity of financial planning), I roamed, tramp-like along the lanes of the Pas-de-Calais.

Speaking French passably well, I lodged with French families; worked in the fields during the harvest; talked with peasants over glasses of *vin rouge*, and with them proposed solutions to the coming war in the Crimea, which appeared unavoidable.

Since grief, for me, has nothing to do with fidelity, I slept with a farmer's wife in Amiens and a baker's in Rouen, and she had the scent of yeast in her young, bright hair.

Purely for nostalgia, I arranged a bank draft with *Crédit Français* and travelled from Rouen to Paris on the railway I had helped to build.

But on that journey, I was beset with another, more vibrant wish – to return to my own country. It was an immediate compulsion that nothing would satisfy.

I recalled with excitement that the fairs would be cramming the streets of the little Welsh towns; it was a clarion call. I ached for the sights and sounds of my country and my people.

After a rough Channel crossing, I took a train to Cardiff, and the first day of April found me at Pontypridd station among the milling celebrants – folks were coming in from the other valleys for Ponty Market Day, and I joined the throng.

Market Street and Taff Street were jammed like herrings in a barrel. Fat porkers and their relatives were being driven squealing to market. Clutches of hens squeaked and ·squawked upside down in batches. There were bread stalls and cheese stalls, egg stalls and sausage stalls, and butter stands with fat women, white-aproned and busty, slapping up the pats.

Hawkers were crying wares, oil men with paraffin, muffin-men ringing handbells, knife-grinders whetting their blades, and packmen with dusky wives carrying silk bales on their heads all the way from Arabia. Wilberforce Negroes, freed from Bristol, were showing the scars of the lash; fine ladies under parasols with trailing gold-turbanned blackamoors; dandy gents, tipsy bruisers, matrons with frilly daughters.

Cripples from the French wars thumped their drumstick amputations on the pavements; old galley slaves escaped from Spain showed their cankered wrists and ankles, begging for alms as Britain's heroes. There were pimps and prostitutes and lay preachers on every corner giving Hell to everybody from Genesis to Revelation. Fire-Eating Job, the Independent Messianic, was giving the brewers a roasting for raising the price of Allsops; two Irish bare-knucklers were hard at it outside the Temperance Hall. All in all, it was a pretty normal Market Day in Ponty, celebrating the Fair.

On my way to a public house for a pint, I paused on the corner of Park Side Lane.

Earlier I'd watched the Judiciary, bewigged, splendid and incorruptible, in procession to the White Hart for the Petty Sessions. And watching this, like me, was a group of tattered people, all with bandaged hands: the sight of them arrested me.

They were sitting in line against a wall; their ages varied from seven to seventy. These were the labourers of the Crawshay Nail-Making Factory in the Brown Lenox compound. Only workers approaching destitution made nails at a time when nails were made by hand. And they sat in their grimed bandages within the trade that injured their fingers into permanent mutilation.

As I walked slowly by I thought I recognised one or two faces within the group; indeed, I paused to stare down at one woman, but she drew up her rags to her mouth like one in purdah. Then another, with a child in her arms, cried:

'Ay ay – so you remember us, do ye, Nick Davies?'

I shook my head, looking down at her.

'Don't the name Rees Evan mean nothing to ye, then?'

Rees Evan . . .? Rees Evan . . .? The name was faintly familiar, and I plundered my brain.

The woman shrieked: 'Got you a start! Got you a start wi' Brown Lenox, didn't he?' Her eyes glared up in her stricken face. 'And you paid him back good, remember?'

'I do not remember,' I said and made to leave, but she cried:

'Ye don't remember my Rees and Tommy No Hands you drowned down Coedcae?'

Realisation came to me with buffeting force, and she added: 'And not content wi' killing him you chucked me and mine out o' Nyth Bran.' She rose to her feet, and her voice was shrill.

People turned to look and a crowd began to gather.

'Ye turned us out – me and my Alby here – three months

237

after my Rees were drowned. And shall I tell you summat more? My chap would walk ten miles to give a man a start, but a lot you did for anyone since you mixed yourself up wi' gentry!'

Accusing faces were turned upon me. I wanted to flee, but was rooted by her vehemence.

'The curses of Baal be upon ye, you bastard! Cursed be your house . . .!'

Automatically, I fumbled in my pockets, found my purse, opened it, poured five sovereigns into my hand, and offered it, saying, 'It . . . it's not too late. Please take it, Mrs Evan . . .'

The workers craned their necks at the gold; someone gasped, but the woman hit out and sent the money flying. 'Not from you, mister. Me and my lad take nothin' from you!'

I stood among the people and knew a loneliness I had never known before. And then, as I pushed my way through them, a voice said into my ear:

'Well, well – there it is! I wouldn't say you're the ale o' the month, lad, but I must say you deserved that. What happened to you since you came into money – lost your soul?'

It was Jasmine. She took my arm and steered me away. 'Come on, you look miserable to death. What you want is a tot o' skull attack. I know a fella called Mr Whisky and he'll talk to anyone.'

I shook her hand away.

'No! I've got to see this through sober.'

'Sober or drunk, the damage is done. Come on, ye daft bugger, this is when ye need a friend,' and she towed me down Taff Street until we got to the Tredegar Arms.

It was dark when I reached Glyntaff with half a bottle of obliterating whisky aboard, dispensed with the love of Jasmine who had taken the contents of my wallet to give to the poor. I staggered drunkenly through the tombstones

238

towards God's little acre and Jewish plots, past the graves of Abe and Mrs Ezra, and stood before Ruth's grave.

Above me were the stars; it was a night of cosmic fires. Venus, I remember, was flashing green and gold.

I had ordered a simple stone for my girl. All over the cemetery were flying angels and cupids kneeling in prayer, but I wanted none of this, and the mason had done it well – a simple marble slab and on it, in Roman lettering:

SOFT SUMMER WIND BLOW GENTLY HERE.
COLD WINTER SUN SHINE WARMLY HERE.
GREEN EARTH ABOVE LIE SOFTLY HERE.
GOOD NIGHT, DEAR HEART. GOOD NIGHT.

On my knees, with my face in my hands, I wept.

It is the small things that hurt on these occasions; the big things are too terrifying for the soul to contemplate. Even with the smallest effort I could have made her existence happier; but now, like everything else in this life, one is always too late.

I would never advise anyone to seek the solace of the bottle to drown grief: it merely sharpens the agony. Besides, alcohol has several ways out of a man, and one is through the eyes.

Still drunk, I swayed down the country paths and made my way over the river to Penycoedcae.

Perhaps it was so soon after my close proximity with death up at the cemetery, but I had the feeling as I took out my key to open the door of the house that I was being watched.

This is the hair-raising dread of the Unknown: the phantasy faces that peer from every bush and thicket. And the whisky did nothing to give me courage as I fumbled with the door key.

Did ghosts of the dead really walk? I wondered. Can mortal events be so impressed upon the atmosphere of a house that they make visible shape and form, and reap a harvest?

The door swung back, exposing the tiled floor of the hall. My riding boots echoed on the cold mosaic.

The first thing I noticed was that the furniture had been moved: as if a mischievous poltergeist had been at work. For the hallstand was on the other wall. The chair where I pulled off my riding-boots was in the middle of the floor. Then waves of alcohol swept over me with nauseating intensity, and I lurched on down to the kitchen, lighting a candle I found on the table.

People had been in here.

As I stood there swaying, I noticed the remains of a meal: crumbs on the kitchen table, a knife on the bread-board, the rind of a half-eaten cheese. But the kettle, standing on the long dead grate was cold under my hand.

Raising the candle-holder, I stared around the empty room, listening; then raised my eyes to the ceiling. A flake of whitewash drifted down in the wavering light. The silence tingled. And then I heard sounds I had heard before – a satin sound, like the slithering of naked feet on the floor above.

Somewhere out in the beechwood, a barn owl shrieked – the right accompaniment, I thought, to the phenomenon of these icy rooms. And then I heard, and clearly now, the usual whispering voices from above. My heart was thudding against my shirt, and, realising my impotency, I was assailed by anger: an inner fury welled up in me – that I should stand like a shivering boy, building within me craven, groundless fears.

I strode out of the kitchen, along the hall, and went up the stairs to the bedroom.

There existed in this room a sanctity. Momentarily, I stood looking at the bed with its high, surmounting tapestry of damask and gilded pillars. I approached it in tears, touching the pillow upon which Ruth had died. A half-empty decanter of whisky was on a nearby sideboard

240

and I seized it, guzzling at it, seeking escape from grief. Then I threw myself down upon the coverlet, drank what was left of the whisky and slipped into a shuddering, sweating drowse.

I do not know what time I awoke; nor, despite my attempts to remember, do I know today what awakened me.

I dreamed of a presence; only this I can recall. I remember, too, the icy coldness of the room; I began to shiver. The shivering began in my hands and spread slowly into my body so that I became transfixed.

I opened my eyes, and the room, taking shape in the guttering candlelight, became in my mind not a room but a restricting prison with barred walls. It was as if I had been pinioned to the bed by unseen hands, and within the nightmare, as my subconsciousness struggled in my mind, I slowly realised that I had been bound hand and foot.

And then I heard faint breathing and turned my eyes.

Abe Jowell was standing beside me.

I fought to be free; I shrieked, but made no sound. And even as I stared in horror, the form moved.

It was the face of dead Abe as I had identified him – a face mutilated by the splintering crash. The blood-soaked and sopping cravat, I saw, the purple waistcoat stained black with blotches of blood. And from the broken face, one side stoved in, a single bulbous eye peered down at me. And on the hand that clutched a hammer was a gold signet ring.

Now the apparition leaned above me, blood dripping from its wounds, splashing on to my face. I was choking now, strangled by an inner paralysis. And I remember thinking that this is how Ruth must have died. Only the strongest heart could stand this visitation of the dead.

But now I was aware of others in the room. Despite my terror, self-preservation controlled me.

I listened. The usual satin slither of naked feet on wood – the old unmistakable sounds – I could hear them clearly, this time within yards of me. Now the usual voices: guttural whispers, half discernible at first, then louder.

241

Opening my eyes, ignoring the bloodstained face above me, I watched the window, seeing dark figures moving across its half-pulled curtains . . . passing and repassing each other against the stars in whispered altercations, their voices sometimes raised in protest, now question and answer, now quiet assent.

The figures approached the bed. Rigid, I stared up at them as they surrounded me . . . indistinct urchins come in from the night. They formed a ring above me, staring down; their tainted breath was upon my face. I saw them as unclean spectres, phantoms from infernal regions.

Now another sound: the soprano protest of a woman. The bass grunts of men made accompaniment as they arranged themselves closer above me, peering down.

'Keep still.' A hoarse whisper.

I kept still.

And a hand reached out of the darkness and touched my face: it was a woman's hand, though calloused and strong. As I lay there, it stroked my cheek.

I was cold, as a man long dead is cold.

I do not know how long I lay there with the woman's hand upon my face, but I heard her say:

'You got it, Dai?'

Scuffling footsteps. A man coming into the room.

It was Dai Bando.

'Aye, and it's the last one, ye realise?' His breathing was heavy. The woman cried, shrill:

'The last seed? Can't be! I counted two there not five minutes ago!'

'Then somebody's been at the bloody tin!'

'Christ! I'll kill the one who has!'

Now a minor panic, a surge of gasps beside the bed, and I saw them looking into a little tin.

'There'll be a bloody stink when Uncle Bobo comes!'

'Ach no! When Bobo comes he'll bring some more,' and I recognised Patsy. She shouted to the room:

'Somebody's been knackerin' the bloody seeds! Now come on! You know what Bobo does to poppy thieves!'

I saw a ring of white faces moving in the shadows of the candlelight. The faces grumbled and denied, staring accusingly at one another.

'I asks ye plain now,' cried Patsy. 'Who's been at the tin?'

'Stop bloody talkin' and give it to him,' commanded Dai, and he snatched the tin from Patsy and held it, precious, against himself. I tried to break free of my ropes, but the knots bit into my flesh.

'Aye, give him it,' said someone, 'or next thing we know he'll be off the bed.'

A high-pitched voice cried from the darkness, 'If he gets free he'll slaughter us!'

'Settle him quick, for God's sake!'

Dai Bando then knelt on one side of the bed, Patsy on the other.

'I'll put him out. Give it 'ere,' said one, and their hands met in front of my face. I saw a little, black pill like a rabbit's dropping pass between their fingers; then the fingers paused, and Patsy said:

'The last seed. Suppose Uncle Bobo don't come?'

'When there's money in it, he arrives.'

'Pull open his mouth.'

Dai leaned over me, gripped my jaws in his hands and tried to force them apart, but I swung my head.

'Hold his nose!'

'Hey, Maria – you there! Come and hold his nose.'

A hand scoured my face, gripping my nose. I fought to breathe, bucking my body, and others ran to the bed, throwing themselves upon me, holding me down in a chorus of threats. I was choking, and I gasped for air. Patsy dropped in the opium seed and Dai clamped a hand across my mouth to keep it there.

'Christ,' someone whispered. 'The last one!'

'What a bloody waste!'

★

I had swallowed devils.

Rancid and bitter, saliva containing opium dripped down my throat. I retched.

'Mind he don't spit it out!'

They held me, gripping every limb.

'Supposing Uncle Bobo don't come, Dai Bando?'

This was quieter, a girl's voice, and I thought it might be Bridget O'Shea, whose father had been hanged on Joe Wortley's testimony. 'I need a dropping, Dai. I'm nigh dead for a dropping . . .' She sounded faint.

'He'll come, I tell ye!'

I lay with clenched eyes while the opium saliva searched my stomach.

They were addicting me.

'What time ye say Bobo's coming?'

'Nine o'clock.'

'Nine? Do ye realise it's nearly midnight?'

'Shut your mouths!' shouted Dai Bando. 'We're all in the same boat, aren't we? Do ye think I don't need a snot? I anna had one for days – shut it!'

With my eyes now accustomed to the flickering light, I raised my head an inch on the pillow and searched the shadows for faces; one by one I recognised them.

Dai and Patsy were still kneeling beside me, watching my face for opium change. Old Soak and Maria, his missus, were squatting on the floor nearby – he as gaunt as a fiddler's flute, Maria still flourishing her three-chinned obesity. Bridget O'Shea, whose voice I had just heard, suddenly moved into the candlelight, and momentarily I saw her face – a once-young face now ravaged by opium. Little Darby the Fuller was there, grown from boyhood; his was a choirboy's expression, a head on a sack of rags and tatters, and his skinny arms were blue with cold. Fat Ma Bopper lay with her head in Billo's lap; Binnie Tooley and Martha Higgins, once classmates in Ruth's school, were sluts with wan faces, their bodies wasted by Bobo's drug.

244

Others were there, too; people I did not know. The room was full of the dregs of the ragged poor, the opium addicts of High Doss. Uncle Bobo's children.

I closed my eyes and lay back, giving myself up to the waves of nausea sweeping up from my stomach, for the opium had found the alcohol, and I knew that I might die. And in a sudden hallucination I saw before me, but a foot away, the face of old Plum Belly, the broken-down Shakespearean actor.

Shorn of the Abe Jowell disguise now, Plum Belly was back to normal, and he grinned at me, his yellow teeth rolling on his gums, and his breath stank. In measured, cultured words, he said, 'Can you hear me in there, Nick Wortley?'

I glared back at him. This was the *doppelgänger* who had stopped Ruth's heart, and I fought the ropes again.

He said, 'You really do have to admit it, Wortley, it was an excellent performance.'

'Perhaps, but you'll hang for it, won't you!' And with a strength that astonished me, I raised myself and shouted at the room. 'You killed her; you murdered Abe Jowell as well, and I'll see you hanged.'

'Oh, no, Nick Wortley,' replied Patsy, 'you got it wrong, boy. An eye for an eye, the good Book says, remember: we'll be doing the hangin', son, when Uncle Bobo comes.'

I do not know how long I lay spreadeagled on the bed, for time has no consequence when the intellect is deranged. A paranoia now contained me; hallucinations were alternating between spasms of clear-headedness.

One moment I walked with Ruth hand in hand in sylvan glades; next I descended into flaming pits that consumed my body. Ensnared by an intense and frenzied madness, I was released into magic, floating upon a yellow and purple cloud; weightless.

In those coloured dreams I died; I died and awoke to live,

245

again. Visions of devils were arranged before the bed; the faces of Dai and Patsy were exchanged for the masks of fiends.

Now came tranquillity for the poppy opiate soothes, and I was chastened into benevolence. Now this forgiveness was shattered by rage, an explosion of hatred: hysteria followed and I remember bucking about on the bed, bawling obscenities. Then came a soothing balm again; serenity and smiles. A halcyon coolness replaced the frenzy; all this is the work of opium, poisoning.

And in that paranoia Ruth came to me, entering by the window.

She same across the room to me with her hand outstretched in sisterly benediction, and the ragged urchins of High Doss shrank away from her in fright. And then as Ruth reached me the bedside candle caught her dress alight and she was enveloped in flames. Ruth made no sound but stood there while the fire consumed her. I saw her features scorch and melt, her limbs wither into sticks; I tried to scream, but made no sound.

I lay there watching while she burned to death.

Next the wraith of her knelt beside the bed and took my hands in hers, and the hands I held were stripped of flesh, the little bones of her fingers stark white and hot.

'Darling,' whispered Ruth, her skeletal face against mine, for she had no face. 'It's only a dream, I tell you, it is only a dream . . .'

I slept, I think, for when I opened my eyes again Ruth had gone and the rays of an early dawn were searching the room with shafts of fire.

In that red dawn Uncle Bobo Bando came.

Chapter thirty-three

I'll say one thing for Uncle Bobo: he might have had no chin, but he had all his marbles about him.

He came off the milk train from Ponty station, driving in a hired trap, and his little pony clip-clopped her way happily along the drive to the entrance of Penycoedcae, and everything happened at once. The bedroom bustled with hurrahs and activity; curtains were pulled, the sun shot in, and I saw the room and its dishevelled occupants clearly for the first time.

Ruth's wardrobe had been raided by the women. They were dressed in whatever finery they could find to fit them. The young ones were in evening gowns, the older women with skirts and bodices slit up the back to make them fit. Patsy was in pink, with frills at the neck and elbows, and all of them, unkempt and filthy, looked like hags of the French Revolution. Even Dai Bando had fitted himself out in my riding-habit: knee-length boots, frock coat and cravat. And in this elegance, with a grimy face, he ran out to meet Uncle Bobo.

The latter arrived with great aplomb: velvet riding coat, bulging fawn stomach, breeches and a tarred pigtail. A massive man, who carried his sixty years or so with a sprightly step.

Approaching the bed where I lay trussed, he removed his yellow straw boater, swept the floor with it in a gracious bow, and said, double bass:

'Uncle Bobo Bando, kind sir, at your service. Very unhappy I am to see you in this predicament,' and he opened his cavernous mouth and bawled stridently, 'Nephew! Come, *come!* And shake ye bones!'

His lower jaw, I noticed, was made of shining brown leather, where the cannon ball, red-hot in flight, had passed across the left side of his face and removed his chin. He was amazingly coherent for a man so terribly injured.

Dai Bando appeared at his elbow, and Bobo bawled in bog Irish:

'Cap'n's respects, me lad, but will ye tell me why this foine gentleman is tied up alongside in this foul manner?'

'If I have him standing, he'll injure the bloody lot of us, Uncle Bobo. Look at the size of the fella.'

'*Faith!* Didn't ye seek his honour that he wouldn't escape? Did you have to luff him up like a bloody topsail?'

'Gi' us a pill, Uncle Bobo,' begged someone. 'Please . . .!'

Coming closer to me, Bobo said, 'Ye'll kindly forgive the risin' generation, Skipper – tying up a foine gent like a lug-sail, turning a bit o' fun into a criminal act.' He paused. 'If I was to release you, ye wouldn't do a bunk now, would ye – you being gentry?'

'Don't bank on it,' I said.

I heard a voice say softly, 'Oh holy Jesus, this was never worth my mother's pain . . .'

Now Bobo roared, 'Come on, you lubbers!' and he waved a silver-knobbed stick. 'Give Dai here a hand to untie the young gent – jump to it or I'll smarten ye. It's a dirty wind ye've blown him, and no mistake, ye bloody scallywags! And the longer ye take, the longer ye wait, remember!'

Six of them were at me now, tearing at the knots that held me, and Bridget O'Shea whimpered, 'Gi' us a dropping, Uncle Bobo – in the name of Jesus, give us a rabbit droppin' . . .!'

'All in good time, me hearties! Full and by, full and by!' Uncle Bobo stamped about and roared like a man on a ship's forecastle. 'Hold him hard at that . . .' as I was pulled off the bed, upright before him, and his blue eyes danced in the puddle of his sweating face.

'Me dear sir, if I loose your hands, ye'd not be attacking poor, crippled Bobo now, would ye? And me injured so terrible in service to the country?'

'No,' I said.

He hit his stick on the floor. 'Ye hear His Honour, do ye?' He sidled up to me. 'Accept me sincere apologies for any inconvenience me relatives 'ave caused ye, for I'd not harm a hair of ye head, me darlin'.'

'Get on with it,' I snapped. 'What do you want?'

He considered this. 'Well now, I've been considerin'. Do ye think we might have a wee talk in private – Captain's cabin, and all that – just you and me . . . away from this dirty crew?'

'About what?'

He opened a snuff box, tapped it on his thumb, sniffed noisily, and said, on the verge of a sneeze, 'Well, me first intention after arrivin' at top speed was to hang ye, you understand? For you and yours 'ave been causing ructions among me poor relatives in High Doss, up Bradford way, they tell me. But I was wonderin' . . .' he looked at the begging faces around him. 'I . . . I was wonderin' if I could attend to me dear relatives first, sir, for the poor souls are in love wi' the poppy . . .'

'Yes, and you addicted them, you wicked old sod!'

'Now that's an unfair judgment, for Uncle Bobo never did harm to a livin' soul.' He drew from his pocket a small, round tin and all present – Dai Bando and Patsy to the fore – craned nearer.

I saw the spit of anticipation bubbling on their lips, their strained, pale faces. Bridget O'Shea was clawing at her throat, leaving upon her skin thin, red scratches. Plum Belly was trembling convulsively. Maria and Old Soak clasping one another were like children before a thrashing. And Uncle Bobo said:

'It's their medicine they're after, ye see, sir, so it's all hands to the capstan. Pipe "Up Spirits", me lucky lads! Get yourselves down on ye knees and I'll serve you with Bobo's communion. Line yourselves astern, me beauties!'

I watched.

They knelt like communicants about him. Heads bent,

they waited, and he served them with an opium pill apiece, ceremoniously patting each head with priestly benediction.

It was a scene I will never forget.

And as each communicant received the opium, he or she shuffled away to lie quietly and await the drug's effect.

They were his slaves: Uncle Bobo commanded them totally. Snapping shut the tin, he replaced it in his pocket. Opening his frock coat, he drew out a flintlock pistol.

I had been expecting this.

'Now don't you alter course one point, Mr Wortley, or I'll blow ye fookin' head off, understand?' And he added hoarsely: 'Easy as she goes, sir. You and me are goin' to have a chat about a wall-safe, so move ye jib forrard. Don't try no funny business, or I'll bloody scupper ye,' and he prodded me with the pistol.

Reluctantly, I went, and he followed, still prodding. 'No boardin' parties, Mr Wortley, or you're bloody shark's meat, get it?'

I nodded, and we left the bedroom. Still prodding me from behind, Uncle Bobo followed me downstairs. In this manner, with my head still swimming from opium and alcohol, we reached the drawing-room. Even from there I heard the snores of the opium-eaters on the floor above.

'We can make a bargain, you and me, can't we, sir?' Bobo leered from his scarred face. 'Ye see, I got to be honest with ye, I've taken to ye no end. Are ye listening?'

'Go on,' I said, watching the pistol.

'Mind, you've done Dai badly, you and yours, like I said. His feyther – me loving brother – got 'is neck cropped because o' your pa, didn't he? False testimony, weren't it? And that Bridget O'Shea, her pa copped it as well. As for your Brandt piece – just look what her dad did to the folks in High Doss! Would ye like to hear more?'

'I'd like to hear it all,' I answered, playing for time; soon,

250

perhaps, he would feel confident and relax.

Bobo continued: 'So they all decided to make Nick Wortley pay – you and the Brandt daughter, too. Now, I 'ad no hand in this, as God's me judge. They followed you to the Woodhead railway, and ye scarpered to Rhymney; they followed ye there, and you scarpered here . . .'

'They were after the Brandt money?'

'Now you're gettin' it, sir. There's no flies on Dai and Patsy. Ye see, they reckoned that if you got all the money, they could blackmail you for it, but the first thing to do was to get you and Miss Brandt together, understand?'

'So they killed Abe Jowell,' I said.

'Well, it were a coach crash – Dai sort o' helped 'im on his way wi' a hammer.'

'Then they scared off the servants.'

'They 'ad to, didn't they? Dangerous old gossips.'

I said, 'And then they brought in Abe's ghost.'

'Did the trick, didn't it? Got rid of your housekeeper and hitched you on to the Brandt piece. Mind, it weren't Dai's fault that they both had weak hearts.'

'And this is where you come into it?'

Uncle Bobo beamed. 'Not quite right, sir – me and you come into it.' He leaned confidentially. 'Ye see, sir, we're a cut above that trash upstairs. You see me all present and correct, and you go free. If not . . .' He drew his finger across his throat. 'Ear to ear . . . Begging ye pardon, sir, but I got no option. But you come under me lee and we can sail off windward together.'

'If I give you the money, I can go free, you mean?'

'As free as air, sir – stiff breeze, tiller and compass!'

'On your word of honour?'

He straightened, clicked his heels and crossed his heart. 'As bosun mariner in service to the Navy, sir. You 'ave the word of a sailor and gentleman.'

'Over here,' said I, and led him to the portrait of Nelson. Pushing the picture aside, I took the safe key from its hiding-place.

'Well now, that's very perceptable of ye, ye lordship!' said Bobo.

Now would come the real danger.

When he saw the money.

I swung back the safe door and brought out the gold.

Bobo's cheeks bulged purple.

I took out five bags, each containing 200 sovereigns, and noticed the pistol falter in his hand as I opened a bag and poured them on to a table. Dawn sunlight flashed on the newly minted coins; Uncle Bobo's eyes rolled.

'How much there, shipmate?' A hoarse whisper.

'A thousand. More where it came from.'

'In the bank?'

'Yes, in Cardiff.'

'How much?'

'About two hundred thousand.'

'Stone the bloody crows! How do we get at it?'

'I'll give you a bill of exchange . . .'

He straightened. No fool, this one; it wasn't going to be easy.

'What then?' he asked suspiciously, and I replied:

'I give you the bill, you take it to the bank, they pay you the money.'

'O aye? You ain't runnin' me before the wind, Cap'n. The marines would bloody 'ave me.'

'The police, you mean? Of course not! It simply means that the money would be transferred to your name.'

'Is that a fact, my beauty?' He prodded me with the gun. 'You have some sent up here, my son, and let's be certain sure, eh?'

'How much?'

'Five thousand.'

I turned away. 'Don't be silly! If I asked them to send me fifty, they'd want to know why I couldn't come myself.'

'Bloody hell, they're right canny with your money, ain't they?'

'They have to be, with buggers like you about.'

It pleased him. He stared at first, getting the sense of it, and then chuckled: then he shouted bass laughter, rearing his head back, and I chopped down with the edge of my right palm on to his wrist, sending the pistol flying.

Bobo howled with rage and pain and leaped to retrieve it, trying to scramble along the floor, but I straightened him with my knee: and as his astonished face swayed before me I got him with a right hand that sent his leather chin flying: stumbling the length of the room, Bobo hit the wall with a thud and sagged down on to the floor.

Picking up the pistol, I laid it on the table. With the curtain girdle I tied Uncle Bobo's hands and feet, trussing him backwards like a chicken with a sailor's running bowline: he'd like that touch, I thought. Then I put fifty sovereigns into my pocket, replaced the other money in the safe, and locked it.

On a second thought, I took Uncle Bobo's opium tin from his pocket, opened and dropped two seeds into his chasm of a mouth during a snore: then, checking the windowbars for strength I locked the drawing-room door and ran up the stairs to the bedroom.

Here was a minor battlefield of sprawled corpses, chins upturned in a symphony of opium snores. Dai and Patsy; Plum Belly and Little Darby; Old Soak and Maria, with Po Betsy in the middle; Binnie and Martha Higgins side by side.

From the wardrobe I took out my discarded navvy clothing which I had kept for nostalgic reasons. Changing into it, I was now in the same state as when I had arrived in Ponty years ago. Indeed, some mud still clung to the purple waistcoat and the navvy boots; the velveteen coat was still ripped at one shoulder, something Abby Nothin had always promised to mend, but never did.

Before I left the house I scribbled a note for the

Superintendent of the Pontypridd police and put it into an envelope:

Something is happening at Penycoedcae Villa up on Beech Hill, which requires investigation.

Getting into Bobo's trap, I reined in the pony, wheeled it, and clip-clopped down the drive to Ponty town.

It was Sunday morning.

I realised this when I went over the Old Bridge after pushing the envelope under the door of the police station in Sardis Road.

Standing on the bridge, remembering the ancients who had stood there in past generations, I listened to the singing from Tabernacle. In lovely harmony – soprano, tenor, contralto and bass – the words of *Calon lân* swept up to me on the clear, mountain-brushed air.

People passed me on their way to church or chapel, in well-ironed dresses, Sunday suits, polished boots and the smell of camphor. Leaning on the bridge I listened, and heard:

Nid wyn gofyn bywyd moethus,
Aur y byd na'i berlau mân,
Gofyn'rwyf am galon Hapus,
Calon onest calon lân.

The wind blew from the river and it was cold on my face, as the dreams of men grow cold within the fires of vain ambitions. With the words of *Calon lân* ringing faintly in my ears, I turned my face to the north, and there was a sadness in me as I left my town and my people.

Chapter thirty-four

There had come upon me the old wild call of freedom; only once before had I experienced this with such intensity, and that was when, as a callow youth, I had left High Doss to be a tunnel tiger. Now it came again, this fever; it snatched me up and carried me back to the wilds of Pikernaze. For there had been reports that they had driven a second tunnel alongside the first one for an up-and-down line, and by reading the newspapers I had become an enthusiastic brother to the planning.

How strange, I thought, that with private capital now exceeding £200,000, I might even have tendered for this second contract!

This time I went by train in comfort.

A little later Pontypridd had the longest railway platform in the world; 250 trains a day entered the station. But even in the 1850s trains were plentiful, and within minutes I was on my way to London and the North.

The sun was going down when I got to Sheffield.

I was surprised to find that it was only with difficulty that I could buy a ticket to Manchester, then I noticed that the carriages were crowded and bedecked with flags and bunting as for a ceremony.

'What's happening?' I asked a porter.

'This is only the second train to go through the new tunnel to Woodhead on the double line!'

'And the first one?'

'Went through this mornin', Mister. The engineers and directors are celebrating at Salter's Brook – last week the navvies toasted a whole ox down there, did ye hear?'

I shook my head.

'You from these parts?'

'Never been here before.'

The train started; it rattled out of Sheffield and I was immediately stuck up with kids licking toffee-apples, blowing sherbet dabs and climbing all over the seats. Buxom young wives hit out heartily, their chastisement adding to the wails and shrieks. Fat ladies with baskets on their chests, comely old gents with rubicund faces, others with the sallow countenances of the labouring poor – all sat as rigid as the new station slot-machines on that bucking. swaying run. *Rat-a-tat-tat! Rat-a-tat-tat!* And one of the urchins knelt beside me and asked:

'Are you a navvy man, mister?'

'Oh, *heist* you!' cried his Irish mother, shocked.

For reply, I gave him a grin and nodded, and he cried to his mates, delighted:

'See, I told you – all the big fellas are tunnel tigers. You got a tail in your trousers, mister?' and his mother cried:

'Wee Shaun, I'll beat the ass's reins off ye when I get you home!' and she swung one that would have settled me had it landed. 'Beg ye pardon, sir, I'm sure,' said she. 'It's the wild, wild tales they're gettin' from school, ye understand?' and her son yelled, tearful:

'If he's a tiger he's got a tail in his trews!'

I said, 'Aye, I have. But it'll cost ye a bright tanner to see it – for we never show tails free. Have you a sixpence?'

His sad, brown eyes drifted over me and he shook his head.

'No tail, unless I see the colour of your money.'

An hour later the children were still howling.

Reaching Dunford we stopped to take on water. Infants, until now lulled to sleep by the womb-motion, awoke and bellowed lustily; young mothers fed them, eyes virtuously downcast, one hand sheltering the breast. I stuck out my legs, stared at the ceiling and pretended I wasn't there, while grandads, privileged by age, cooed and pinched the cheeks of the sucklers. Closing my eyes, I dreamed.

In the hissing escape valve steam and belching of the firebox, I dreamed of starlight, and Abby Nothin. And I saw through the carriage window the criss-cross, crazy remains of skeletal roofs – the shants where I'd done up poor old Tabor. Finger Silence Street lay rutted and silent, for the navvies had gone. Gone with the cholera, some said.

'O, aye!' said an old man opposite me, and munched his whiskers. 'They 'ad the Black Death some'ut terrible on the second tunnel, mind.'

'Nigh thirty dead, I heard tell,' said a grandma, and I saw in her eyes the hungers of her generation. 'I lost a son, that's why I come, see?'

I nodded. 'A pilgrimage . . .?'

'No, I lost me son, see? That Dr Harrison were no good, mind. My lad was on the tramp – John Collins was his name, he were only twenty-five.'

I said I was sorry.

'Ain't started to live, really speakin'.'

Yes, and there was Jim Green, who died in a barn; and old Peg Leg, the nurse with one leg, she died, too; and Mrs Foulkes, who followed her, she turned blue; likely she caught it off Thomas Fiddler, patient No. 245. Dr Harrison was at his best when the Black Death came to Woodhead – port wine, hot coffee and strength of character was his prescription. I knew all this from the newspapers, but didn't let on.

'He were my only son,' said the old girl, her eyes wet.

'Who?' asked someone.

The train started again with a lurch; the children began to scamper about again.

'My lad,' said the gran. 'John Collins, I just told ye.'

'O, aye?'

'Mind, they was cruel old places to work,' said a man, 'them Woodhead tunnels.'

You can say that again, I thought.

Where, I wondered, was Abby?

The train lurched into the tunnel entrance for Manchester, and the calm evening was exchanged for rumbling darkness and flashing lights.

Did the ghost of Little Bert walk here between the rails, waving to passing trains? Did the shades of Gaffer and Educated Ifan stand in the safety niches as the carriages rattled by? Was Byron of the club foot here, soaked with the water of Woodhead reservoir?

Old Zeke, the purple man, was he still alive? I wondered. Where was the wraith of Tom Ostler who shot like a bullet up the shaft. Is Jake O'Hara still listening to the ships' propellers in Southampton? Does he sleep soundly, his now infant body, the Christ in concrete?

And Cat-Eater, what of him? Is he still living on dinners of boiled tabbies and Persians? Does Hairy Ambler walk the roads on his newspaper ticket? Who bathes his feet now that Abby is not there?

The brakes slammed on; the carriage shot from darkness to light again, and the train lurched to a stop at Woodhead Station: the hissing steam blipped off as the fireman shovelled the box.

The children about me were asleep now; birdsong I heard coming faintly over the moors. I should have travelled on, for my ticket was to Manchester, but impelled by something greater than myself, I got up, opened the carriage door and stepped out on to the platform. Brandy snaps of sun were playing in the elms, I remember. Sheep called faintly; a dog barked. It was like standing at the end of the world.

I was the only one to alight; the guard blew his whistle. The train shunted off, leaving me alone with the tunnel.

I could hear faint music; it came on the summer wind. And then I remembered the old Crown Inn and made my way along the line towards it.

The music became louder as I approached; bats were

swooping around the tunnel mouth. In these parts the dusk falls like the drop of a sorcerer's cape. I glanced upward. The sky was blue-gold, the stars swimming with a milky sickness, and the full moon was dozing on his back with his arms folded and his legs cocked up, as Abby used to say. Distant windows glinted in the pale light; the wind kissed my face, the music surged.

Light and smoke hit me as I opened the door of the Crown Inn, and there was a right old palaver going on inside. I remember that it was the night of eight-weeks' pay, and they always paid out in the publics. But I'd never seen this taproom so full, with a leprechaun up on a table beating time with a quart of stout, and as I came in, he sang to an accordion:

Our new foreman was Mike McCan.
Take it from me, he were a bloody mean man!
Last week a premature charge goes off,
And a mile in the sky went old Joe Goff!

Pots were tossed up, pewters waved and the ale went down as the chorus came up – deafening, battering off the walls:

So dig, ye bastards, *dig!*
Dig ye bastards, *dig!*
For it's work like a bee for the sugar in ye tea,
So dig, ye bastards, *dig!*

The Irish midget beat the time, the squeeze boxes soared, and he shouted:

Come the eight-week-pay report,
Jim Goff found he were ten bob short.
I'm ten bob short, will ye tell me why?
You've been docked for the time you was up in the sky!

So dig, ye bastards, *dig!*

Dig, ye bastards, *dig!*
For it's work till ye drop or Ganger says 'Stop',
So dig, ye bastards, *dig!*

The lads were well into it: about forty bruisers, and according to the barmaid, as she pushed me a quart, they'd only just begun the randy.

From 'Blow Up' to 'Yo Ho' they'd be at it now for days, finishing up in Glossop, likely, drinking the publics dry, chasing the women and fighting among themselves, so I reckoned it was no place for me.

Also, the barmaid was a doe-eyed, watery piece with a come-hither look that frightened me to death, so I made for the door with my glass, but never reached it, for a voice cried through the din:

'Well, well, I never did! *Jawch*, lads, look what the rooster's found!' and I turned in time to see old Cushy Cuddlecome climbing over the tap showing fat legs and garters, and she rushed me, collared me, swung me round in a circle and smacked a kiss on me that stuck me up with her rouge and powder.

'*Jawch!* Look, the love of me heart! Have you ever seen such a big, handsome fella? You come to stay, me charmer?'

'Just passing, Cushy.'

She winked a mascara'd lid, batted her bright blue eyes, and sidled up to me, whispering:

'Sure, there's always a bed in Cushy's place for the likes of you.'

Ham Bone and Swillikin Jock, her two pansy minders, were hovering near, looking terrified.

'Where's Abby?' I asked.

She was affronted. 'Now, who wants Abby Nothin when you're surrounded with the fruits of the entire establishment? Come on, lad, shiver up your herring roes!'

'You seen her, Cushy?' I asked.

The singing stopped. Irish faces peered: little elfin faces; bulbous red noses like gnomes; handsome faces; ugly faces soiled by ale and hard living, but every man there was with honour, for he was a navvy man. They peered from Cushy to me, and back. It's not that the Irish are nosey; they just want to know what's going on.

And Cushy was weighing me for size; her expression changed:

'You walked out on her, Welsh Taff – d'you care where she is?'

'She walked out on me!'

'Ach, what the hell! It were only when the moon was full.'

'We jumped the brooms fair and legal – she's me wife, but she roosted off!'

'Jesus!' Cushy clapped her hands. 'A woman's entitled to a change o' scenery, too, ye know!'

The men guffawed, shouting her encouragement.

I said, levelly, 'I'm askin' you again – where is she?'

'If I knew I wouldn't be tellin' ye. Last time I saw her she'd had her fill o' men, you in particular. So she'd hied herself back to Connemara, and she put her nose so high she'd have drowned in a storm.

But I knew old Cushy: she was fanning her wrath to keep it warm. The Irish navvies, the drama unfolding, watched and listened.

I asked, 'Is The Hermitage still up on the hill?'

'Unless someone's lifted it.'

'I wouldn't mind seeing the old place again.'

'Aye, but watch it, for they've got a gang o' Scandies up there now, and they don't like Ponty Welshmen.'

I nodded. 'I'll chance it. Give us another quart o' your watered Allsops and I'll sup it up there for old time's sake.'

'As long as ye know what I water it with,' said Cushy, and threw back her head and cackled, sending the place into stitches.

I was tiring of her. Sadness was besetting me, knowing that Abby was gone. People went home from Woodhead to die, especially to Connemara. I slapped down threepence and the barmaid poured me another quart.

'I'll be back,' I said and pushed my way out into the night.

I walked slowly up the hill to Shaft One. The corrugated iron roofs of the derelict shanty town I knew so well creaked and groaned in a little wind from Salter's Brook. And I thought of Tom Ostler and Alf Posh and the rest, and of Gaffer, who died.

I thought, too, of the silicosis navvies who choked up their lungs after years in the filth of Woodhead; of the missionaries who pestered us for our souls while the shareholders pestered us for profits. I thought of old Surgeon Pomfret who infuriated the Woodhead directors by giving details of the accidents – a report that finished up as a Parliamentary question and was then shelved after the usual democratic white-wash . . . by a House of Commons where scores of Members had financial interests in railway companies.

All the magic names came flooding back to me – Pigtail, Punch and Fanny, Dolly Leg and Gravey, Coffee Joe and the brothers Lock and Key, Charlie Frisky who only drank whisky. A shovel was called a 'navvy's prayer-book', a pick was called a 'dick' and the lads called themselves 'thick-legs' and 'muckers', and I thought of the navvy poet Alexander Anderson, and of Pat MacGill, who wrote:

As a bullock falls in the crooked ruts,
He fell when the day was o'er.
The hunger gripping his stinted guts,
His body shaken and sore.
They pulled it out of the ditch in the dark
As a brute is pulled from its lair.
The corpse of a navvy, stiff and stark,
With clay on its face and hair.
Will ever a one remember,
The times when our voices rung:
When you were limber and lissom,

And I was lusty and young?
Remember the jobs we've laboured,
And the beautiful songs we've sung?

I thought of the vomiting and rice-water bowels of the cholera; of Joey Monkey who died of bleeding from the mouth, and how I picked up a bit of his tongue. I thought of the navvy children in the brat-cages, and of Lucy Kenning, aged two, who fell down No. 1 shaft. And I thought of the directors of the Sheffield-to-Manchester who dined on roast veal, ate peacocks' tongues, drank champagne and sang *Non nobis domine* after completing a job well done, and we called them a set of unforgivable bastards. I still did – with special reference to Lord Wharncliffe and his directors who refused us tents and lengthened our hours, and Purdon who shortened our fuses and got away with it at the official inquiry.

One navvy died for every mile of track laid in Britain, but this never came into their statistics of profit and loss. In years to come, the tame historians will write of the labouring man. Employed by the Establishment to put the Establishment case, they will denounce us for striking and despise us for our lack of education. But the trouble with official history books is that they lie by omission: they are written by the educated for the wealth-owning class, and there's never been anyone educated enough to put our case.

Woodhead Tunnel, for me, stands as a criminal indictment of the industrialist's disregard for the labourer.

One day it will all be changed. Meanwhile, I am filled with a lively and desirable loathing of those who exploit the poor, and put railway company directors at the head of the queue.

I made a mental note to write to Doherty of the National Protection of Labour; for I intended to transfer through him to the Miners' Association the entire wealth of Farrer Enterprises – Gaffer would like that, I thought, and so would Ruth.

The sky was alight with candlefire now. Remembering Ruth, I wanted to weep, but could not. And it was a pity about Abby, too, God help her; no woman could stay alive at the rate she was setting herself . . . I walked slowly, careful of slopping the Allsops, and found myself at the entrance of the Hermitage.

The door opened to a touch and I went inside; the moon came in with me, bowing first.

I stood there looking at the truckle beds.

Over there on the right is where I slept beside Gaffer; next door but three was Cat-Eater's bunk; Ezekiel's praying mat was still on the floor, and I thought of Byron who drowned and Little Bert who evaporated.

Turning, I looked through the door of the skiv's bunk at the bed where I had made love to Abby. It seemed a century ago, out of another age.

Wandering down the middle of the shant now, I turned to the slur of a footstep.

At first I thought I was back in Penycoedcae Villa again, and seeing ghosts – for the wraith that had entered the shant door was Abby.

'Holy Jesus, Nick, me heart's been scalding for ye,' said she.

But it was not the Abby I knew.

Life had taken her, starved her, racked her, hammered her into skin and bone. She was a woman aged. With her thin arms by her sides, she stood there and I swear it was the old pink dress she was still wearing, tattered and torn.

'*Abby!*' I said, and approached her.

The moon looked, too, and I saw her more clearly. How old would she be? I wondered. Twenty-seven?

Call it seventy-two.

God in Heaven!

She said simply, her face with the pallor of illness, 'Cushy sent me up, see? Ham Bone and Swillikin Jock brought me in her trap. I . . . I been down at the Crown Inn for months. I've had the cholera.'

'Oh, Jesus, *no!*'

'Then I heard you was down at Salter's, and I wanted to see ye.' She held her throat. 'Can you hear me wheezing like an old black hog?'

A shadow moved like a bear feasting behind her, and a star went out in the sky. A man came into the shant. Pushing Abby aside, he said, 'If you're on your feet again ye can get back to work, skiv, or you'll collect a thumping,' and to me he said, 'What you doin' here?'

It was Cat-Eating Scan.

Reaching out for Abby, I pulled her behind me and we backed deeper into the hut.

Cats said, 'Ay, ay! The Welsh nance come back, has he? What you up to with our skiv? Snatchin' her again?'

Abby whispered, 'Run, Nick, run! Tabor's comin' up, behind!'

Cat-Eater seemed to have grown, or perhaps it was the light. He was bearded, too, and as he clutched at me in the moonlight I hooked a left to his chin, but whiskered it, because of the beard.

Pushing Abby away to the wall, I circled, awaiting his rush; strange purring sounds were coming from his throat. I once heard of a man who ate bear's meat, and in his delirium roared and growled like a bear.

Cats shrieked falsetto, and rushed. I stood my ground and hooked a left to his body. This brought his head down; momentarily, he tottered, and I went in, hitting him for holes, finally knocking him up with a right smash to the chin. Cat's heels lifted, his buttocks followed and he landed with a crash. But rose instantly with blood on his face and snarling like an animal.

Abby stepped in and hit him with the poker.

'*Ham Bone! Swillikin!*' she shrieked.

More men were coming through the door. Abby got the

first one, the second tripped over Cat-Eater and floundered past me, and I waited, fists clenched, for the third, who had ducked his head under the shant door, but the man advanced only slowly.

It was Tabor.

'Oho! The Welshman come back, eh?'

I lowered my hands and he pushed me gently before him to the wall while his butties crowded in behind him. Somewhere out in the darkness I heard Ham Bone gibbering with fright, and Swillikin, bearded and ferocious, put his head round the door, and said, broken:

'For Gawd'd sake, give up, old Nick. Last time we was here I got hit up something cruel . . .'

Tabor said. 'You want Abby Nothin? Half a woman?'

'Try stopping me.'

The room glowed; somebody had lit a lamp.

Tabor ran his fingers through his mop-gold hair. 'All right, you take her. Later you will put her in a dustbin, and save me the trouble?' He prodded me in the chest. 'But you come once more, Welshman, and Tabor will kill you.'

He was within range and his big, square chin was begging for it. Abby whispered, 'Nick, please . . .'

I held her against me, and she was trembling. Thinking she was going to fall, I swung her up into my arms.

Glowering, the Tabor gang made way as I took her through the door. And the moment I got her within reach of Ham Bone and Swillikin at the trap, she shrieked:

'Ye uselesss pair o' bloody pansies! Runnin' gunks! Didn't ye hear me yelling for ye?' and she swiped at them with the poker.

She'll live, I thought, as I lifted her into the trap.

Later, I held her in the bed at Cushy's place. The night was quiet over Pikernaze, for all the Crown casks were dry and the lads were away on a randy to Glossop. And just when I thought Abby was sleeping she rose in the bed like a revived corpse, saying, 'Did ye know I took me holy vows in a convent while you were away, Old Nick?'

'No, you didn't mention it.' I sighed like a woman in labour.

'Ay ay. I joined the Jesuits o' Jerusalem up in Manchester – I became an apprentice nun, ye know.'

'A novice, you mean?'

'That's right. They wanted to make me the Mother Superior after a twelve-month, but the Pope were against it because I was only twenty-six, and you've got to be thirty before you can be Mother Superior.'

Jesus, I thought, she hasn't changed much, and said, 'Sleep now, for God's sake!'

'But I did me holy pilgrimage – I was received in audience at the Vatican, as I expect you read in the newspapers.'

Faintly on the wind I heard a distant tolling bell, probably from Crowden, like a processional hymn of monks; but it appeared to come from within the tunnel entrance; it called me out of an errant dream.

Kissing Abby's face, I got out of the bed and went to the window. Woodhead station was deserted, save for moonlight; its signal lights glowed red and green, and the black entrance of the tunnel gaped at me like the mouth of a carnivorous animal that awaited its nightly feed of men. For the losses in building Woodhead were higher in percentage than the deaths in action of four great battles – Salamanca, Vittoria, Talavera and Waterloo.

And, as I watched in disbelief, I saw a column of walking dead emerge from the tunnel's mouth.

Rank on rank it came, a tattered army of wraiths. As if they had opened the lids of their coffins and gathered to abuse the world, they marched out, the ghosts of the slaughterhouse called Woodhead.

★

Before them danced the children of the brat cages; some, in tatterdemalion groups, were doing cartwheels at the head of the emerging, deathless legion.

Preceded by their little scrags of wives and skivs they came: men with picks and shovels on their shoulders.

The gnomes of the North Country barrow runs were there; giants from Scandinavia with wheelbarrows on their backs: in bright arrays of coloured waistcoats and mud-stained yorks, they marched: timeless ones of the great Darlington and Settle. Now they spewed their bulging ranks out on the double line, and I heard their marching feet above a sudden blustering wind, for the night mist was clearing and I stared down, trapped by the vision.

I saw masons and revetters, plate-layers and spikers, rail-hauliers and shot-firers, and these were carrying the fatal iron stemmers. As plain as day I saw this ghostly army; a vast concourse of dead came thronging out of the tunnel.

They came by their trades, arrogant with pride of place: cutters from Olive Mount on the Liverpool–Manchester: Church Tunnel men were there, risen from the shallow graves of the London–Birmingham.

They came from the mass graves of the Woodhead cholera, and these marched with military precision to the clanking of their tools: they came from the viaduct of Dinting Vale, that vast gravestone to their courage: they came under the orders of men like Locke and Brunel who secretly despised them, and in the love of others like Brassey and Peto, who respected them. Tunnel tigers were there, the wraiths of Boxmore, also the record-breakers of Tring. From Camden and Kilsby tunnel to the Dutton Viaduct on Grand Junction they marched, many who were soon to die.

Now they filled the whole of Woodhead, marching in their thousands – one man killed for every mile of track in Britain laid – and the clinking of their tools and thunder of their boots beat about me in the little room. And, even as I stared down at the phenomenon, another ghost came out of the past, and this was Ruth.

I fashioned her from imagination into reality; seeing her first on the edge of the marching men. Disengaging from the mass, she came slowly up the slope from the line, dressed as I had seen her years before in my violent, adolescent dreams of High Doss. With her arms outstretched to me she came, a vision in white; nearer, nearer to me; now she stood outside the window, and moved through it into my arms, and the touch of her brought to me a coldness, as a man is cold within a tomb. But the moment her lips sought mine, I knew warmth; leading her to the bed I lay there with her in a strange rhapsodic dream.

In the room's faint light I saw her face, and behind her eyes was the grain of the pillow, but her mouth was sweet to me; her arms dark stains upon my shoulders. There was a richness in the opening of her body to my touch and I entered her with joy, and the thunder of the marching army died within our gusty breathing. In the panic of that love-making I called her name. And, as if in expiation for all the longings of our lost youth, she lay in a strange transmuted silence while I enjoyed her. As in a fraud of death she lay, like one at peace, but broken in my hands to bring me the gift of absolute possession. All the fevered nights of waiting returned in utmost consolations. While in life she had robbed my manhood, in death she returned it to me whole.

'*Ruth!*'

As one who had died she lay, and in the bright explosion of my youth I made my son in her. And suddenly came transfiguration; the shade of Ruth dissolved and slowly merged into a lifeless changeling; the waist I embraced was thinner, the full red lips of one became the bloodless mouth of another; and the fevered bloom of Ruth's cheeks died into a stricken pallor. In a moment the moonlight's wand replaced youth with age. Ruth had gone, leaving behind a husk of a woman. And this was Abby.

As from a great distance, the bell of Crowden began to toll in my head. Within its peculiar sound it warned of the milk train coming through at speed from Sheffield. And in gathering panic I rose from the bed and leaped to the window, to stare down at the marching army, and this was of men packed shoulder to shoulder now, oblivious of the coming danger. I saw their bobbing heads and swaying shoulders, and opened my mouth to shout warnings as the signal lights of Woodhead changed with a crash from red to green. But I knew I was already too late, for I could hear the tell-tale subterranean rumblings in the tunnel as the express came clattering onward. On, on it came while I stood petrified, waving arms that would not move, bawling warnings that made no sound. The milk train thundered closer, closer; the room beneath me trembled to the shock waves of the rails. And in the moment before I covered my face to a scene of carnage, I saw the billowing smoke that precedes an emerging locomotive. Fire-shot, it belched out of the tunnel followed by a myriad sparks as the fire-box glowed, blazing into the darkness, instantly lighting Woodhead's midnight into day. And in my head I saw the track of mutilation as the engine ploughed into the packed ranks of men; I heard the shriek of brakes, the screams of injured people, a panorama of dead and dying . . . but when I uncovered my eyes, Woodhead was empty save for the milk train's red lamp receding into the distance and its wheels dying into fainter rumblings.

As the vision of Ruth's beauty had died within the bed, so the pageant of the marching army had vanished in its brief phantasmagoria.

The Woodhead tunnel, starved of its daily feed of the living bodies of men, gaped blankly at the moon.

'You all right, Nick?'

270

It was Abby's voice; stirring in the bed, she sat up, putting out a hand to me, and her presence raked me back to reality.

I nodded.

'Come back in, boyo, you'll catch your death.'

Now I lay beside her. She lay with her head in the crook of my arm and her breathing, though listless with weakness, was rhythmic upon my face, and in the pin-drop silence I listened to the beating of her heart. She said:

'If you wanted me that bad just now, Nick Farrer, why didn't ye take me? I anna that far gone, ye know.'

'Hush, Abby – sleep now, is it?'

She said, 'You'm a queer old fella, ye know. A woman never knows where she is with you from minute to minute. One moment you're like a bloody cock belting after the roosters, next moment you go dozy in the nut and tell a woman to sleep. One thing's sure, ye Dai Dafto, I knew where I was with that bloody old Tabor.'

'*Heisht*, you,' I said, going Welsh.

She whispered, 'I'm all right for lovin', ye know, although I'm a skinny. And I'm your missus, remember. I ain't just anybody.'

Because she was only a relic of a woman I did not pester her, but held her as I had done before on the moors of Pikernaze . . . so long ago that I can scarce remember.

Abby said. 'Just now you said some funny things. You come big for me and held me like loving me, and called a name, but it weren't my name you called, Nick Farrer . . .'

I did not reply to this, and she added, 'And you spoke in a language I didn't understand. Welsh, were it?' She peered. 'Who're Ruth?'

'You were dreaming, kid.'

'Oh no I weren't, Old Nick. It was you doin' the dreaming. Don't dream of anyone no more, just dream of Abby, eh?'

I thought, Oh God, Ruth, *Ruth!*

Taking my hand, Abby put it on her little breast, saying, 'Dunna go all huffy cool on me, Nicko. I ain't so bad. I'll fatten, ye know.'

'Christ, you need to.'

'Mind, I've been sick and sad and sorry for walkin' out on ye, and more a-feared o' meeting up with you again than the bishop in all his anger,' and she crossed herself. 'Perhaps you don't go for me now since I'm a skinny and you're a great boast of a fella.'

'You'll do,' I said. 'It's a skiv I'm after, ain't it?'

'So ye'll take me on again?'

I nodded against her. 'If you walk the roads with me and not slope off again.'

'Where are ye taking me, then?'

'To the second stop to Nowhere, but Jesus pours pints for the folks who live there, and there's a welcome in that valley, even for Connemara Irish.'

She whispered, 'Would ye have slates in mind? For it's a roof I'm after. I'm sick and tired of runnin' . . .'

'Ay ay,' I said, taking off her Irish. 'I'll settle ye there, Abby Nothin, and fatten you up with starch bread, faggots and mushy peas in the markets, and when you've a decent pair o' thighs on ye and milking breasts, I'm going into ye after sōns. Do you fancy that?'

And she laughed at the ceiling crying, 'Ach, I do, I *do!*'

'Providin' you promise not to slope off again when the moon comes full.'

'Snakes alive!' cried she, sitting up. 'What pledges do ye want, for God's sake? A woman's only human. Anyway, the moon's full now, Nick Farrer, and there's a thousand children in the stars, and I'm still abed with ye, ain't I?'

'That's so, and you're staying,' I answered. 'Try moving your left leg.'

She did so, and shouted to wake the dead.

'*Quiet!*' I whispered, 'or you'll have old Cushy in!'

'Ye damned savage, you've tied me toe to the bedrail!'

'And that's how it's going to be in future,' I said, and her

272

arms went about me and she sighed deep in her throat, saying:

'*Jeez!* You're a mad, mad Welshman, but you're one hell of a man at six-foot-three. Now I'm not goin' I'll stay with you to eternity – I swear it by the livin' God.'

'I bet,' I said. 'Sleep now, Abby, for you're ill. Sleep . . .' And I pushed her gently down into the bed, but she came up again like a woman scalded, saying:

'Look, are ye saying I've got one foot in the grave, or somethin'? Sleep? I can do that any time!'

'Sleep, girl,' I said, and kissed her lips, and put her back on the pillow.

Further reading

ADDY, *The Textile Revolution*. Longman, London.

ANDERSON, ALEXANDER. *Songs of the Rail*. Simpkin Marshall, London, 1878.

BAINES, *The Woollen Manufacture of England*. Sale Public Library, Cheshire.

COLEMAN, TERRY. *The Railway Navvies*. Penguin Books, Harmondsworth, 1968.

DEVEY, JOSEPH. *The Life of Joseph Locke*. Bentley, London, 1862.

EDWARDS, E. E. *Echoes of Rhymney*. Starling Press, Risca, 1974.

ENGELS, FRIEDRICH, *The Condition of the Working Class in England*. Progress Publishers, 1973.

EVANS, E. W. *The Miners of South Wales*. University of Wales Press, Cardiff, 1961.

EVANS, R. MEURIG. *Children Working Underground*. National Museum of Wales, 1979.

KENRICK, G. S. *Disturbed Districts* (Pontypool). Pontypool Public Library, 1840.

MACGILL, PATRICK. *Children of the Dead End: The Autobiography of a Navvy*. Herbert Jenkins, London, 1914.

MORGAN, OWEN ('MORIEN'). *History of Pontypridd and Rhondda Valleys*. Pontypridd Public Library, 1903.

PICTON-TURBERVILLE, EDITH. *I Saw Them Build a Railway* (personal reminiscence). Mid-Glamorgan County Library, Bridgend.

REES, DAVID J. *The Gateway to the Rhondda* (reminiscences and history of the Rhondda Ward). Vanguard Press, Treforest.

Social Conditions (1850) in the Llynfi Valley (Chapter 18). Mid-Glamorgan County Library, Bridgend.

STAMP, A. H. *A Social and Economic History of England, 1700 to 1970*. Research Publishing Co., London, 1979.
SULLIVAN, DICK. *Navvyman*. Coracle Books, London, 1983.